CW01646310

IMPRINT OF WAR

Birth of the Rim - Book Two

Phil Huddleston

CONTENTS

Imprint of War: Birth of the Rim Series, Book Two
By Phil Huddleston

This is a work of fiction. All of the characters, locations, organizations, and events portrayed in this work are either products of the author's creative imagination or used fictitiously. Any resemblance to actual events, businesses, locales, or persons is coincidental and not intended to infringe on any copyright or trademark.

Copyright © 2019 by Phil Huddleston
Cover created by Christian Kallias

The distribution of this work without permission is a theft of the author's intellectual property. If you would like permission to use material from this work (other than for review purposes), contact Phil@PhilHuddleston.com. Thank you for your support of author's rights.

USEFUL TERMS

AI – Artificial Intelligence. Can be sentient (conscious) or non-sentient.

AU – Astronomical Unit, commonly used to specify distances inside a solar system; about 150,000,000 km. The Earth is 1 AU from the Sun.

Compensator – a device on a starship which reduces the effects of g-force on the inside of the ship when the ship is under heavy acceleration (accel) or deceleration (decel).

Corvette – the smallest class of armed warship, or a similar civilian vessel.

FTL – faster than light.

G-force (or g) – the force of gravity. When standing on Earth, you experience 1g of weight. If you were experiencing 8g, you would weigh eight times as much.

Holo – holotank, a 3D display allowing the view of complex situations.

IFF- identification friend or foe – codes used to separate enemy ships from friendlies.

KPS – kilometers per second. Escape velocity to leave Earth is roughly 11.19 kps. To reach the Moon in 1 minute, you'd average 6,407 kps.

MEMSAI – Military-Grade Enhanced Matched Semi-Sentient Artificial Intelligence. A personal assistant and security device which has a limited ability to read projected thoughts and take action. It cannot read normal thoughts, only those intentionally projected.

QE Buoy – a small device stationed at a (relatively) fixed location in space, using Quantum Entanglement (QE) to send data to a distant point. Usually used by the military as an early-warning device or to monitor a planet.

XO - Executive Officer, the second in command of a ship, usually responsible for the day-to-day operation of the ship, leaving the captain to concentrate on overall strategy.

PART ONE - SWORD - 2185

DIRGE

Aronte is the capital city of the Aeolian Empire. With a population of well over 5 million, it is the largest city in the Empire. Located on the planet Aeolis in the Helios System, it sits on the banks of the Thermodon River about 3 kilometers from the Pontus Axeinos, the ocean covering most of the western hemisphere of Aeolis. The use of Greek and Amazon names for features of the Empire is a testament to the Earth origins of the Aeolians.
- RimWiki, 2230 Edition

63 Years After Pandora's Visit
12 March 2185
Aeolian Empire - City of Aronte

The shuttle settled slowly to the ground, and with a hissing release of vapor the engines spooled down. On the pad in front of the hatch, an honor guard of Aeolian Marines stood, their brass and braid glittering in the sun. The hatch extended; the Sergeant barked, "Present...arms!" Gracefully, the honor guard's rifles moved to the formal position.

Standing to one side, Princess-Captain Hecate Andromache Aronte waited. She was a tall, well-muscled woman of twenty-seven, showing none of the dissipation so common among the Aeolian nobility. Her hair was cut short, so that it didn't show beneath her dress cap. Her uniform, the white formal dress of a serving Fleet officer, was immaculate in the late afternoon sun. The medals on her breast showed she was no desk commander. They included the Star of Aronte, given to officers who have captured or destroyed an enemy ship, and the Blood Mark, from a wound taken in combat.

In the hatch, eight Marines appeared, shouldering a coffin covered with the flag of the House Aronte. In somber unison, they slow marched off the shuttle with her father's body. Hecate lifted her hand to her left shoulder in the Naval salute and held it.

Behind Hecate, shielded from the afternoon sun by a pavilion, stood Hecate's aunt - Hippolyta Lysippe Aronte, Empress of the Aeolian Empire, Protector of the Faith, Guardian of the Relics and Bow, and High Priestess of the Golden Temple. Beside her stood her daughter, Kantilla, the Princess Imperial.

On Hippolyta's other side – and slightly behind – was Hecate's mother, Princess Deinomache, her face like stone.

Separated by a barricade and hundreds of Palace Guards, thousands of commoners stood behind, silent except for occasional murmurs.

Out in front of the pavilion and the lines of bodyguards, Hecate stood alone, facing the coffin that carried the body of her father, Prince Alexander. The sun, on such a clear day, burned hot against the fabric of her uniform.

Despite herself, a small tear moved slowly down her cheek; she gritted her teeth to stop the tears.

I will not cry. I will not! He wouldn't stand for it!

A muffled sobbing came from the crowd behind the ropes. Slow marching, the Marine escort carried the coffin to a caisson pulled by four black horses. Gently they laid it down. With a soft command, they stepped back and saluted. The Naval Band began a bagpipe dirge.

Hecate marched forward to the coffin and placed her palms flat on the top, bowing her head. And there she stayed, minute after minute. Her lips moved slightly as she said the Prayer for the Dead. Finally, as the watching crowd stood in silence, she took a step back; and resuming her military bearing, stood rigidly as the caisson was drawn away.

After many minutes, behind her she heard movement as the Imperial party turned and made their departure, followed by the thousands who turned out to see a dead Prince brought back from space. But still Hecate stayed, fixed in her grief, eyes closed against the sun setting in the East.

*****

Three days later, in Naval Headquarters, a half-dozen ranking officers gathered. Hecate sat at the end of the table, waiting impatiently, her fingers tapping. Chief of Naval Operations Admiral Maya Aronte leaned forward.

"Princess-Captain, are you sure you want to go through with this? It will be difficult..."

Hecate stared at her stonily. "I am ready, Mum. Please proceed."

Maya sighed. "Very well." She signaled silently via her AI. <Go ahead>

A second later, the room disappeared as the invisible comms embedded in their heads, manifested by a small blue bead glowing on their left temples, created a virtual space around them. It was called a sensorium; and it used all their senses to completely duplicate a virtual reality. They found themselves on the bridge of a small corvette. The scene was viewed from the front right of the bridge, with the Captain directly in view. Prince Alexander, Hecate's father, sat to the left side of the Captain. In the center of the bridge was a 3D tactical holotank. Officers and crew sat at their stations in a circle around the holo, consoles in front of them.

Prominent in the holo was a starship. It was wedge-shaped, with striations down the sides and cross-hatching on the top. A dull matte black, it showed no obvious weapons or sensors. It was running hard, dead away from them.

"They're still accelerating," said the Captain. "Hail them again."

"Aye, sir." said the Comm Officer. She touched her screen and spoke.

"Unknown ship near Ptolema, please talk to us. We will not harm you; we only wish to speak with you. We are a research vessel, not a warship. We only wish to communicate with you."

They paused, watching. There was no change in aspect. The black ship continued to run.

The Captain spoke again: "No chance of catching them, Tac?"

"No, Mum. They are quite a bit faster than us in 3-space. They mean to make the mass limit and sink out."

"Yes," said Prince Alexander. "But why? Why won't they talk to us?"

"Sir, I've never seen a ship like that. Nothing in the Empire looks like that," said the Captain. "But we'll never catch her."

The Tactical Officer suddenly jumped in her seat. "Aspect change! Mum! She's coming about!"

"What?" asked the Captain. "Why?"

In the holotank, the black ship ceased acceleration and spun back toward them. As her nose came around to bear, pale blue fire came from a beamer. There was a flash - and the bridge disappeared in fire and screaming.

Hecate sat frozen. Maya stood up and walked to her. She placed her hand on Hecate's shoulder. "We'll find them, Hecate," she said. "I promise you - we'll find them."

Hecate looked at her steadily. "No, Admiral," she said. "I'll find them. And then I'll kill them."

*****

An hour later, in Maya's office, Hecate slammed her palm against the arm of the chair. "No!"

"Please, Hecate!" said Maya. "You are a destroyer captain! How could I give you a frigate? Tell me - how?"

Hecate bared her teeth. "Tell Command exactly what I'm going to do...which is track down the bitches who killed my father and tear them to shreds. But I need a frigate! You saw the size of that...that...Black Ship! It's at least a frigate! If I go out there with a destroyer, I'm hopelessly outgunned!"

Maya sighed. "It's a good thing we're cousins, dear. I couldn't tolerate this kind of outburst from just any destroyer captain, you know."

Hecate shook her head. "Maya, you know I wouldn't take advantage of my position under normal circumstances. Have I ever done that before? In my entire career? You know I've stuck to the standard officer track. But this is different...this is family! This was my father!"

Maya shook her head. "Hecate. I want to help. But I can't give you a frigate."

Hecate rose from her chair. "Then I'll go with a destroyer."

Maya pointed a finger. "Hecate, don't make me pull rank on you. You can't go without orders. I already have a full task force out at Ptolema looking for this so-called 'Black Ship'. You need to stay here and let them do their job."

"Maya, I'm going. If you can't cut me orders to go - as much as I would hate it, I would have to ask my mother to help. And she'll ask Auntie..."

"Oh, Hecate," sighed Maya. "For Stars' sake, let's not get Auntie Empress involved. You know that never ends well. And remember - she hates the Earther myth! She warned your father to give it up, not to go out there looking for ghosts..."

Hecate grimaced. "Maya, that was his dream...to find some evidence of the ones that went before. Earthers, or whatever the legends say. He died for that dream. And he found something, all right. Some kind of ship we've never seen before. I'm going, with your help or with Auntie's..."

Maya surrendered, throwing up her hands. "OK, OK already. I'll cut you orders to go help in the search for the...whatever...Black Ship. But...and I mean this...you are limited to six weeks. Back here in six weeks, regardless. Got it?"

Hecate grinned. "Aye, Aye, Mum."

"Good," said Maya. "Now...get the hell out of here!"

Hecate stood to attention and saluted. With a smart turn, she left the office.

Outside, her Executive Officer, Commander Andrea Iona Satra, waited for her in the hallway. "Well?" she asked, “Did we get a frigate?"

Hecate shook her head. "No. But we got orders to go look. That will have to do."

Andrea grinned, a fierce and wolfish grin. "Good. Let's go kill somebody."

Hecate laughed, a hard thing to do so soon after her father's funeral, but if there was one thing she loved, it was Andrea Iona's bloodthirsty sense of humor. "Yes, Andrea. Let's go kill somebody. But first we have to find them!"

MATADOR

There is no avoiding war; it can only be postponed to the advantage of others.
- Niccolo Machiavelli

620 Light Years from Earth
Past the Pipe Nebula
Planet Danek

Fleet Admiral Brunt stood on the Flag Bridge of the Bat Empire Navy battleship BEN *Warmonger*, looking through his viewer at the destroyed city of Kedan on the planet below. Little was left; the skeleton of an occasional building jutting crookedly into the sky, with here and there a stone wall that had survived the onslaught. Roiling destruction covered the landscape – the city was little but fire, smoke, ashes. He grinned, his bat-like ears perking up at the sight. "By the Stars, I live for this," he thought.

Brunt was a typical upper-caste Bat. About two meters tall, he was lean and wiry, with light brown skin and dark gray fur - fur so short as to be almost invisible, as befitted a noble. His uniform was gray with red piping on the collar and sleeves, and stripes down the trouser legs. His cape was blood-red - worn only by officers who had conquered a planet and colonized it with new Bats.

In one hand, he held a baton, used frequently to strike slaves and subordinate officers. In the other hand, he held a cup of a'kaff, the stiff, bitter drink almost every BEN officer drank constantly.

"Sir," called his Chief of Staff, Captain Orantel, "All but one of the escaping ships have been destroyed. One of them got away, though."

Brunt turned and looked across the bridge at him. "No matter. No planet to come back to. No place to go. Won't survive a week out there." He grinned even wider. "Let them go!" He laughed.

His staff laughed with him. As soon as the fires and smoke died down, they would call for the colony ships. Then a myriad of young Bats would be building their dwellings on the planet below, living off the frozen, stacked corpses of the former inhabitants.

Even now, gangs of slaves roamed the planet, collecting bodies and preparing them for refrigeration and storage. The young Bats brought in by the colony ships could live for two years on those stored bodies, giving them ample time to establish their colony.

Brunt turned back to the viewer. It had taken them two days, but they had finally broken through the defenses of the Daneki. And then, once the defenses collapsed, they had spent another week tracking down and killing all the remaining inhabitants of the planet. Except for a few starships that ran at the last minute, none were left. And even those starships were pursued and destroyed.

Except one. Brunt grunted. "No matter," he said. "They'll die in the Pipe!"

*****

Far away, the small Daneki corvette *Matador* plummeted toward the Pipe Nebula, running cold and silent. Two dozen creatures huddled inside, short of food, air, and water, praying to their Creator. Their star system had been only 50 light years from the Pipe Nebula, so they called themselves the Daneki - which in their language, meant 'People by the Smoke'. But their location near the nebula was not enough to escape the expanding empire of the Bats.

An officer sat splay-legged on the floor of the corvette, giving up his seat to a pregnant female. His uniform, once gray, was covered with soot and ash. One of his arms was in a sling; his three-fingered hand was matted with dried blood. Not much different from a Human in appearance, with mostly the same things in the same places, he was five and a half feet tall under normal circumstances. But now he looked like a folded wet rag. Gazing wearily around the ship at the others, he sighed. Getting to his feet, he went up the passageway to the cockpit and entered, sitting on a small jump seat behind the pilots.

"Are we safe?" he asked.

"Aye, sir," replied the Pilot. "We lost 'em."

The officer - a Captain - hung his head for a moment, folding his hands in front of him. Then he looked up. "Where are we headed?"

"Right now, just straight away from them, deeper into the Rim. But we need to make a decision on a destination."

"What are our reserves?" asked the Captain.

"About..." the Pilot looked at the instruments overhead. "About ten days, at minimum use. We're tight on oxygen, a little better on food and water."

"OK. Where do you recommend we go?"

"Well...," the Pilot rubbed his face. "Anywhere but back toward the Bats. So, I'm thinking, we just keep going as we are, straight away from them."

"Any viable planets on that path?"

"Unknown. What with the Pipe Nebula in the way, we don't have much data on the other side, and we've never explored much out that way."

"But we can't go back toward home."

"Only if you want to become Bat fodder".

"OK," sighed the Captain. "Keep a course to the other side of the Pipe, then surface and take some bearings. We need to find someplace we can get air, water, and food. We don't have long in this tin can."

"Understood, sir. We'll do our best."

The Captain clapped a hand on the Pilot's shoulder. "I know

you will."

Captain Cassian went back to the passenger cabin and sank back down in his spot on the floor. A young child stared at him from across the cabin. He smiled a wan smile at the boy, who had lost his parents in the Bat attack on the Daneki Science Hall just a few hours before.

"Are we going to die, sir?" asked the young orphan, Vitus his name.

Cassian shook his head. "No, son. We're not going to die. We're going to find us a planet and then we're going to be just fine."

*****

"Sir?"

Cassian heard the voice from a far distance. He had been watching the Bats snuff out the lives of his squadron again, one by one, in blood and flame. His friends dying, crashing, exploding, buying him the time to get these few survivors out...

"Sir?"

Slowly he roused. Another bad dream. The Copilot was gently shaking his shoulder. "Sir, we have found a planet."

Cassian sat up, shaking off the stiffness of lying on the floor.

"What?"

"Sir, we've found a planet. We think it has water and air, possibly some food."

Cassian, shaking away the last cobwebs from his brain, stood up. The cabin was dark, everyone around him sleeping. "Show me," he said quietly.

They had been running for a week, on short rations. The air was starting to smell bad; they were running out of time.

The Copilot led him to the cockpit. On the small tactical holo between the two pilots was a system display, showing a large gas giant, any number of smaller moons and asteroids, and one rocky world, highlighted.

"That one, sir," pointed the Pilot. "It's in the habitable zone, shows water, oxygen, nitrogen, no concentrations of dangerous gases. There's some chlorophyll, so at least basic plant life."

Cassian clapped the Pilot on the shoulder. "Good work, men. How long until we can be there?"

"Another ten hours, sir. But we'll have to run a close-in survey to see if we can land."

Cassian slapped the Pilot on the shoulder once again, reached over and tapped the Copilot as well. "Excellent job, men. Let me know when we reach orbit. There'll be some happy folks in back if this works out."

*****

Hours later, in orbit around the smallish planet, Cassian was gratified to see clear signs of plant life covering most of the surface of a continent, one sandwiched between two oceans. Remote sensors showed a breathable atmosphere. There was no evidence of dangerous trace gases. There was no sign of civilization.

They decided to put down on the coast of the larger ocean, giving them access to both land and sea.

"Everybody buckle in!" yelled Cassian, standing in the middle of the *Matador's* troop section, hanging on to a strap. "Might get a little bumpy!"

The young boy, Vitus, that Cassian remembered from the escape through the Pipe Nebula was sitting close by him. The boy looked up at him, uncertainly. Cassian winked at him. "Gonna be just fine, son. Just buckle up and hang on!"

In minutes, the corvette started to rock and pitch as they hit the upper atmosphere. For a good ten minutes, it was a roller-coaster ride - corvettes were not really designed to land on planets, although they had the capability in an emergency - but eventually it started to settle down. A few minutes later, the pilots announced over the PA, "Landing in one minute!". A small, half-hearted cheer went up from the passengers.

Aside from Cassian and the pilots, everyone on the ship was

civilian. Cassian had been given orders to evacuate key scientists and their families from the Science Hall – the central scientific facility on Danek. He had barely gotten even this small group out. They had cleared the facility just as it exploded behind them, with a squadron of Bat assault craft right on their tail. Weaving for their lives, they broke atmosphere right into the teeth of a Bat destroyer - and only their speed, and the surprise of their sudden appearance, had caused the destroyer's shots to go wide as they sped away.

Now, as the *Matador* grounded on the beach of this alien planet, sixty light years from their former home, they rose wearily to their feet and opened the hatch. Orange light from the K0 star poured in, not as bright as their home world - but a welcome relief from the dim environment in the ship.

Cassian stepped out and breathed in the cool, crisp air. He sighed. His stomach rumbled with hunger, and his mouth was dry with thirst, but at least he would not suffocate to death.

Following basic military protocol, he unslung a rifle from his shoulder and began a slow walk around the corvette, looking for danger.

He saw bird-like animals flying in the air, not too different from the ones of his home world. A few small beach creatures scuttled away as his footsteps approached. He couldn't help but smile. As he finished his walk round, the Copilot came up to him excitedly.

"Sir! The water is a bit salty, but within limits. Our water processor can handle it!"

"Good, fantastic," said Cassian. "Let's get to it, then."

"Aye, sir!" said the excited Copilot, who turned and yelled at the dazed civilians wandering aimlessly around the beach. "All able-bodied males come with me! We need to run a hose down to the water!'

Cassian turned toward the females and children, who had stopped at the sound and were looking toward him.

Cassian shouted to them, "Everyone who isn't working on the water treatment, come with me! Let's find out if anything is edible here!"

He turned and walked toward the verge of grass and plants set back from the beach. Behind him he heard the footsteps of the females and children following. Together they walked up the sand until they came to an area of plant life, just short of a forest. Many of the plants bore flowers - some carried things that looked like fruit.

"Here, take these," said Cassian, handing several of the older females a small stick-like plant tester. "Each of you with a tester, stay here in one place." He turned to the others.

"Everyone else, spread out and bring back samples of the plant life - leaves or fruit or flowers, whatever looks like it might be edible - to the testers."

"Testers! Test each plant item they bring you by poking the test probe into the surface of the leaves or fruit. You'll get a readout that shows if the item is safe to eat. No guarantee of taste, of course. Just an indicator that it won't kill you. If it tests dangerous, throw it into a pile behind you, over there." He pointed.

"And if it tests safe, give it a taste. Anything that tastes too horrible to eat, throw into another pile behind you, on the other side, here..." Once again, he pointed.

"And anything you can tolerate to eat, put into a third pile, right in front of you." He pointed again. "When you have a few good items, set everybody to gathering in those things."

Cassian turned and scanned the ocean. Far away, he saw a huge marine animal broach the surface, blow air and sink back down again.

Cassian felt a small twinge of hope. They were still probably dead, he thought, like the rest of his people.

But there was a slight chance of life - if the stars aligned.

NEMESIS

AEN Nemesis – *a destroyer of the Aeolian Empire Navy (AEN), named after the ancient Greek god of retribution.* Nemesis *was laid down on 6 May 2181 at Nyx Shipyards on Aeolis and was launched on 25 March 2182. After additional outfitting, she was commissioned on 27 October 2182, Princess-Captain Hecate Aronte in command.*

- *RimWiki, 2230 Edition*

12 April 2185
Beehive Cluster - Planet Marinas
AEN Spacedock *Hercules*

"*Hercules* Approach, Destroyer *Nemesis,* ready for docking," intoned Comm Officer Atropos.

Hecate slumped wearily in the captain's chair, looking at the holotank before her as they approached the space station floating above the planet.

"Three damn weeks," she spat. "Three damn weeks and not a damn thing to show for it."

Her XO, Andrea Iona, commiserated with her. "I know, Skipper. And we're all tired. But we'll feel better after this shore stop."

"I don't want to stop!" exclaimed Hecate.

"I know, Skip," said Andrea. "But we need to re-supply. And the crew could use a break."

Hecate growled. "I know. But I don't have to like it."

Andrea smiled as a loud "clunk" signaled the docking maneuver was complete. "C'mon, Skipper. Let's go get our supplies. And maybe a drink at a bar?"

"Not for me, thanks," said Hecate. "I'm going to stay aboard and work on some charts. That black daughter of Hell has got to be around here somewhere."

"Mum," said Comm Officer Atropos. "I've just received a strange message. It has our codes, but it's not from Fleet. Looks like it came from the planet."

"What?" exclaimed Hecate and Andrea at the same time.

Atropos flicked the message to them. Hecate read the message in her vision holo and looked at Andrea, puzzled.

Muttering, Andrea finished her scan of the message. "If you want the Black Ship, come to Minerva's Temple at 10 pm. Sit in back, order a Red Death." Andrea looked around at the officers on the bridge. "What's a Red Death?"

Lt. Atropos grinned. "9-parts vodka and 1-part red coolant fluid from the engine room of a starship. At least that's the claim, I've never had one."

Andrea looked back at Hecate. "What the hell you think this means?"

Hecate bared her teeth. "I think it means I'll go ashore after all."

Two hours later, Hecate and Andrea stood outside the bar called Minerva's Temple on the planet Marinas, gazing at the neon-lit entrance. She and Andrea were dressed in civvies, nothing too flashy – well, at least for Hecate. Andrea didn't have a non-flashy civilian outfit in her wardrobe, but Hecate had persuaded her to choose one that could possibly pass as conservative, at least in the dark.

Andrea Iona Satra was near six feet tall, with jet-black hair and flashing brown eyes, and a body hard as nails. From a minor branch of the Aronte dynasty - no longer in the line of succession - the Satra clan were all pure warriors, and nothing but. Raised as a ward of the Imperial family after both her parents were killed in the Fringe Rebellion, Andrea was a distant cousin to Hecate. There was not another person in the Empire Hecate would prefer beside her in time of trouble.

But conservative clothing was not in her vocabulary.

In contrast, Hecate was not as dark, her hair a light brown, almost red, and her complexion much lighter – an anomaly among Amazons. Although an inch shorter than Andrea, like most Imperials she carried herself like the royalty she was, even if unconsciously. It was an inbred trait she never considered. Due simply to the way they moved and spoke, it was unlikely either Hecate or Andrea could pass for commoners.

Placed discreetly at key points around the building was a squad of Hecate's Marines. Another squad, in plain clothes, had wandered into the bar over the course of the last couple of hours, their weapons tucked discreetly out of sight.

"Well, shall we?" asked Andrea.

"We shall," responded Hecate. They walked into the bar, pausing inside the entrance to let their eyes adjust.

Tucked in one corner was a live band. In the center of the room was a dance floor, with couples writhing to a hard-driving song. They noted their Marine bodyguards spaced randomly around the club, avoiding eye contact.

On the right side of the room was a row of tables, filled with couples hanging out near the dance floor. On the left side were booths with patrons eating dinner. At the back of the club were a few booths out of the direct hubbub.

"I've been here before," said Andrea. "It's a hot place! Wish we could stay!"

Hecate grinned at her. Andrea's reputation as a hell-raiser was legend in the Fleet. She knew if Andrea had been here before, she had probably shut the place down and spent the night in jail.

Snaking their way through the club, avoiding the press of people around the dance floor, they came to a vacant booth in the back row. Hardly had they sat when a slave appeared.

"What can I get the fine ladies?" he said, bowing low, his eyes averted.

"Bring me a Red Death," said Hecate.

"I'll have the same," said Andrea.

The slave's eyes twitched, but he said only, "It shall be done, my ladies," and turned quickly away.

Andrea watched him scuttle back toward the kitchen; her eyes narrowed.

"He's as nervous as a chicken on Prophecy Day," she said.

The band finished up their song and launched into an even louder one, the music blaring. As they waited, tolerating the noise, a woman appeared next to the booth. She leaned over and spoke just loudly enough to be heard.

"Follow me," she said. Without another word, she turned and walked down the hallway toward the kitchen.

With a quick glance at Hecate, Andrea left the booth and followed, Hecate close behind her. The woman ahead of them never looked back. She crossed the kitchen area, passed through, and continued down the hallway beyond. There she pressed a wall panel on the left side and a door popped open. She went through and turned, gesturing for Andrea and Hecate to follow her.

Stepping through the panel, Hecate and Andrea emerged into another hallway. Following this for several meters, the woman stopped at another doorway.

"In here," she said.

Andrea and Hecate paused at the door. "You are safe," said the woman, with a slight smile. "No one here wants to hurt you, and your Marines can track you even back here. Please enter, Minerva would like to speak with you."

Andrea looked at Hecate, who nodded. Andrea pressed a small button on her wrist comm, signifying to their security team all was well, and they stepped through the doorway to find a large room, with a wooden table running nearly the full length. An older woman, richly dressed with jewels in her hair and draped around her neck, sat placidly awaiting them, seated at the table.

Hecate smiled at her. "Hello. You must be Minerva," she said.

"I am," said the woman. She looked to be seventy-five or eighty years old and wore the traditional *peplos* of the most conservative members of Aeolian female society - ancient Greek clothing long abandoned by most of the population.

Hecate sat across from her. She felt Andrea take a protective position behind. Minerva said nothing, merely staring at Hecate, until Hecate decided to speak first.

"You sent me a message?"

"You look a bit like him," said Minerva.

"What? Like who?" asked Hecate.

"Your grandfather," said Minerva.

Hecate was confused. "My grandfather? You mean, Prince Themistius?"

Minerva smiled enigmatically. "No, I mean Zeno."

Hecate held a puzzled expression on her face. "Zeno? Zeno died over forty years ago. He was killed on Barcam."

"Ah." Minerva cocked her head. "Is that what they told you? Well, a good story, that is. But nevertheless, he has left you a message. Do you want to hear it?"

Behind her, Andrea spoke up. "What are you playing at? Spirit messages from the dead?"

Without turning her face away from the old woman, Hecate held up a hand, stopping Andrea. "Let her speak, XO," she said. Looking directly at the old woman, she went on. "There were rumors he survived that attack. There was even an old story when I was a child..."

Here Hecate paused. Minerva grinned. "An old story, indeed, there was. That he came from someplace far from here...and that he returned there, still living."

Andrea gasped behind Hecate. Hecate looked stonily at the old woman. "Speak your piece then, old woman, and be done with it."

"Aye, I will." said Minerva. "I have a message from your grandfather, you may take it or disregard it, I care not. He says, 'If you want the Black Ship, you'll find it at Pestilence Port. But take care that it's the true enemy and not a true friend.' "

Hecate stared. "Pestilence Port? That's a pirate's den, to be sure, but we have already had...people...report back to us. There is nothing there."

Minerva laughed. "Your spies, you mean? I doubt they would be able to see the Black Ship if it were docked in front of them."

Andrea, behind Hecate, spoke up. "How can you say this message came from Hecate's grandfather?"

Minerva frowned. "I have delivered the message as I was asked. I have nothing more to tell you. And you should be careful on your way back to your ship – there are many in this port who would do you harm. I suggest you leave by the back door."

Hecate sat in thought for a moment, then rose from her chair. "Thank you, Minerva Mistress. I will take your message to heart."

Turning to Andrea, she touched her elbow. "Let's go."

But as they headed for the door, Hecate heard Minerva's last whisper: "Surely, you do look like him."

*****

Slipping out the back door of the bar, Hecate and Andrea headed back to the ship, keeping a wary eye out for trouble. As they entered the port area, Andrea turned towards Hecate. "What the hell was that all about? How could your grandfather still be alive?"

"I don't know," replied Hecate. "My mother Deinomache always told me he was exiled to Barcam after she was born - and died there the following year."

"But why was he exiled?" asked Andrea, walking beside her.

"He was not of the Blood," said Hecate. "He could not remain on Aeolis. As soon as my mother Deinomache was born, he was sent into exile. He was from Barcam, so that is where he was returned. He was reported killed in the Rebellion when the fleet bombarded Barcam."

Andrea mused on that information. "So, he could not be alive now to give you a message."

Hecate paused for a bit before replying. "There was a rumor, which was always denied by my Auntie...that he survived."

Andrea nodded. "But why would Auntie Empress deny it, if

he was still alive?"

Hecate grimaced. "You don't know my Auntie. She would stonewall on something like that forever, before she would admit that a commoner who fathered a child on an Imperial Princess still lived and breathed somewhere at the end of the Empire."

Andrea thought on this for a while. "So... he could be alive yet. But he would be, what...at least 70 or 80 years old."

"I guess anything is possible."

They walked for a while. Finally, Hecate said, "You didn't ask about the other."

"What?"

"I heard you gasp when Minerva mentioned that he came from someplace far away. So, I guess you've heard that rumor also."

Andrea snorted. "That he was an Earther? More nonsense from the Earther Cults?"

"Careful, Andrea. My father died trying to prove the existence of the Earthers." But Hecate had a smile on her face as she said it. She knew Andrea would always be her staunchest ally, regardless of her outspoken nature.

"I just meant...well, I know that your father was a believer in the Earther legends, and he was chasing after that Black Ship trying to prove something about them. And I wouldn't say anything bad about him, you know that. But nobody puts much stock in that silly rumor...that your grandfather was an Earther, I mean."

Hecate nodded. "I never did before..." But her voice trailed off, and she walked lost in thought the rest of the way to the shuttle. She never noticed the quiet little man following them, his comm bead flashing briefly from time to time.

*****

Aboard ship, Hecate gave orders to prep the ship for departure as soon as supplies were loaded, and the crew returned from shore leave. Then she asked Andrea to accompany her to her quarters. Sitting at her desk, she motioned Andrea to a chair and said, "I want to watch it again."

Andrea sighed. "Hecate..."

"I know, I know," said Hecate.

Andrea shook her head. "It hurts you so. I can't stand to see you in such pain.

"It's OK," said Hecate. "Something is still bothering me. And now I keep thinking about what Minerva said."

"What do you mean?" asked Andrea.

" 'Take care that it's the true enemy and not a true friend.' I want to see it again."

"Oh, Hecate...please don't." said Andrea.

Hecate spoke: "Sensorium, activate."

<Activated> replied the AI.

"Show us the record from my father's last mission," she ordered.

The room disappeared around her and Andrea. Once again, as several times before, they found themselves on the bridge of her father's ship just before it was destroyed. She had re-lived this scenario many times since her father's death, and each time it cut her more. But something was nagging at her now.

The sensorium was as real as if they were there. She saw the bridge, with the captain and her father seated behind the holotank, and the consoles arranged around it. She saw the Black Ship in the holotank, running hard away from her father's research vessel, pulling away - it was faster. It was clearly headed for empty space away from the star, so it could hit FTL and be gone.

"They're still accelerating," said the Captain. "Hail them again."

"Aye, sir." said the Comm Officer. She touched her screen and spoke.

"Unknown ship near Ptolema, please talk to us. We will not harm you; we only wish to speak with you. We are a research vessel, not a warship. We only wish to communicate with you."

They paused, watching. There was no change in aspect. The black ship continued to run.

The Captain spoke again: "No chance of catching them, Tac?"

"No, Mum. They are quite a bit faster than us in 3-space. They mean to make the mass limit and sink out."

"Yes," said Prince Alexander. "But why? Why won't they talk to us?"

"Sir, I've never seen a ship like that. Nothing in the Empire looks like that," said the Captain. "But we'll never catch her."

The Tactical Officer suddenly jumped in her seat. "Aspect change! Mum! She's coming about!"

"What?" asked the Captain. "Why?"

In the holotank, the black ship ceased acceleration and spun back toward them. As her nose came around to bear, pale blue fire came from a beamer. There was a flash - and the bridge disappeared in fire and screaming.

* * * * *

Hecate bowed her head, tears rolling down her cheeks. Andrea came over to her and placed a hand on her shoulder. Hecate placed her own fingers on top of Andrea's for a few seconds, but then took them away, straightened her head and dabbed at her eyes.

"I'm OK," she said. "I'm OK."

"Did you see anything different this time?" asked Andrea bitterly.

"No." said Hecate. "It's always the same." She hesitated. "But...there's something."

"What?" said Andrea.

"I don't know. I can't put my finger on it. But it has something to do with the beamer fire..."

"What about it?" asked Andrea.

"The beamer from the Black Ship. It almost looks like they fired before they were fully around."

"Agreed," said Andrea. "We've talked about this."

"Bear with me," said Hecate. "They fired early. Clearly, they have good tech - their frigate was faster than a corvette - but still they fired early. Why?

"Again, agreed," said Andrea. "But still, they hit the corvette and destroyed it."

Hecate nodded. "OK. But that weapon looks awfully like the beam weapons used in our frigates and cruisers. Slightly different pulse components, but essentially the same technology."

"Yep," said Andrea.

"And our beam weapons are phenomenally accurate at that range, but they have a pretty tight beam. You have to be right on target. If that weapon is basically similar to our beams, I'm just not sure she had enough bearing on target to hit the corvette."

"So, they have more spread than we do." said Andrea. "We've talked about this."

Hecate thought. "And the other thing that bothers me is they had just passed that little moon off to the left." She stopped.

Andrea nodded.

"It almost looks like they were firing toward the moon, not the corvette."

Andrea shook her head. "And why would they do that?"

Hecate mused. "Because there was another ship there?"

Andrea grimaced. "They shot at another ship? But then..."

Hecate looked at her. "Then the other ship killed my father."

"Hecate, we can't know that. Every indication we have is that the Black Ship was shooting at the corvette. We have to act on that assumption. If we find that ship, we have to treat it as an enemy."

Hecate nodded. "OK, I get that. But...if we find it...I don't want to shoot first and ask questions later. I want to at least give them a chance to talk to us."

"Dangerous," said Andrea. "Not by the book. You're either going to get us shot up, court-martialed, or killed."

Hecate smiled. "Just let me handle the court-martial part. And you handle the part about not getting us shot up or killed."

DISCOVERED

War does not determine who is right, only who is left.
- Bertrand Russell, Philosopher

550 Light Years from Earth
Near the Pipe Nebula

Later in the evening, the refugees from Danek had a bonfire by the sea. They had found several suitable plants and one of them was a potato-like item, quite tasty when roasted. Wrapped in a succulent leaf, it felt like heaven to their empty bellies when they had them cooked and were able to wolf them down.

They had packed away hundreds of pounds of these and other edible items, in the reefer on the corvette. Their water tanks were full.

His passengers had asked Cassian why they could not just remain on the planet; but Cassian reminded them that they were only days away from the newly enlarged Bat dominions.

"A planet like this," he said, "will be scouted by them soon enough. They're moving in this direction now. We were safe for hundreds of years while they went Coreward, but now they've turned back toward the Rim. So, we can't stay here; we have to put a lot more distance between us and the Bats if we want to survive."

There was a silence as they absorbed that.

"But what if we don't find another planet that we can live on?" asked the young boy, Vitus.

Cassian rubbed the stubble on his cheeks. "We have stores now for a bit over a month of travel. We'll go another two weeks out toward the Rim, see what we can find. If we find nothing in that time, we'll sneak back in here, replenish, and set off in a different direction. But we don't have much choice. If we stay here, we die. That's the reality of it."

Vitus nodded. "So which direction will we go?"

"The pilots have picked out a system a little over two weeks from here, which looks promising. We won't know for sure until we get closer, of course, but we're going to give it a try." Cassian turned and squinted up into the clear night sky. "About there, I think," he said, pointing.

Young Vitus turned and squinted up into the sky, as if he could see 250 light years. Cassian grinned.

Soon they would know - if they would live, or if they would die. But tonight, they were alive. It was good.

*****

Next morning, the early light of their new planet shone brightly in the cockpit windows. The ocean surf thundered to their left, and the green forest stood to their right.

Cassian watched as another of the large marine creatures broached far offshore, its back rolling blackly as it crested and returned to the deep, a sign of the life they were leaving behind in this temporary haven.

"Ready to depart the planet, sir," said the Pilot.

"Good," said Cassian. "Cabin's ready, everybody strapped in. Let's go." He settled deeper into the jump seat and tugged his belts tighter, anticipating a rough ride out of the atmosphere.

The *Matador* groaned a bit as it lifted from the soil and slowly began moving upward, not really designed for the work it was doing. After a dozen minutes, they began to reach thinner air and the corvette accelerated, breaking out into space a minute later.

"Contact!" yelled the CoPilot. "Bat destroyer, coming around the planet!"

"Dammit!" cursed Cassian. "Get us out of here, guys!"

The Pilot slammed the throttles forward past the emergency

stop and the *Matador* jumped like a racehorse, slamming Cassian back into the jump seat and banging his head against a fire extinguisher mounted on the back wall of the cockpit. He saw stars in his vision; but managed to stay conscious.

"Go, go, go!" he shouted, as a beamer blast zipped by the cockpit, not more than fifty meters away. He could feel the heat from it. The pilot juked, and Cassian was once more slammed against the back of the cockpit. As everything went black, he could only think, "We came so close."

*****

Slowly, his awareness returned. Cassian realized he was still strapped into the jump seat. Something was dripping down his face and eye. He touched it and realized it was blood, mostly congealed. He tried to pull the mess away but was not very successful.

"What happened?" he mumbled.

The Pilot turned and looked at him. "Back with us, eh?" He turned in his seat and took a cloth from his flight jacket, dabbing at Cassian's eyes until the cloth was red with blood - but at least Cassian could see again.

Cassian managed to lift himself and look around. Outside the cockpit, he could see the fuzzy black nothingness of six-space and knew they had sunk out and were running. "Where are we?" he asked.

The Pilot nodded, "We're on a random vector. I couldn't take us to the system we planned, the destroyer was right on our tail, and he saw our vector when we came out of atmosphere. That was my mistake, I should have come out on a random vector, but I didn't think that far ahead.

Anyway, I did a couple of random jukes, put the planet in between us, and ran for the mass limit. By the time they came around the planet and got on our tail again, we were out of their beamer range. They shot four missiles at us, but I managed to dodge them. As soon as we hit the mass limit, I sank out, then ran for a bit, surfaced, took a random vector, and sank out again. I had to do it several times before we finally lost them."

Cassian held the cloth against his head, staunching the blood. "So where are we headed?"

The Pilot shook his head. "Nowhere. They'll be searching all the nearby F, G, K, M type stars looking for us. I had to take a vector to the most unlikely place possible to lose them. I just picked a random A-type, a system not likely to have any habitable planets. I thought that might work to lose them. Maybe we can find a moon on a gas giant there with some atmosphere. If not, I think we'll have to try to sneak back to the planet we just left, but they'll be watching there for sure. We don't have a lot of options."

Cassian's head thudded from an enormous headache. "What's the chances of finding a moon with an atmosphere in an A-type system?"

The Pilot looked at the Copilot grimly. "Not worth a damn, sir. Not worth a damn."

Cassian sighed. "Do we have enough consumables to make it there and then back here?"

"Just barely," said the Pilot.

"OK, we'll go take a look," said Cassian. "When we get there, we'll survey the area for any other systems we can reach which might have a habitable planet. If none are within our range, we'll come back here and try to sneak in long enough to re-supply."

"Sir, I think you should go clean up, take care of that head wound," said the Pilot. "Nothing is going to happen for a long while now."

"Roger that," said Cassian. Slowly he got up from his seat and went back to the cabin.

* * * * *

Later, Cassian lay sleeping on the floor of the corvette. Young Vitus had somehow found him a few rags for a pillow.

In his dreams, Cassian saw the Bat assault craft at the

Science Hall, firing their cannons into the building. He saw his squadron cut down, ships crashing to the ground and exploding, as they bought him time to get these precious scientists away. He trembled in his sleep.

Vitus lay down beside him and reached over and placed his arm around the sleeping officer. Together they slept fitfully, in dreams of their own.

BLACK SHIP

The soldier above all others prays for peace, for it is the soldier who must suffer and bear the deepest wounds and scars of war.
- General Douglas MacArthur

22 April 2185
Beehive Cluster - Near Pestilence Port

"Out of six-space, Captain." said the Tac Officer.

"Very good, Reah," said Hecate. "Set a course for Pestilence Port and keep us stealthed. If anybody is going to be surprised out here, I want it to be the other guys."

"Roger, Mum," confirmed Reah.

Andrea grinned. "Like a lion lurking among the sheep."

"A small lion," said Hecate. "Let's not pick on anybody bigger than us."

Turning back to the Tac Officer, Hecate asked, "What do we have in the system, Reah?"

"Well," said Reah, "We have the A5-class star, two small rocky planets in close that are too hot for habitation, three gas giants out in the edge of the system with a lot of moons, and a ton of junk all around. It's a really cluttered-up system. Pestilence Port is on the largest moon of the innermost gas giant, basically a mining colony, low population. We have about a twelve-hour run-in to the port."

"OK. Any threat areas I should be aware of, maybe a good place for an ambush?"

"Oh, tons of them," said Reah. "Just take your pick. Like I said, a very cluttered up, junky system. Rocks everywhere."

Hecate sighed. "OK. Keep your eyes peeled. This could very

well be an ambush scenario. Let's not get caught with our knickers down."

"Roger, Skipper." agreed the Tactical Officer.

As the *Nemesis* moved into the system, Hecate sat loosely in her command chair, while Andrea paced the bridge from console to console, looking over shoulders, cocked for action.

Hecate smiled. That is why they were such a good team. She was the relaxed, thoughtful one, Andrea was the tightly wound spring. But if anything happened, both knew exactly how the other would react and how to use that to their advantage.

Hecate was no protected, cosseted Princess of the Blood. Princess Deinomache, her mother, had also been a Fleet Navy Officer, and had worked her way up to Frigate Captain. Throughout Hecate's childhood, it had been understood she would serve in the Navy, and she had been prepared accordingly. Like all members of the Imperial family, she had trained in hand-to-hand combat from the age of six, mastered hand weapons and armor by ten, started flying her own flitter at thirteen, and flew her first space shuttle at fourteen. By the age of eighteen she had graduated from the Imperial Naval College at Aronte and entered the Fleet.

And she had worked her way up the hard way - never once using her blood or her title for advancement. Now, at twenty-seven, she was a destroyer Captain, and would soon be in line for a frigate.

"Contact!" yelled the Tac Officer. "I have a stealthed destroyer, barely visible, coming out from that big asteroid behind us, vectoring for our six, I designate DD1."

"Battle Stations!" yelled Andrea. She turned to Hecate. "It's an ambush, for sure."

As the klaxon sounded both overhead and in their internal comms, Hecate assessed the picture in the holo.

"Bring us about forty-five degrees to the left, Helm, and make for that big moon over there by the outermost gas giant. Up to max standard. Let's get some protection behind that moon. Get our weapons hot, Guns. Comm, hail this bitch and see if she wants to talk."

"Aye, Mum," said the Weapons Officer and Comm Officer simultaneously.

"No response, ma'am. Still coming on, still stealthed. If we didn't have the new Mark II detectors, we wouldn't even know she was there."

"Thank God's thumb for that," said Andrea. She glanced at Hecate briefly. "I wonder if Auntie knows we have those..."

Hecate shushed her. "Not now, Andrea. What's it looking like, Tac?"

"Still coming hard, ma'am. She's gonna have us right about the time we get to that moon. Whoever she is, she's got a Mark II also. She's right on us."

"OK, let's plan on a tight perigee with a vector change as we go around that moon, I want to scrape dirt off the tops of the mountains and come around it with enough vector change to make exit a good 20 degrees off vector from our inbound track. Let's see if we can fox this lady. Prepare for excess g's."

The klaxon, which had stopped, sounded again with the singsong of the excess g warning, letting crew members know they were about to exceed the limits of the compensator.

"Contact!" yelled the Tac Officer. "I have another stealthed destroyer, coming from behind the moon we're making for, designate DD2. It's a setup!"

"Damn!" yelled Hecate. "I walked right into it!"

Andrea yelled at the Helm, "Roll our belly armor to the bitch in front of us, she's closer, and get us the hell out of here!"

"Aye, Mum!"

"Guns, open fire with everything!" yelled Andrea.

“Too close for missiles, Mum,” yelled the Weapons Officer. “They won’t arm before they hit!”

"We're gonna get pounded," observed Hecate. "Hang on, everybody."

The *Nemesis*’ railgun cannon let loose their first shots with deep thumps that shook the whole ship. At the same time, the Tac Officer yelled, "Incoming!" and then the sharp, metallic clang of a cannon round striking the armored belly of the destroyer nearly knocked everyone off their feet.

"This bitch can shoot," yelled Andrea. "Waggle and Wobble, Helm. Guns, anything?"

"Aye, mum, we hit her once. No obvious damage, but she knows we're here."

"Let's do a little better than that. Keep firing!"

Deep thumps from the aft cannons showed that the Weapons Officer had already decided that. But that was immediately followed by two more incoming cannon rounds striking their belly, in quick succession.

"They've both got our range now." said Tac. "We're bracketed."

"Max Emergency, Helm!" yelled Andrea, diving for her command chair, and immediately got knocked to the floor as the Helm rather enthusiastically firewalled the engines to full emergency power, the initial 202g thrust exceeding the limits of the compensator by 2gs, then rising quickly as the AI piled on as much as it thought the Humans inside the tin can could tolerate.

With the destroyer on a random walk course away from the two enemy ships, the g-forces pushed Hecate deep into her seat while the random walk from the AI jerked her back and forth against her straps. As the g-force built to the destroyer's max of 207g - 7 g over the limit of the compensator, crushing them into their seats - Andrea managed to finish crawling into her combat chair and strap herself in, blood oozing from her nose but otherwise seemingly OK.

Hecate wondered how many broken bones this battle would cost the crew; but there was no choice. She was in a crossfire between two ships of equal size and firepower to hers, and both had her range. She had to change the equation. "Be ready, Guns!" she grunted.

"Aye, ma'am" groaned Guns under the g-force. As their relative angle to the pursuers behind them opened a bit, Hecate heard her own aft cannons blazing away, alternating between the two pursuers. All three ships pounded each other for several seconds as Hecate rushed away from the battle line and the other ships twisted toward her.

"Contact!" groaned the Tac Officer. "Another one, right in front of us, in stealth, just waiting for us, DD3!"

"Crap!" spat Andrea.

Hecate smiled grimly, shaking her head. "They've really got us in a box, Andy. Our only choice is to go right through this one. Helm - ram that bitch in front of us!"

"Aye, mum!" yelled the Helm, her voice quavering.

The Weapons officer launched all four of the *Nemesis*' missiles at the destroyer in front of them, but they were so close that only one of them armed before reaching the target. It exploded near the other destroyer, but somewhat behind it, not doing any real damage.

With her aft cannons alternating between the two pursuers now boxing her in from behind, the *Nemesis* charged toward the new enemy, firing both forward cannons as fast as possible at the ship before her, alarms flashing across the board.

"Overheat on all cannon, Captain!" yelled Guns, her face shiny with sweat.

"Keep firing, keep firing!" yelled Hecate as the ships rushed together.

"Mum..." called the Helm, as they were a few seconds from collision.

"Do! Not! Flinch!" yelled Hecate. At that moment, a tremendous explosion struck their ship, as the destroyer closest behind them scored a direct hit on their engines. The blast spun them to the side, an instant before they flicked by the ship in front, missing by less than a hundred meters. The lights went out, and every screen on the bridge went dark.

The force of the explosion had knocked Hecate hard against the side of the command chair; she thought a rib was probably broken. Overhead, the emergency battle lights came on, building slowly to full intensity. The holotank flickered and resumed operation on battery power. But the picture it painted was not good.

Andrea grunted in pain beside her, then whispered bitterly, "They've got us."

Hecate nodded. "Yep. We're dead in the water. Guns are disabled, main engines are out, and we're just coasting along like so much junk. They'll come in and finish us off."

*****

Minutes later, smoke lay over the bridge, drifting in the light of the emergency battle lamps. They had managed to get the spin of the ship under control using docking thrusters; but everything else was out.

Andrea stood behind the auxiliary command console and laid two rifles on top, facing the bridge entry. She shook her head. "Hecate, think what you are saying."

Hecate paused from stacking extra ammo charges behind her own console and stared at Andrea. "Andrea, think about it. We get ambushed by three destroyers. All three clearly had Mark II detectors. A perfect setup. This is Navy."

In the holotank, the three enemy destroyers approached cautiously, a few minutes from boarding them.

Andrea shuddered. "Hecate, no...it can't be..."

Hecate glared at her. "Let's be realistic. You know Auntie. You know she's capable of anything. And now...I think we know who set up the ambush for my father, too."

Andrea put her hands over her ears, as if to block out the sound. Then, taking her hands away, Andrea went on. "Why? Why would Auntie Empress want to kill you? Or your father? He was no threat to her - why would she do that? He was about as disinterested in Palace business as anyone I've ever known. All he wanted to do was to pursue his stupid Earther theories. And you - you're what, third in line?"

Hecate sighed. "Actually, second. But my Mom is young. So, I’m a long way from a threat to Auntie. But this is a crazy world we live in. This is a setup, and it’s Navy, and that means it's Auntie."

Andrea thought out loud. "I take it that means, there'll be no survivors."

Hecate grimaced. "You got it. That's why they're boarding us, to make sure."

Commander Andrea Iona Satra gave a big smile. "Good, then I don't have to worry about accidentally killing any good guys!" She hefted her pulse rifle, checking the charge for the second time since they had passed out weapons for their last-ditch stand.

Hecate gestured to the Tac Officer. "Make sure everybody has spare ammunition and..."

"Contact!" yelled the Tac Officer. "Frigate, designate FF1. I think...it's the Black Ship!"

Hecate turned to the holotank. The wedge-shaped Black Ship appeared well above and off their port beam, moving backwards in a hard combat decel, just coming into range equidistant between the three enemy destroyers. Before Hecate could even think, the much larger frigate class beam weapons and cannon of the Black Ship lashed out multiple times in succession, faster than any destroyer could hope to return fire. Within seconds, all three enemy destroyers were hit, and hit hard. The one closest to them, off their tail, shed several large fragments. Firing back, the three destroyers hit the frigate but with no apparent effect, their rounds glancing off the front wedge of the frigate while making bright yellow flashes.

Hecate yelled. "Guns - get me a weapon! Anything!"

The Weapons Officer stared at her. "If I drop life support, comp and lights, I think I can get one rail gun up for about thirty seconds."

"Do it!" yelled Hecate.

The lights dropped, and gravity went away. The Weapons console powered up. Hecate stared at the holo. The black frigate fired again at the destroyer directly in front of them, and it began to turn away, preparing to run.

Hecate yelled at Guns. "That one! The instant you see her ass, let her have it!"

As the fleeing destroyer made its turn, its engines came into view. Instantly the Weapons Officer fired the rail gun. Too fast for the eye to follow, a huge railgun slug entered the starboard engine of the enemy destroyer. The destroyer exploded in a fireball, shredding metal in every direction, including dozens of fragments that came back toward the *Nemesis,* pounding against the hull like rain.

Seconds later, as the other two enemy destroyers were lashed hard by the black frigate's fire, they tried to accelerate away from the action. As they powered away, another one exploded in a fireball. The Black Ship continued to fire at the third enemy destroyer as it departed, taking bits and pieces off it - until suddenly its engines quit and it coasted, bleeding air and debris, on a course to nowhere.

* * * * *

Inside the bridge, Guns powered down the rail gun and her console. Slowly the battle lamps came back on, dim and barely visible, gravity came back, and the air handlers started up again.

“Zeus’s Balls!” breathed Andrea Iona. She hit the "Off" switch on the pulse rifle she was holding, and it began whining down as it returned to an inactive status. Hecate realized she was also still holding a powered pulse rifle and hit the "Off" switch on it as well.

The Comm officer lifted her head. "Mum, we're being hailed!"

Hecate looked at her, in shock. "Put it on," she said.

A female voice came over their comms: "...assistance? Repeating, Rim Defense Force Frigate *Paris* to Aeolian Destroyer *Nemesis*, may we offer assistance? Over."

FRIGATE

Only the laws of the spirit remain always the same.
- Native American Proverb

Onboard the Frigate RDF Paris

Hecate stepped off the AEN *Nemesis* onto the improvised docking adapter. She took another two steps; the third took her off the docking adapter onto the RDF *Paris*. Close behind her came Andrea Iona.

A strange warbling sounded as she entered the Black Ship; two ratings and two officers on each side snapped to attention and saluted her as she entered the bay; she was shocked to see one of the officers was male. Behind her, she heard Andrea Iona gasp at the sight.

A man on one end of the honor guard was holding a whistle in his mouth, blowing the warbling tone. A tall female officer standing next to him stepped forward and spoke in perfect Aeolian. "Welcome aboard, Princess-Captain. I'm the XO, Commander Prentiss. If you'll follow me, I'll take you to the Admiral's day cabin."

Hecate nodded curtly and followed her out of the entrance bay, down a passageway and then, after a turn, along another passageway to a stairwell. Up the stairwell they went, and directly onto the bridge of the starship.

Hecate had little time to look around; but she noted this bridge was much larger than the one on the *Nemesis*. Several command chairs sat to the rear of a large central holotank, easily three times the size of the one on her destroyer. Operational consoles were arranged in rows behind the holotank, facing forward. Before she could register more, Commander Prentiss led them through a hatch into a cabin on the port side of the bridge.

The cabin contained a conference room. As they entered, a man stood up from the far side of the table. His uniform was remarkably like that of the Aeolian Navy dress uniform, white, with gold trim and buttons. His shoulder boards contained four gold stripes.

Commander Prentiss announced her. "Captain Egan, Princess-Captain Hecate Andromache Aronte and her XO, Commander Andrea Iona Satra."

Captain Egan stepped forward and reached out a hand to Hecate in a strange gesture. In something of a daze, she extended hers forward also. He shook her hand up and down.

How strange, she thought, to see male officers – and a Captain at that! She couldn't help but turn to look at Andrea, who was standing beside her with her mouth open.

"Welcome to the *Paris*, Princess-Captain," Captain Egan said in perfect Aeolian. "Please, take a seat and make yourself comfortable. We have a lot to talk about."

Hecate lowered herself carefully into one of the chairs on the side of the table, her ribs still sore and tightly bandaged. Andrea sat beside her. Captain Egan sat across the table from Hecate, looking at her intently. He seemed to be studying her face; but then abruptly spoke.

"We have sent all available personnel to your ship to help your damage control teams. I trust they are being helpful?"

Hecate nodded. "Thank you very much."

The Captain grimaced. "Well, it's certainly not enough to make up for us being late to the party. We had originally intended to be here waiting for you when you came into the system, but we were unavoidably delayed a few minutes. Please accept my deepest apologies for what happened to you and your crew."

Hecate nodded. "I understand. We're just grateful that you came when you did. Another ten minutes and we'd have been fighting hand-to-hand in the passageways."

Captain Egan nodded in turn. "Yes, I know. Again, my sincere regrets that we couldn't get here sooner."

"But where...where did you come from?" burst out Andrea.

Captain Egan grinned at her. "You mean originally? Or just recently?"

Andrea grinned back and exclaimed, "Both!"

"Most recently, we've been en route from Pestuda. We had to make an emergency stop there due to an injured crew member, and it threw us just a bit later than anticipated to get back over here to Pestilence Port."

Hecate breathed, "And originally?"

"Earth, of course," said Captain Egan.

There was dead silence in the room.

Captain Egan looked at them askance. "You seem surprised," he said.

Hecate frowned. "Earth is just a legend to us, a myth. I never believed it was real."

Now it was Captain Egan's turn to look puzzled. "But...I thought your father was a firm believer in the Earther legends, and in fact devoted the best part of his adult life trying to prove them!"

Hecate shook her head. "That doesn't mean I took them seriously. It's the official policy of our government that those are just myths, with no basis in fact."

"Ah," said Captain Egan.

"So...I... I never believed in them like my father did. I just thought he was chasing ghosts...just a hobby..."

Hecate stopped. She lowered her head. Tears came into her eyes.

Andrea Iona placed a hand on Hecate's shoulder lightly. "Let's talk about something else," she said. "You have males in your officer corps! How is that possible?"

Captain Egan smiled. "We have a different society than yours, and in our society, both males and females have equal opportunity for advancement. Everything is based on merit, especially in our Navy."

Andrea made a "wow" with her mouth. "That is going to take some getting used to!" she exclaimed.

Hecate nodded. "Definitely."

Captain Egan continued to smile. "I'm sure you'll get used to it in time, but for now, we'll make every effort to have our best female officers attend to you, just to reduce the culture shock."

Hecate nodded.

"Now," said Captain Egan. "About the intact destroyer that tried to run - we have boarded her with our Marines and taken all remaining survivors into custody. The crew has been locked up in one of our cargo holds, and the officers are in our brig. I suggest that you question them to determine why they attacked you."

Hecate smiled a feral smile. "I'll question them, Captain. But I already know the answer."

Beside Hecate, Andrea agreed. "Auntie Empress."

"We can take the Captain and XO aboard the *Nemesis* and put them in our brig," said Hecate. "But we don't have room for the rest of the prisoners."

Andrea looked at Hecate. "It really depends on what you are going to do next, Skipper."

"I'm going to Aronte and kill an Empress," growled Hecate.

A short silence ensued as each person thought through the implications of what had just been said.

Captain Egan spoke first. "We can retain the rest of your crew onboard and ferry them to Aronte, or any other location you wish, Princess-Captain."

"Good, thank you," said Hecate. "Andrea and I will put our heads together and formulate a plan, and let you know."

At that moment, the Chief Petty Officer guarding the door called out, "Attention on deck!"

Captain Egan stood to a loose attention. Hecate glanced at Andrea, then both followed suit.

Through the hatch came a large man, also in dress whites. He walked to the head of the table and stood behind the chair, resting his hands on the back of it.

"Stand easy, please," he said. He looked at Hecate. His uniform was similar to Captain Egan's but had five gold stars on the shoulder boards.

"Hello, Granddaughter," he said.

*****

Hecate stared at the big man in the white uniform standing at the head of the conference table.

In her Mother's chambers at the Imperial Palace, there was a picture. It was a picture of a man dressed in the uniform of a Palace Guard, with black beard, blue eyes, and a sword at his side. It was her grandfather Zeno.

Hecate knew the story well - how Grandmother Antiope was widowed at a young age when her first husband, Prince Hyginus, died after their first child, now Empress Hippolyta, was born. And how Grandmother Antiope had taken a second husband, a commoner from the Palace Guard - a large man with a sword. The man in the picture. And how Grandmother Antiope had become pregnant again with her mother, Princess Deinomache, and upon her birth, by Imperial law, the commoner - her grandfather Zeno - had been banished. Imperial law did not allow a commoner husband to remain in the Imperial Household if a female child – a Princess - was born.

The man had been allowed to hold the newborn baby once; and to kiss her once; and then he was whisked away, never to see or touch her again.

The man standing in the conference room in front of her was a big man. He had no beard; but he had the same blue eyes. And the same smile.

Hecate breathed, "But you can't be him..."

The Admiral - because Hecate realized that must be the rank she saw on his shoulders - merely continued to smile as she processed.

"My Grandfather was exiled to Barcam...he is dead. They

reported him dead..."

The man tilted his head wryly. "The rumors of my death were greatly exaggerated, I'm afraid."

"But," came from Andrea. "You would be...what...70 or 80 years old!"

Admiral Jake Hammett grinned. "Well, actually, that's not even close. But let's not talk about that. I try to keep my age a secret from most of my staff."

Hecate protested. "This is not possible!"

Jake waved Hecate to her chair and sat down. "It is possible, Granddaughter. I will explain it all to you in good time - perhaps at dinner this evening. But for now, just accept that I have a method of staying young. And that I am, indeed, the same man from the picture in your mother's bedroom. How is your mother, by the way?"

"No - wait - how do you know about the picture?" asked Hecate.

Jake smiled at her. "Let's just say, my exile has not been as strict as some would think it, Hecate dear. But really - how is Deinomache?"

"As well as can be expected, considering her husband was just murdered by that bitch of a sister of hers," growled Hecate. Andrea nodded.

"Wait!" Hecate exclaimed, as a sudden realization struck her. "If you are my grandfather...and you are from Earth...then..." she stopped.

"Yes, Hecate dear," said Admiral Jake Hammett, Chief of Naval Operations of the Rim Defense Force, with a huge grin. "You are one-fourth Earther. You are part legend."

* * * * *

Hecate sat, trying to comprehend what she had heard. Beside her, Andrea Iona could no longer restrain herself.

"How is it that you look like us, talk like us?"

Jake looked at her. "What do your Earther legends say?"

Andrea stared at him. "They say that the Aeolians originally came from another planet, called Earth."

Jake smiled. "And that is the truth."

"No!" exclaimed Andrea.

"Yes," said Jake. "It is true."

Hecate grimaced. "But how?"

Jake leaned back in his chair. "Approximately 3,300 years ago, a rogue ship stopped by Earth and abducted several hundred people. It transported them to Aeolis and abandoned them there. Over time, they survived and prospered. The rest is history. At least, your history."

Andrea thought. "So - you're saying, we are descended from you?"

"Not exactly," said Jake. "A better way to put it would be that we are all descended from the same ancestors. But 3,300 years ago, your ancestors split off from ours. Since that time, we've evolved separately."

"Oh, Stars!" said Andrea. "I have a thousand questions."

"Me, too!" said Hecate. "Starting with, do all Earthers live as long as you?"

"No, I regret to say, they do not," replied Jake. "I am the only one so far, and that because of a very special circumstance, not likely to be repeated."

"What circumstance?" asked Andrea.

Jake glanced at Captain Egan, then back to Andrea. "Let's save that conversation for dinner tonight, shall we?"

He rose from the table. As he did, Captain Egan stood to attention again, as did Andrea. Hecate, however, was too shocked by the events of the last few minutes to respond in kind.

"I'm sure you would like to get cleaned up and rest a bit after the battle," said Jake. "Let's get together in – say, ninety minutes - for dinner, and I'll answer as many of your questions as I can. Will that suffice for now?"

Hecate belatedly stood and nodded. "That would be good. I could use a bit of time to process all this."

"Good!" said Jake. "I'll see you at dinner. Captain Egan will take care of you."

Nodding at Egan, Jake left the room.

Captain Egan turned to Hecate. "Is there anything I can get for you or your crew at the moment?" he asked.

Hecate shook her head. "No, Captain. Perhaps we should just regroup for now. This is all new and strange to us."

Captain Egan nodded and led them from the room. They passed through the bridge again, down the stairs, and to a cross-corridor which led into Officer Country.

Egan paused before a door, and with a touch against the pad, it opened.

"For you, Princess-Captain," he said. "Commander Satra will be next door." Hecate nodded, glanced at Andrea with an unspoken thought, and entered. She knew her quick glance at Andrea was all that was needed to remind her XO to stay on her toes. Behind her, she heard Egan continue down the passageway with Andrea, and the door slid shut behind her.

Looking around, Hecate found a rather large cabin - compared to her cabin on the destroyer, it was huge - with a bed, desk and chairs arranged neatly. Pale peaceful colors were present throughout, and on one wall was a large viewer, with curtains hung on the sides, made to look like a picture window.

The scene looked out on a beautiful green meadow, with mountains towering in the background. Hecate assumed it was a scene from Earth. Strange animals ate grass in the meadow, four-legged with brown pelts and white tails. Some of them had antlers.

On the left was a door; peeking through, Hecate saw a bathroom, with a big, beautiful tub and shower. She hadn't seen an actual tub since leaving Aronte. She wasted no time putting it to use.

An hour and a half later, Hecate finished dressing. While she had been in the bath, someone had cleaned and pressed her uniform, which now looked a bit less like it had been through a battle. She looked in the mirror on the bathroom door. "Presentable," she thought.

A soft knock on the door brought her attention back from the mirror. "Come," she said loudly, then thought, "What if they don't understand Aeolian?"

But evidently, they did, as the door opened, and a female orderly came in, taking two steps into the room and then bowing in the Aeolian fashion. Hecate was taken aback.

"Dinner is served in the Admiral's cabin, Mum," said the orderly. "I can take you there when you are ready."

"I'm ready now," said Hecate. She followed the orderly out of the cabin and down the passageway, back toward the Bridge.

"How is it that you speak Aeolian?" she asked.

The orderly looked at her, smiling. "Compressed learning, Mum. Any crew working in the Aeolian Empire must master the language."

Hecate puzzled over this as they crossed past the stairwell up to the Bridge and over to another door, which the orderly palmed open. She then stood aside for Hecate to enter.

Hecate found herself in an anteroom, with a couch on one side and a couple of overstuffed chairs on the other. Through a door she could see the Admiral's cabin. A lace tablecloth covered a heavily laden table, and standing awaiting her arrival were the Admiral, Captain Egan, and Andrea Iona.

Hecate entered the cabin and stood behind the only vacant chair. All three bowed to her in the Aeolian fashion. She blushed. "I'm sorry, am I late?"

"A Princess is never late," smiled Jake. "Please, sit."

Hecate sat and then the others followed suit. An orderly appeared out of nowhere and suddenly wine was in her glass, followed quickly by the others. Jake picked up his glass and raised it in a toast. "The Navy!" he announced.

Joining in the toast, Hecate couldn't help a quick glance at Andrea Iona. She was not quite sure which Navy he meant.

Andrea spoke. "Admiral Hammett. You said you would tell us how you came to be...well...Hecate's grandfather. And how you have lived so long. And what the hell you are doing here in Aeolian space!"

"I did promise that, didn't I?" said Jake. "Very well. This is a bit of a long story, so please settle back and get comfortable."

GRANDFATHER

The pessimist sees difficulty in every opportunity. The optimist sees opportunity in every difficulty.
- Winston Churchill

Onboard the Frigate *Paris*

"In our year 2121 – your year 2871 – an intelligent AI starship we called *Pandora* landed on Earth and warned us about a vicious empire of aliens 805 light years away from our planet. We call these aliens the "Bats"; because to us, they look like a small animal we have on Earth – thin, light fur, pointed ears on top of their heads, fangs."

Jake waved his hand at his personal holo and it expanded, becoming visible to all, and showed a rotating, 3D image of a Bat.

Jake saw Hecate shudder; but Andrea grinned at the thought of a new enemy to fight. Jake grinned back at her.

"*Pandora* called for three people: me, an air force pilot named Teresa, and a scientist named Kirsten. *Pandora* declared that by her computation and simulations, we were the three people who were destined to lead Earth into the future by creating a Space Navy.

"Nobody at the time understood this; there was tremendous resistance. Everyone – including us – thought *Pandora* was crazy. But, in the event, she put us on a path that we couldn't change. She provided funding, technology, and knowledge to us so that we could get our Navy going – what we now call the Rim Defense Force, or the RDF."

Jake waved his hands in a circle. "Everything you see around us – this frigate, all the technology, all our knowledge about the

Bats and about your Empire, started with *Pandora*. Her name fit her well – she truly opened a box of troubles for us."

Jake grinned, took some coffee, put the cup down in the saucer, and continued.

"The Bats are a vicious, genocidal race. If they discover any sentient race nearby, they immediately assault the planet and destroy every intelligent creature on it. They do not allow other sentient races to exist near them. Right now, the edge of their Empire is about 100 lights from the edge of Rim Space, our border. They are slowly but surely heading our way."

Andrea did some quick computations in her head. "So even if they don't accidentally stumble on you with a scout ship, you'll be fighting them in about 25 years, because your radio emissions will meet the boundary of their Empire. There won't be any hiding from them after that."

"Exactly," nodded Jake. "We estimate about 28 years plus or minus five years, and that's if they don't stumble on us by accident. But we are aggressive in our scouting, so we believe we can intercept any scouts before they find us. We're working on the assumption we'll fight them in about twenty years."

Hecate interrupted. "Are you ready? To fight them?"

Jake shook his head. "Not yet. If the war started today, we would not survive. But we are working as hard as we can to get ready."

Hecate looked at Andrea. Both were thinking the same thing. If the Bats destroyed the Earthers, it would only be a matter of time before they came for the Aeolians.

Jake continued. "In 2140 by our calendar – 2890 by yours – I came to Aronte in secret, hoping to find a way to create an alliance with your people. During that time, I met your grandmother, Hecate – Princess Antiope."

"You saved her life when she was attacked by assassins," interrupted Hecate.

"Yes," said Jake. "That's right."

"And then you married her," Hecate added.

"Yes. I loved her very much. I grieve her death to this day,

Hecate. She was truly one of a kind."

There was a quiet period around the table for a few moments. Finally, Hecate broke the silence. "And then my mother was born, and you were exiled."

"Yes," nodded Jake. "I was exiled back to Barcam, but of course I was not really from there. I returned to our headquarters on a planet called Kamilaroi, not too far from Earth. And I've been there for the last forty-four years, building up the RDF and preparing for the war that is coming."

"So, you were here in the Great Raid of 2890?" asked Andrea. "By our calendar, I mean."

Jake bowed his head slightly. "I was, Andrea. And I know what your grandmother, Ligeia, did that day. She saved the city. Antiope cried for her. As did the entire nation."

Andrea nodded. "I wish I could have known her," she said. A single small tear came out of her eye and slid down her cheek.

By now dinner had been completed, and the four sat around the table in the Admiral's cabin, having coffee and dessert. Hecate was not sure she liked coffee, so she sipped slowly. Andrea Iona, on the other hand, was taking to it like a duck to water - she was already on her second cup.

Hecate was slowly coming to terms with the story Jake was relating. Everything he had told them meshed. And Jake had made an exceptional offer. He had given a DNA sample to Hecate's ship's doctor, who had taken it back to the *Nemesis* for analysis. The doctor had returned shortly and, with a brief nod to Hecate, told her all she needed to know.

This man was her grandfather.

"But why haven't you tried to form an alliance with us sooner?" asked Hecate. "It seems to me the danger is imminent. The Bats are nearly upon you!"

"I agree," replied Jake. "But let's be realistic. You know as well as I do that if your Empress Hippolyta, with her hatred of the Earther Myth, got definite proof of our existence, she would immediately use it as an excuse to invade us and make us into a colony of Aeolis. Quite frankly, up until recently, we wouldn't have had the means to resist your Navy. It's only within the last couple of years that we've reached a point where we feel we could negotiate as equals and defend ourselves if your Empress decided to attack. So, we were on the cusp of sending a mission to approach your government and establish a diplomatic channel – when this happened."

"You mean Hippolyta's attacks...," said Andrea.

"Yes. One of our frigates witnessed the attack on your father, Hecate. They realized too late that the stealthed destroyer slipping up behind your father's corvette was opening fire on it. I'm so sorry that they weren't in time to save him."

Hecate spoke bitterly. "Someone will pay for that, I promise."

Jake nodded. "And then we received intelligence that you were the next target."

"How?" exclaimed Andrea. "Do you have spies in our Navy? You do, don't you!"

Jake looked at her, with a slight smile on his face. "You know I can't answer that, Commander. But even if it were true, let me assure you it would be purely as a defensive measure. We have no animosity toward you or your people. We are only trying to survive."

Hecate glared at Jake. "How many?"

Jake shook his head. "Can we please just defer that discussion to a later time? If we form an alliance, then I promise you, we'll clear all that up."

Hecate was not satisfied. "How many spies do you have in our Navy, *Grandfather*?" she said sarcastically.

Jake leaned forward, put his elbows on the table, and looked sternly at Hecate.

"*Granddaughter*, don't make me send you to your room!"

There was a short silence. Then Andrea burst into laughter, and the rest of the table soon followed, Hecate included. Finally, after a moment of hilarity, they settled down.

"OK," said Hecate. "I'll defer that question. But not forever."

Jake agreed. "That's fine. Let's work on our survival first, then we'll get to the smaller issues."

Jake leaned back and went on. "So basically, that's the story. We received intelligence that you were on your way to Marinas for re-supply and that you were being shadowed by three destroyers. I left the message with Minerva on Marinas to have you meet us here. And we were just a few minutes late making our arrival - for which I am very sorry."

"But...how...have you lived so long? You look to be about forty years old!" said Andrea Iona.

Jake nodded. "When the Machine Ship *Pandora* came to Earth, one of the first things she did was make some modifications to my genetic structure, which froze my age at thirty-eight. I haven't aged since then."

"But why did she do that? Not that you're complaining, I imagine." asked Andrea.

Jake continued, "*Pandora* stated the only chance for Humanity to prevail against the Bats was for me to survive long enough to lead the RDF all the way to the final battle, for both technological and strategic reasons. I've never fully understood it myself, but over the years, I've come to accept it. It's really hard to argue with *Pandora*."

"And is *Pandora* still around?" asked Hecate.

"Well, yes and no," said Jake. "She roams about our part of the galaxy, and you never know where she is. But occasionally she'll stop by to say hello. The last time I saw her was about...oh, I guess twenty years ago. She suddenly popped up one day in orbit around...well, one of our planets...and sent me a message. I went up and visited with her for a couple of hours, then she was gone again. I haven't seen her since."

Hecate set her coffee cup down in the saucer. "I want to talk about these Bats more. You say they are about 800 lights from Earth?"

Jake hesitated. "Yes, their capital planet is about that distance from us. You realize, I can't give you too much information right now. Your government...your aunt Hippolyta...is quite antagonistic to the concept of Earth."

Hecate nodded. "I understand. But what I need to know is,

are these Bats a danger to us as well?"

"They are," said Jake. "If they overrun Earth, then you will be next."

Trying to formulate which of her many questions she wanted to ask next, Hecate was momentarily silent. Andrea glanced at her, then jumped in.

"Why are your ships wedge-shaped? It seems like an inefficient use of space."

Jake nodded. "It is, but we use a technology called a grav deflector – a strong, artificial gravity gradient – to deflect incoming cannon rounds and beamers. A grav deflector works best when the ship is wedge-shaped. By putting it right at the front of the ship and fighting nose-first, incoming rounds, beamers, missiles can be deflected back along the side of the ship instead of penetrating."

"Most of the time," added Captain Egan with a wry smile.

"Just so," said Jake. "No system is perfect, so if the round is fast enough, massive enough, hits at just the right angle, it can penetrate. Same with a beamer, if it hits at precisely the right angle, it can get through. Still, though, most of the time, even if it penetrates, the gravity gradient will deflect it down the side of the ship, making it an in-and-out shot through the less critical parts of the structure. On a good day..."

"And," added Captain Egan, "We also use the grav deflector when we travel at high speeds in three-space, to deflect radiation, small particles, even some larger rocks. That allows us to get up to about point-six light speed in three-space, as long as the system is not too cluttered up."

"Wow!" said Andrea. "Incredible! We can only handle point-three, maybe point-four in a really clean system we've already surveyed. And we armor up our ships, armor up the belly and try to fight belly toward the enemy. Your system is better, I think."

Hecate nodded. "And what's the chances of us getting that technology?"

Jake looked at her. "Better than you think. If we can negotiate an alliance with you, then you'll get all our technology."

Hecate looked at him. “Empress Hippolyta will never consider it. She’ll shoot first and ask questions later.”

Jake grinned. “Then let’s toast to the success of your trip back to Aronte.”

*****

Early the next morning, Hecate stood at the front of the cargo bay, facing the surviving crew of the Aeolian starship *Metis* - the lone survivor of the three AEN destroyers that had ambushed her.

The crew had been locked in the cargo hold of the *Paris* since being recovered from the derelict ship. Now they stared at Hecate sullenly, not sure if they would live or die.

This morning, onboard the *Nemesis*, Hecate and Andrea had questioned the Captain and the XO of the *Metis*. The two officers had survived the questioning – but only just. Hecate was in no mood to be merciful.

Now she paced in front of the remainder of the crew, collecting her thoughts.

"People. You've been told what really happened yesterday. I know you thought, in good faith, you were attacking a ship that had been taken by pirates. But now you know that your Captain and XO were attempting to assassinate a Princess of the Blood. They are now locked in the brig on the *Nemesis*, and they'll be taken back to Aronte to answer for their crimes. And they’ve admitted that you were innocent of this, that they lied to you about your mission."

Hecate paced at the front of the group, ill at ease.

"I wish I could tell you that you can just go back to Aeolis, and all will be forgiven. But alas, it isn't quite that simple. You see," and Hecate hesitated.

"This attack was ordered by the Empress." A gasp went through the crowd.

Hecate faced them. "Tomorrow, my ship will be repaired enough to start back to Aeolis. And I will go back to face the

Empress. It will most likely be a battle to the death, a Blood Match by the rules of the House of Aronte. Only one of us can walk away. And the reality is, if I lose this battle, you should know...the Empress will not let any witnesses to this attack remain alive."

The assembled crew muttered, as they comprehended the situation.

"Therefore," Hecate continued, "Captain Egan of this frigate has made a gracious offer. He will follow me back to Aeolis, keeping his distance and maintaining stealth. He will stand off from the planet, hiding in the Kuiper belt, while I face the Empress."

The crew stood silent. Hecate looked at them with sympathy in her face, but iron in her voice.

"If I lose the battle, then Captain Egan will offer you a choice. He will either drop you off on a planet of your choice in the Empire - or you can choose to go back to his star nation with him and make a new life there. You will all be offered places in their Navy. The choice will be yours. But I must tell you in all honesty, if I lose this fight, and you stay in the Empire, you will not survive. The Empress has many means of finding people and killing them. And I can tell you with absolute certainty, if I lose the Blood Match, and you stay, she will track each one of you down and kill you."

An officer in the front row spoke up. "Where is the home system of this ship? Where would we end up?"

Hecate shook her head. "I can't tell you just now. If I lose the battle, Captain Egan will provide you that information after you make your choices. If I win...well, then I'll tell you personally."

A voice in the back spoke up. "Who's in charge, after you leave?"

Hecate gestured at a young Lieutenant Commander standing beside her. "Lt. Commander Thelestris will be your commanding officer in the interim. I expect each one of you to provide her with the same respect and attention as if I were standing here personally. Woe betide the person who gives her any grief, people. Got it?"

A chorus of “Aye, Mum” went around the crew as they all looked at Thelestris. Hecate held her gaze on them for a long moment, then nodded.

"Best of luck to all of us, then," she said. "Godspeed."

MARFIK

If you fell down yesterday, stand up today.
- H. G. Wells

Daneki Corvette *Matador*

Cassian stood over the pilots, staring at the holotank. They had been traveling for two weeks. They had surfaced just outside the mass limit of a large A-type star and were accelerating inward at an economical 75g. Soon the sensors started to clarify the layout of the system.

"One...gas giant," said the Copilot. "...there's another...nothing in the hab zone, as we expected... That's it."

"OK, we know where we need to go. How long to get to the first gas giant and check out the moons?" asked Cassian.

"About thirteen hours, sir," said the Copilot.

"Awesome," said Cassian. "I'll tell the folks."

Walking back into the crew bay, Cassian told the waiting civilians about the system. "Let me emphasize to you all, there is no way to tell at this distance what we will find. You should all plan to be disappointed, and if it turns out better than that, then, well, that's gravy."

Cassian turned and resumed his sitting position on the floor of the crew bay, as he had spent the last two weeks when he wasn't up pacing around or doing exercise in the limited space in the engine room. A few minutes later, he was just about to doze off when the Copilot came back and touched his shoulder.

"Sir?"

Cassian snapped awake. "Yes?"

"Sir, better come up front."

Cassian glanced up at him. His face showed a worried look.

"OK," he grunted, and unfolding once again from the deck, walked stiffly down the passageway to the cockpit again.

When he got there, the Copilot resumed his seat, while the Pilot turned to him.

"We've got company, sir." he said, as Cassian sat down in the jump seat.

"What?"

"Two rather large ships. Right behind us."

Cassian focused on the holo. Sure enough, there were two ships running close behind them, not more than a hundred klicks in trail. The sensors rendered the ships as black wedges. They were easily ten times the size of the corvette.

"Are they broadcasting?"

"No, sir," said the Pilot. "We haven't tried contact yet."

Cassian thought hard. "Those are not Bat ships."

"No, sir," said the Pilot. "No, sir, they are not."

"If they wanted to harm us, they would have already..." Cassian continued.

He glanced at the Pilot. "...and I doubt very seriously if we could out-run them."

The Pilot nodded. Cassian gestured with his hand. "Stop all accel."

Reaching for the controls, the Pilot pulled the throttles. The black ships matched them, staying exactly in place. The three ships coasted through space in formation.

Now what? thought Cassian. He waved a hand at the Pilot. "Send a contact signal."

"Contact signal?" The Copilot looked puzzled. "What does that mean?"

Cassian sighed. "I don't know. Try...ah...try the first one hundred prime numbers."

*****

Three hours later, Cassian grunted in frustration. All their attempts to communicate with the two black, wedge-shaped ships following them had come to naught. The two ships simply hung in space, one on either side of their rear, in perfect firing position. Cassian and the pilots had started by transmitting the first one hundred prime numbers, then moved on to simple words and sentences, trying to elicit any kind of response from the others. Finally, in frustration, he had ordered the Pilot to just start transmitting historical videos. Either the ships did not receive their signals, did not understand them, or simply did not want to talk. Now, after hours of trying, he was at his wit's end.

"I'm going to go out there," he said.

"Sir? No, sir! Don't do it!" said the Copilot.

"Have to," said Cassian. "We have to get this resolved."

Cassian stepped back into the main cabin and pulled a spacesuit out of a locker. He started putting it on when the Pilot stuck his head through the bridge hatchway.

"Sir...they've responded."

Cassian, stunned, dropped the spacesuit on the floor and ran back to the bridge.

The video screen between the Pilot and CoPilot had come to life. It showed a creature from the other ships. The creature had the same general physical arrangement as his own people - a similar head, eyes, nose, mouth, ears, neck...and what he could see of the upper body looked similar. It seemed to be taller, larger overall, but not that different from him. And it wasn't a Bat!

The creature looked at him out of the video and smiled - a gesture Cassian recognized, as it was like that of his own people. It spoke in a strange language, then paused.

"Hello, Daneki corvette," said an artificial voice, clearly an AI, in passable Daneki. "Sorry for the delay. It took our AI a while to parse your language. You appear to have come a long way. Can we talk?"

*****

Many hours later, Cassian sat across from the alien creature, which called itself 'Human'. The Human AI had translated that into Daneki with words that came out as 'monkey men', which Cassian thought was hilarious. He bit his tongue to hide his smile, thinking about the little monkey creatures of his home planet. Clearly their AI had not yet fully mastered his language.

The Humans had exchanged data with Cassian and determined that their environmental conditions were adequate to support Daneki life; biological tests showed that pathogens were unlikely to be an issue between the two life forms, at least in the short term; with that information in hand, Cassian had consented to journey over to the Human ship for a conference.

Now the Human spoke at length, and Cassian waited patiently for the AI to translate. Finally, the Human stopped, and the AI began.

"We understand you are running from the Bats. I am sorry to hear that they have destroyed your civilization. You may be sure that we will help you in any way that we can. But also, please understand, we cannot take any chances that you might, in fact, be spies for the Bat Empire. We do not know very much about the Bat Empire, and thus we must be careful. For that reason, we are going to ask you to come with us. We will escort you to another location, where we can communicate at length in comfort and safety. It will take about three weeks to reach our destination. We will re-provision your ship and provide you with vectors. We will be happy to transfer some or all of your passengers to our larger ships for the journey. Will this be satisfactory to you?"

Cassian thought for a moment. These creatures were quite leery of the Bats, he could tell. And in his mind, that made them potential allies. And he had to admit, if the tables were turned, he would probably act in the same cautious manner.

He was sure that, wherever they were going, it wouldn't be anywhere close to the home planet of these creatures. Not unless they were completely stupid, and they didn't strike him in that vein.

So, they would take him to a neutral location, far from their own space, and then there would be an interrogation - they might call it something else, but that's what it would be. And they would pick his brain for anything they could use against the Bats.

Cassian could see the gleam in the eye of the officer across the table from him. When the Human officer realized that Cassian and his people were refugees from the Bat Empire, the Human nearly salivated at the thought of obtaining intelligence from them.

But Cassian didn't care. He would tell them anything they wanted to know if they gave him just one thing. Just one thing he wanted from these Humans, after he saved his people in the corvette. Just one thing...

A chance to kill Bats...

Marfik System - RDF Forward Scout Base Twelve

It had been a long three-week trip. But they had finally arrived.

The shuttle settled slowly into a dock outside the dome, and with a mutter and a pop the engines stopped. Cassian sat in the sudden silence.

It was over. At least this part of it. Cassian had successfully brought a remnant of his people from certain death to what was, at least, a chance of a future.

He bowed his head and said a short prayer to the Creator. Then he got up, brushed off his uniform, and stepped forward to the hatch.

Captain Martin, his host on the journey from Zeta Ophiuchi, smiled and gestured, providing him leave to precede him. Cassian walked down a short boarding tunnel and emerged outside.

He saw a sparse, rocky moon. Above his head was a dome, with the shuttle docked next to the dome. Overhead he saw a smallish gas giant. A half-dozen corvettes and shuttles were clustered at other docking ports around the edge of the dome, and overhead he saw larger ships in orbit. There were low, gray buildings arranged neatly in a military manner.

A squad of armed Humans waited quietly to one side, their rifles raised in a guard of honor.

A figure walked from one of the buildings toward Cassian. The...Human, they had called themselves...was about three centimeters taller than he - and Cassian was a tall male for his race. He had earlier noticed four fingers on Captain Martin's hands, rather than the normal three; but otherwise there were very few differences between them. As this one got closer, though, he could see that his nose and eyes were different than Captain Martin's.

"Greetings, Captain Cassian," said the Human, in near-perfect Daneki. Cassian was taken aback.

"How...how can you know our language?" he asked.

The Human smiled. "We have an advanced AI which can perform machine learning while you sleep. It's called compressed learning. It only takes about three nights to learn a new language, and I started working on it as soon as I heard you were on the way. Let me introduce myself - I am Captain Saigo Takamori, but everybody calls me 'Sam'. Let me welcome you to our little home away from home here."

Cassian touched his forehead in the Daneki salute, and the Human - a “male”, he realized, as he recognized the sex of the stranger - did likewise. Clearly, “Sam” had gotten a good briefing from the black frigates escorting them.

Behind Cassian, the Pilot and Copilot stood in awe, speechless. And behind them, Cassian's other charges gazed around in wonder.

"Captain Cassian, I'm sure you and your people are tired and would like to eat and rest. If you'll follow me, I'll show you to quarters which I think you'll find very agreeable." With a gesture, Captain Takamori turned and walked back toward the complex of buildings. Cassian and his people followed.

As they walked, Cassian looked up at the dome over them. It was not high, and he could see there was an atmosphere outside the dome, because there were plants growing outside the dome.

But the plants did not look very inviting, and Cassian suspected the atmosphere outside the dome was not very inviting either.

Far away, he could see a ring system around the planet overhead, shining whitely in the light from the distant Class A star.

*****

A week later, Cassian and Sam sat at breakfast, Cassian enjoying the new-found flavors of Human food. Tests had confirmed their biology was remarkably similar - they could breathe the same atmosphere, eat the same food - and drink the same liquor, much to Cassian's delight.

After a week of meetings, Cassian had convinced the Humans of his sincerity and honesty. In his descriptions of the Bats, he held nothing back. He told them everything he knew of their warfighting capability, their colonizing methods, and the little that he knew of their home planet, society, and culture.

Importantly, Cassian had told them that the Bats recently turned their explorations back toward the Pipe Nebula – which meant in the same general direction as Earth.

"Your radio emissions – your EMF – started on Earth about 1910, I believe," said Cassian.

Sam - short for 'Samurai', Cassian had learned, a nickname given to him because of his Japanese warrior ancestry – nodded.

"That's correct. That puts our radius of electronic noise at 275 light years from Earth now. And based on your information, we know the Bat Empire is now about 420 light years in radius from their home world. So, as of this moment, there's a margin of about 108 light years separating us."

Cassian considered. "You need to be fully ready to fight them about twenty to twenty-five years from now. That's assuming you can fend off any of their scouts that might come this direction."

"I think we can do that. We have an aggressive scouting program, as you saw when you came into the Zeta Ophiuchi system."

Cassian smiled. "I hope you can stand behind that. There's a lot of space out there."

Sam nodded. "Believe me, we understand. But we've seeded the frontier between us and the Bats with millions of QE buoys, so we have a solid tripwire system that lets us know the instant a ship enters any system we are monitoring. Beyond that, all we can do is prepare for the future war; and our Chief of Naval Operations, Admiral Hammett, makes damn sure we do that every day, believe me."

Sam continued. "Not to change the subject, Cass, but as you know, you'll be leaving tomorrow for Tolleson Base, our main military headquarters. I think you'll like it there. We have a fine R&D facility there. Your experience developing attack fighters will be put to good use. All your scientists will have important roles to play in the future. The folks at the R&D lab are excited to have you and your people come and work with them."

Cassian nodded. "I can't thank you enough, Sam. Without your people, we'd all be dead now, drifting through space on a trip to nowhere. I'll never forget what you have done."

Sam smiled. "Cassian, just go and do good things for us all. I'm sure I'll see you again. And it's been a pleasure." Rising, he said, "I'm sorry I have to run, but I have a meeting."

Cassian nodded, looking around the cafeteria. In the corner, he saw the main part of his group having breakfast, smiling and happy. He saw young Vitus just coming into the cafeteria. Vitus got his food and came over, and Cassian waved him to a seat. Vitus nodded, sitting, quiet for a change. Cassian understood.

"Vitus, you know we're going to another place, where the Humans will give us housing, jobs, a new life."

"Yes, sir," said Vitus.

"I bet you're thinking about where you will live."

"Yes, sir," said Vitus. "I don't have anybody. On the ship, it was OK, because I was with everyone. But there, I'll be alone."

"No, Vitus, you won't," said Cassian. "I've made arrangements for you to live with me."

Vitus jumped in his chair for joy. "You have? Oh, thank you, sir!" he practically yelled.

Cassian laughed, his first real laugh in a long time. "Vitus, you are now my adopted son. Welcome to our little family!"

COUNCIL

Acinaces – *a type of Scythian sword used by the Aeolian matriarchy; it appears to have been one of the weapons used by the original twelve Amazon warriors deposited on the planet Aeolis in 1184 BC. This type of sword ultimately became a symbolic weapon used only for executions and challenges. An ancient version of this sword was known as the Sword of Penthesilea and could only be touched by a member of the Imperial Family.*
- *RimWiki, 2230 Edition*

City of Aronte

The Empress Hippolyta sat at the end of the council table, her chair a simplified version of her throne at the other end of the room. Her robe was covered in tiny pearls, luminescent in the light of the room. The dress was beautiful, but did little to improve the pinched, bitter look of the forty-nine-year-old Empress.

On her left sat her daughter, Princess Kantilla. On her right was Princess Deinomache, Hippolyta's younger half-sister - and Hecate's mother.

The chair next to Deinomache was empty - Princess Hecate's place in the council room. The remaining chairs around the table were filled with the other members of the Imperial Council – five of the most senior women of the Aeolian nobility, advisors to the Empress.

Behind the Empress, against the back wall of the council chamber, two Palace Guards stood silently. Spaced evenly around the room were another four of the burly, kilted men.

The Empress cleared her throat. "It appears, Sisters, that our niece Hecate has met with an accident in space. It is necessary to choose a replacement for her on the Council."

Deinomache, her eyes still reddened by tears, objected. "Sister, it's been only six weeks. Surely we can give her more time."

Empress Hippolyta sniffed. "We will give her no more time. The Navy has searched thoroughly. Much debris from her ship has been found. It seems her fusion reactor exploded. Princess Hecate is declared dead."

With a bang, the door to the Council room slammed open. In the doorway stood Princess-Captain Hecate Andromache Aronte. In her hand was the Sword of Penthesilea - the sword passed down for countless generations of the Aronte dynasty, and which could only be removed from its mount in the Palace for one purpose.

A gasp escaped her mother, Deinomache. Other than that, dead silence held the paralyzed Council members in thrall as Hecate stalked to the Council table, the sword held before her, upright in both hands, in the time-honored tradition of a challenge to the death. Stepping up behind her empty chair, she reversed the sword and slammed it down point-first into the thick wood of the council table, with a 'thunk' that shook the entire structure of it.

There it stood, vibrating, as she glared at Hippolyta.

“I accuse the Empress of treason,” she said, “and demand satisfaction.”

*****

Stunned, the members of the Imperial Council stared at Princess Hecate as she stood behind her empty chair, the sword still vibrating in the wood of the heavy council table. On one side of the blade, just below the hilt, was the ancient symbol “Heta’. On the other side of the blade was the ancient symbol “Pi’.

This was the Sword of Penthesilea. It was the formal symbol of a challenge to the death.

With a shriek, Empress Hippolyta waved at the Palace Guards behind her: "Arrest her! She dares bring a weapon into the Council! Arrest her!"

The Guards made no move, other than a slight nod from the Captain to Hecate.

"I'm afraid your Guards will not be helping you today, Hippolyta," said Hecate. "It appears those loyal to your murder cult have disappeared."

Across the table, Hippolyta's supporter, Areximacha, snarled at Hecate: "How dare you! What is the meaning of this outrage?"

Hecate smiled a little cat smile at Areximacha. "I have here..." Hecate tossed a data cube on the table..."complete evidence that Empress Hippolyta and Princess Kantilla killed my father, Prince Alexander, and laid an ambush for me to assure my death as well."

The sudden intake of breath around the table was audible.

Hecate pressed on. "As you know, the murder of a Prince of the Blood, and the attempted murder of a Princess of the Blood, are both treason under the Imperial code. Thus, I may challenge for a fight to the death."

Hecate reached out and slapped the sword handle, sending it back into vibration against the table. She glared at Empress Hippolyta, still sitting in shock at the head of the table. "I so challenge."

Areximacha stuttered, "But...but...that cannot apply to the Empress!"

Hecate jerked the lone empty chair away from the table, knocking it over backwards, stepped forward and slammed her hand against the wooden surface.

She hissed to Areximacha, "I can easily handle two challenges today, Areximacha! Do you want to go get your sword as well?"

Areximacha froze, suddenly silent. Beside Hecate, her mother Deinomache placed a calming hand on Hecate's back. Hecate turned to the Empress, and spat, "I have the evidence on those cubes, Hippolyta. It has been reviewed by CNO Maya

Aronte and members of her staff. It has been reviewed by the Captain of the Palace Guard. They realize you have played them for fools. You'll get no more help from the Navy. And no help from the Palace Guard. It's just you and me, Hippolyta. Go get your sword!"

Hippolyta seemed to diminish in size, and looked away from Hecate, toward the Palace Guardsmen lining the wall. All stared at her in silence, their faces cast in stone, their eyes bitter. Hecate was well loved in the Palace, and Hippolyta began to realize the futility of help from that quarter.

The Empress gazed around the Council table, at the noble women who had been her loyal supporters. Some seemed to be fascinated by the glittering sword, still swaying slightly in the table. Some looked down at the table. None looked back at her.

"I see," said Hippolyta. "I doubt I could stand against you, Hecate, for more than a few seconds. I see no point in fulfilling the challenge. What do you want?"

Hecate glared at her. "You will accept exile. Or you will die. The choice is yours."

Hippolyta sat silent for a matter of seconds, her face still. Then she spoke, her eyes staring blankly at the other end of the table. "I accept exile." Tiredly, slowly, she removed her tiara and placed it on the table in front of her.

“So be it, Hippolyta,” breathed Hecate. “But first, you will tell me why. Why did you kill my father? Why try to kill me?”

Hippolyta looked at Hecate with fury in her eyes, and then at Deinomache. She practically spat as she answered, “Because you have polluted blood! You have Earther blood! I had to kill the rumors, destroy any chance that you or your Mother could ever take the throne! You know why!”

Deinomache gasped beside Hecate. Hecate looked at Hippolyta stonily. “How do you know that?” she asked.

Hippolyta shook her head. “I've always known it; I overheard my mother, Antiope, talking to Zeno about it once when I was a child.” She gestured to Deinomache. “Ask her! She knows it too!”

Hecate glanced at her mother, Deinomache. Deinomache's

head was lowered, staring at the table. At that moment, Hecate knew it was true. Slowly, Deinomache raised her head and looked at Hecate.

“I’m sorry, daughter. I always intended to tell you. But I should have told you sooner.”

Furious, Hecate gestured to the Captain of the Guard at the back wall, who had heard everything. He marched forward.

"The Empress has abdicated the throne, Captain Pramis. She wishes to go into exile. Find a suitable planet for her, far away from Aeolis, and take her there. Now. Today. She can spend an hour packing and then begone with her. And take her back-stabbing daughter with her." Hecate wheeled on Princess Kantilla. "Unless you want to go get your sword, Kantilla!"

Kantilla bowed her head meekly and got to her feet to follow her mother.

Captain Pramis bowed deeply. "It shall be done, Princess." Gently, he touched Hippolyta's elbow. Hippolyta rose slowly to her feet. She looked at Hecate.

"In spite of it all, Hecate, you...I see now you are a true Aronte. A fierce and worthy warrior. I’m sorry."

Still angry, Hecate turned her back and ignored them as Captain Pramis escorted Hippolyta and Kantilla out of the room. When the door had closed behind them, Hecate turned back to the table. She let her gaze sweep around the assembled council for a moment, then stepped around to retrieve the Imperial Tiara from the head of the table. She returned to stand behind her mother and made to place the Tiara on Deinomache’s head; but before she could do so, Deinomache turned, grabbed her arm, and stood.

Hecate paused, confused. "Mother? You are next in line for the throne. You are our new Empress."

Deinomache shook her head. "I am too old, and too settled in my ways, to take on a new job now," she said. "This is a job for younger blood than mine. I refuse the crown."

Gasps went around the table as realization settled in for the council members. Hecate looked puzzled. "Mother! Please...you must do this!"

"No, Hecate." said Deinomache firmly. "I refuse the crown."

From the end of the table, Hecate's friend Xanthippe spoke firmly.

"Long live Empress Hecate."

TIARA

From the end spring new beginnings.
- Pliny the Elder

In dismay, Hecate held the Tiara in her hand. It was the symbol of the Empress of the Aeolian Empire, and the person who wore it was the absolute ruler of that Empire. And now she stood before the Imperial Council, next in line for the throne.

"No!" exclaimed Hecate. "I'm a Naval Officer! I belong in the Navy!"

Her friend Xanthippe spoke quietly. "Hecate. Look at who is next in line."

Hecate looked around the table. She realized that after her, Areximacha was next in line of succession. Areximacha – Hippolyta's strongest ally, and Hecate's worst enemy.

It came to Hecate that if she refused the throne, Areximacha would make sure neither Hecate nor her mother Deinomache survived the day. Hippolyta would be back in power by the morning. Hundreds, if not thousands, of Hecate's friends and allies would die in the bloodbath. Every one of the Palace Guardsmen who stood in the room with her now. Her cousin, Maya. Her friend, Xanthippe, who had defended her in this room. Every member of her crew on the *Nemesis*.

Slowly she realized this was not something she could avoid. Her life as a starship captain was over.

Quietly, slowly, Hecate walked back to the head of the table and laid the Tiara down again.

"First, I must speak," she said. "As you just heard from Hippolyta's lips, the Earther legend is true. Our ancestors came here more than three thousand years ago from another planet called Earth, just as the legend states. This week, I encountered people from that planet. I have met them. I have spoken to them. I assure you they are real, and they are our relatives."

Hecate gestured toward her mother, Deinomache. "And also, as Hippolyta said, my grandmother Antiope took a man to husband, Zeno. It turns out that Zeno was from Earth. Therefore, my mother is one-half Earther. And I am one-fourth."

Hecate looked around the table. "If I take this crown, understand that I intend to reconcile with the people of Earth. We have a common enemy; an alien race called the Bats. They are advancing on both Earth and us; if they discover us before we are ready, they will destroy us completely.

"Only by joining forces with the rest of our Human family can we survive this threat. Therefore, by taking this crown, I not only accept the leadership of our Empire; but I also accept the responsibility of joining the separate halves of Humanity back into a common family."

Once more Hecate swept her gaze around the table. Then she quite deliberately returned her stare to Areximacha, holding her eyes on her.

"I am willing to begin by forgiving all past wrongs of those at this table; but let me assure you that future wrongs will not be so easily forgiven. Any attempt to undermine my rule, to prevent joining our Empire with our lost relatives, or to interfere with any other steps I take to assure our future, will be met with unconditional destruction. Do I make myself crystal clear?"

One by one, the Council members around the table nodded, starting with Hecate's mother, Deinomache, until only Areximacha remained. Hecate stared at her, and somehow, without moving her gaze at all, managed to bring the still glittering sword sunk into the top of the council table into the moment passing between them.

Areximacha nodded, silently.

Hecate reached down and picked up the Tiara. She held it in her hand while her mother came around the council table to stand behind her. Hecate bowed her head and began a whispered prayer.

Deinomache took the Tiara from her and slowly placed it on Hecate's head, adjusting it in place. Hecate completed her prayer and then slowly sank down into the throne at the head of the table.

"Now we will pray together. For my father. For the souls of the people on the ships that were destroyed. And for the Empress of our Empire to have wisdom, compassion, and justice in her actions."

PART TWO - TRAITOR - 2188

PARTY OF GOD

Troy shall overturn the Grecian state, and sweet revenge her conqu'ring sons shall call, to crush the people that conspir'd her fall.
- Virgil - The Aeneid

12 October 2188
Beyond HD 38858 - Empty Space

Commodore James Lafferty Cobb, RDF, looked at the repeater holotank in his day cabin, which showed a corvette approaching. Cobb rubbed his chin, thinking, then queried his MEMSAI.

<How long until our visitor arrives?>

<Lady Pesculi's shuttle will dock in ten minutes. She should be in your day cabin in fifteen minutes>

<Good. Bring in the refreshments as soon as she arrives>

Cobb leaned back in his chair, contemplating his visitor. Lorna Pesculi - Lady Lorna Pesculi, as she liked to call herself, especially since some "evidence" had recently been discovered of her "noble" heritage - was the Senior Mistress of Hanoverian Prime Minister Gustav Blucher. And Gustav Blucher was the leader of the Party of God - the ultra-religious fascist group that took over Hanover four years ago. The 'Saints', as they were derisively known, had dismembered the parliamentary government of Hanover, instituting a reign of terror that included forced re-education camps which killed "heretics" - basically, anyone who disagreed with them - by the thousands.

More recently, in 2186, huge taxes imposed on the citizenry for "religious requirements" - i.e. building secret warships - had triggered a tax rebellion, resulting in another 20,000 killed before Blucher and his junta had put it down. Blucher and

Pesculi together were two very dangerous people.

And Cobb liked dangerous people. Because James Lafferty Cobb was an extremely dangerous person himself.

Few knew it - Cobb was a master at blending in, working the system, and sliding his way to the top without suspicion.

It was a miracle Cobb had made it through the rigorous screening of the RDF that identified and removed fanatics of any kind - religious or otherwise - but no system was perfect, and Cobb had a secret advantage. He was a complete sociopath. When he told a lie, it was the truth to him. No machine or AI could detect it. And when it came to emotion - he had none. Or almost none.

Only one emotion drove Cobb - the desire to be on top.

It was this hidden drive, to control and to be at the top, that had made Cobb decide to take this meeting. It was a dangerous meeting. Even the whiff of contact with Pesculi would be enough to discredit him, have him recalled to Tolleson Base and re-screened, and probably cashiered back to Earth.

Cobb was one of the few North American Alliance Earthers who had advanced to senior rank in the RDF Officer Corps. The NAA – the recently merged fundamentalist government of the old United States, Canada, and Mexico - produced too many fanatics for the RDF's taste; any NAA citizen who applied to the RDF was thoroughly screened, by both Human and AI testers. Although thousands of them had passed the screening and were part of the RDF, they remained a minority.

Even fewer were in the Officer Corps. In the entire RDF, there were only a couple of hundred NAA natives at the rank of Commander or above.

And worse, Cobb was charged with enforcing the Hanover Ostracization. When the Saints had taken over Hanover and dismissed the Parliament, instituting a religious dictatorship, the RimFed Basic Rules kicked in. Hanover was immediately ostracized - isolated from the rest of RimFed. No starships were allowed in or out. All QE boxes on the planet were remotely disabled. Any communication or contact with Hanover became illegal.

And Cobb, as the Commander of the Tau Ceti sector including Hanover, was responsible for enforcing the blockade. The Ostracization had been in place since mid-2184 now.

Very few attempts to run the blockade were made; and Cobb caught all of them. There was no better position to be in, as far as Cobb was concerned. Because he had built a well-concealed underground economy of smuggling to and from Hanover, on the very warships charged with enforcing the embargo - and he didn't take kindly to competition.

But now his chief silent partner, Gustav Blucher, had sent Pesculi to see him. Cobb didn't like it. He had never trusted Blucher. There was no telling what the bastard wanted.

His MEMSAI pinged. <Lady Pesculi is here.>

<Send her in>

The door opened, and Lorna Pesculi walked in. She was a beautiful woman, to be sure. Cobb could see that. But she wore too much makeup and was covered in furs that had cost a small fortune - so many that he could only just make out the color of the dress beneath. She wore an elegant hat, like something from the early years of the 20th century on Earth - which was pretty much where Hanoverian society was locked.

"Lady Pesculi," Cobb greeted her, bowing to almost-kiss her hand, in the Hanoverian fashion.

"Commodore Cobb," Pesculi said, in a voice that surprised him. It was throaty, husky, and intelligent. He waved to a chair.

"Please, sit and be comfortable. Would you like some tea?" The door opened, and his aide came in, with a tea tray.

"Yes, that would be excellent, Commodore," said Pesculi, removing her hat to reveal a perfectly coiffed head, her hair strewn with pearls and diamonds.

Cobb sat in front of her as his aide poured the tea and departed. "Please, call me James," he said. "No need for formalities between friends. How was your trip?"

Sipping her tea, Pesculi frowned. "Very uncomfortable. But I understand the need for discretion. Still, two days to get out of the gravity well on a conventional shuttle and then another day on a tiny corvette to meet you here is not my idea of a fun time."

"My apologies, Lady Pesculi. But the need for discretion is uttermost. Even the slightest hint that I'm not enforcing the embargo would cause my instant recall and dismissal from the RDF. And the next commander might not be so understanding of your position on Hanover. It would be a long, cold dry spell."

Pesculi nodded. "I understand."

Cobb took his tea, then cocked his head at Pesculi. "So, how can I help you, Lady Pesculi?"

Pesculi sat her tea down and looked at him. Then she smiled. "We're going to take over the RDF and RimFed, Commodore Cobb. And we'd like you to be the new head of the RDF. Chief of Naval Operations, Fleet Admiral James Lafferty Cobb...how does that sound?"

* * * * *

Some days later, in his day cabin on the battleship *Taizong*, Commodore Cobb looked down the conference table at the holos of his most trusted confederates - a dozen officers who had lied, bribed, and killed their way to the top of the food chain in his organization, and whom he knew he could trust completely - as long as the money and power was there for them.

Now a bigger prize was at hand - all of RimFed. Cobb had briefed them. It was time to call for a vote.

"Gentlemen, keep in mind that once we commit to this coup - this rebellion - there is no going back. This is a once in a lifetime opportunity. But failure is not an option. We win, or we will most likely die unpleasantly. However, our chances are excellent. No plan is foolproof, of course, but as I've laid out for you, we will take them totally by surprise. We'll outnumber them in space by 2 to 1, and on the ground by 20 to 1. And we'll have the advantage that they will not believe such a thing is even possible."

Cobb scanned around the table, fixing each of his

subordinates with his gaze. One by one, they nodded. When the last one had agreed, Cobb smiled.

"Excellent. Then the next order of business is to cover our backsides. We need to identify every officer and man that might betray us and get them out of our way. What are your suggestions?"

"Just kill them all," said Li Gui, commander of the frigate *Kolkata*.

Cobb shook his head. "Gentlemen, that would create far too much attention and confusion. We need to find a subtler way."

Captain Rurik of the cruiser *Samara* gestured. "Transfer them to a single ship, then send them to Hanover on blockade patrol."

Flag Captain Oleg of the *Taizong* shook his head. "Couldn't get them all into one ship. Have to use at least two, maybe three."

Cobb objected. "But we've already got most of them on the cruiser *Strasbourg*, we've been working on that for years. How many are left on other ships?"

Oleg scratched his chin. "Maybe 50 - 75 on other ships."

"Let's just abandon them on the moon," said Li Gui.

Cobb shook his head again. "Same problem - attracts too much attention too soon."

Li Gui pressed on. "Make it a rescue mission - we land a destroyer on the moon, then blow the engines. We send all the suspect crew down as the rescue party, then we just leave. That puts them all in one place with no hope of rescue for a while."

Cobb shook his head. "Basic idea is sound but pulling crew randomly from a bunch of different ships for that kind of mission would make no sense. Somebody would get suspicious, and something would get back to HQ. I want something a bit more...subtle, at least in the early stages."

Rurik raised a hand. "Move as many of the suspect crew as possible onto two destroyers over the next few months. When we've got it down to those two ships, we send them on patrol to Hanover. When they get there, their QE boxes and tDrives all fail. Then we send the *Strasbourg* to rescue them, it goes down too, and viola - all our bad eggs are in one basket."

Oleg laughed. "Devious. I like it."

Li Gui and the others nodded. "That could work."

Cobb spread his hands, then tapped the table. "OK, do it. Pick the two oldest destroyers and start transferring your unwanted crew to them or the *Strasbourg*. Bring back only the crew that you're sure you can trust - or at least intimidate. And be discreet about it! We've got most of three months to do this. Don't get in a rush!"

"Aye, sir," came a chorus of voices.

"Rurik, put together the plan to disable their QE boxes and tDrives when they get to Hanover. Also, while you're at it, better disable their weapons too. Maybe the Hanoverians can come out and take them over."

"Aye, sir," said Rurik.

"And don't forget, you'll need to disable all the QE boxes and tDrives on Leeds when we pull out."

Rurik nodded.

Cobb focused on Rurik again. "Rurik, please put together a training program for our fire control officers for the situation we'll encounter at Kamilaroi. Remember, our missiles will be useless – they won't arm if fired at an RDF ship. But railguns and beamers are dumb. We'll be limited to those only. But we can do this."

Cobb stood. "Right. Wish us luck, gentlemen. Dismissed."

14 October 2188
Kamilaroi - Tolleson Base

<Commander Walker is here, sir>

Jake Hammett nodded, a habit that he knew annoyed his MEMSAI, Zoe.

<Does that mean send him in? Or wait?> Zoe sounded annoyed.

Jake smiled. Annoying Zoe gave him a tiny bit of pleasure, and he never missed the opportunity.

<Send him in>

The door opened, and Commander Robert Walker stepped forward smartly, came to a precise stop in front of Jake's desk, and snapped a perfect salute.

"Commander Walker reporting, sir!"

Jake waved a hand. "Relax, Rob, take a seat." He gestured at the overstuffed chair in front of his desk.

"Yes, sir," said the officer, sitting down.

Jake looked him up and down. "You're looking good, Rob. I haven't seen you since, what? About the time you went to the *Wellington*?"

"Yes, sir. Eighteen months ago."

"And now you've made Commander. Congratulations!"

"Thank you, sir. And thanks for the recommendation."

Jake grinned. "You deserved it. A while since you were 'Guns' on the *Paris*, eh?"

Rob also grinned. "Yes, sir. Just a green Lieutenant then. Still trying to figure out which buttons to push."

Jake laughed. "I doubt that. You took out those destroyers like you did it every day. Something I'll never forget."

"Thank you, sir."

Jake leaned back in his chair, tapping his pencil on his desk. He no longer used a pencil - and neither did anyone else - but he always kept some in a cup on his desk. He said it reminded him of the 21st Century of his youth - a time when people still occasionally used pens and pencils.

"Rob, I know you expect an XO slot now on a first-rate ship. And you deserve it. You're a damn fine ops officer. And you'll get it, I promise you. Just not right now. I need you on my staff right now."

"I'll be happy to do it, Admiral," said Rob.

Jake smiled. "Good poker face, Rob. I almost didn't see the tears."

Rob grinned. "Sir, I'll be where you need me. If you need me here, that's where I'll be."

"Well, I need you here, Rob. I need an Assistant Base

Commander. We haven’t had one for over a year, and it’s more than Ginger and I can handle. We've got some stuff going on that is building to a head, and I don't have enough hands to deal with it all. I need someone who can get the job done."

"I'll do my best, sir."

Jake stood and put out his hand. "That's all anyone can ask. OK, Commander Walker. Get with Ginger, my Chief of Staff, and she’ll get you billeted, and run you through your assignments. And welcome aboard."

Rob stood and shook hands. Then he snapped to attention and saluted, and Jake returned it. Sharply, Rob turned and marched out of the office, closing the door behind him.

<They don't make many like that anymore> Jake sent to Zoe.

<Sir?>

*****

Outside Jake’s office, Captain Ginger Barnett waited for Rob, with a smile on her face.

“Well, Mr. Walker, did he give you the honey along with the castor oil?”

Rob smiled. “Yes, Mum, I believe he did.”

“Good,” said Ginger. “Well, come with me and we’ll get you billeted.” They started walking, headed for the Bachelor Officer’s Quarters, or BOQ.

As they walked across the parade ground, Rob’s curiosity got the best of him.

“Pardon me for asking, Mum, but aren’t you Commander Barnett’s granddaughter? The one who helped Jake when he was on Aeolis, back in the 40’s?”

Ginger smiled at Rob. “Yes, good memory, Mr. Walker.”

Rob thought for a second. “So, your grandfather was Prince Adrian?”

“Correct, Mr. Walker,” said Ginger. “My mother was Alexia Aronte, daughter of Prince Adrian and Metrodora…or as most knew her, Ginger Barnett the first. My grandmother.”

"How did you end up here?" asked Rob.

"Well," said Ginger, "When the mutual defense treaty was finalized, one of the conditions was that as many Aeolian Naval Officers be placed in the RDF as possible. So far, we have roughly thirty thousand Aeolians in the RDF, and that number is growing every day. In fact, starting next year, we'll have an entire fleet made up of Aeolian ships and crews, although there will be Earthers mixed in with the crews to help kick-start the long-term integration process."

"So that will be Second Fleet?"

"No, actually, it will be First Fleet," said Ginger. "Jake agreed with Empress Hecate that giving it that name would help the Earthers understand the AEN is here to stay, and is to be fully integrated with the RDF. What is now called Home Fleet will be renamed Second Fleet."

"Damn," said Rob. "Things are happening fast."

Ginger nodded. "Yes. We're getting awfully close to the end game now."

Rob paused. But he couldn't resist his natural curiosity.

"Can I ask, why you don't use the Imperial name Aronte? Your grandfather and mother were both Aronte, so it seems like you would use that name."

Ginger glanced at him, smiling. "I try not to let too many people know about that connection. It makes them act differently. I just want to be Ginger Barnett, a simple Chief of Staff for the RDF."

ROB WALKER

Dost thou love life? Then do not squander time, for that is the stuff life is made of.
- Benjamin Franklin

Sol System - MarsDock

Rob Walker was late. He ran down the boarding dock to the shuttle, in time to see the flight attendant reaching for the door to close it.

"Wait!" he yelled, and the attendant paused, looking at him. Rob threw himself forward, squeezing through the half-shut door before the attendant could close it. "Thanks!" he spoke over his shoulder, panting, as he started down the aisle past the galley. He glanced at his boarding pass and noted his seat - 1C. The first row of seats. He threw his case and hat into the overhead and sat down, dropping his tablet into the slot in front of him and fumbling for his seat belt.

"Here you go, Commander," said a voice. He looked to his left and saw the officer next to him was holding his seat belt for him to take. Grabbing it, he strapped in.

"Thanks, uh...Commander," he said, looking more closely at her. She was in Aeolian uniform, which was almost identical to that of the RDF, with slight differences in cut and trim. For the sake of consistency, Aeolians in service with the RDF used RDF collar emblems and shoulder boards, making it easy for him to judge her rank.

The shuttle lurched as it released from the dock. A slight gravity pulse told Rob it had left the influence of the dock plates and internal plates were taking over. Then it yawed away from the dock and powered away, gently at first, then with increasing accel as it cleared the speed limits near MarsBase. Within five minutes he felt a slight change in the whine of the engines and knew the accel had maxed out at 150g.

Coming to the front of the cabin, the flight attendant made the standard welcoming announcement.

"Good evening, ladies and gentlemen and welcome aboard. If there is anything the crew can do to make your trip better, please ask. Fortunately, Mars is nearly at Earth opposition today, so our flight time to EarthPort will be approximately 2 hours and 30 minutes. Please lean back, relax, and enjoy the flight. Thank you."

With that, the attendant leaned over to Rob and his seatmate and asked, "Can I get you anything to drink?"

Rob looked at the woman, who pursed her lips and thought for a second, then said, "I'll take champagne, I think."

Rob grinned, then nodded to the attendant. "Same for me." The attendant moved on down the aisle, taking the drink orders of the personnel in the front compartment - which on a civilian craft would be called first class, but on this military shuttle was just referred to as the "brass cage".

"I've never had it before," said the woman next to him.

Rob looked at her. "You mean champagne?"

"Yes," she said. "I understand it's quite good."

"Most people think so," said Rob. "I'm Rob Walker. Nice to meet you."

The woman extended a hand, showing that she knew Earther customs. "Nice to meet you, Rob." said the woman. "I'm Phoebe."

"Hi, Phoebe. Hey, that's one of the few names that has survived from ancient Greek all the way to the present day. We still use that name on Earth!"

Phoebe smiled. "Yes, I've heard that before."

Rob was silent for a bit, but this woman was beautiful. He didn't want to let the conversation drop. So, he said, "Two weeks leave on Earth, then Strat School, maybe?"

The woman looked at him suspiciously, then nodded. "Yes, how do you know?"

Rob smiled at her. "I make the roster for Strat School. And I remember a 'Phoebe' on the list."

Phoebe relaxed. "Yes, I am scheduled for...Strat School, you call it?...in two weeks. And you? Why do you go to Earth?"

"Well, actually, I have to take Strat School this session myself. So, I'm doing the same thing - two weeks of leave, then back to Strat School!"

Phoebe looked puzzled. "But if you make up the list for Strat School, why do you have to take it?"

"My boss," said Rob. "She said I have to take it, so I'll understand what the students go through. Then I can do a better job of administering it."

Phoebe nodded. "Oh, OK. Makes sense, I guess."

Phoebe's gaze dropped, and suddenly Rob felt something push into his left chest, right where his ribbons were mounted. He realized Phoebe had her index finger sticking directly into a light blue ribbon on his campaign ribbon mount. She was pushing hard.

"That ribbon..." she spoke, then paused, scowling, and then pushed him even harder. "...That ribbon is Aeolian. How..." Then her touch relaxed, drifted upward to rest on the topmost ribbon on his chest, a light maroon ribbon with a star mounted in the center, and she poked him again, hard enough to rock him back in his seat.

"And that one, I know for certain no Earther can wear. That is the Star of Aronte." She looked at him accusingly, her finger still poking him back in his seat.

Rob grinned. "Now, think about it. Has there ever been an action where the RDF and Aeolians were in the same fight?"

Phoebe shook her head. "I think not."

Rob kept grinning. "Think about it. RDF ship. Aeolian ship. Same action."

Phoebe's mouth made a little moue of surprise, and she removed her finger and stuck it right in Rob's face.

"Pestilence Port!" she exclaimed.

"Correct," Rob smiled at her.

"You were on the *Paris*!" said the woman.

"Gunnery Officer," said Rob.

Phoebe was so excited, she turned in her seat and almost came out of her seat belt.

"You took out three destroyers!"

Rob shook his head. "Nope. Two destroyers. The *Nemesis* took out one."

Phoebe shook her head in wonder. "You took out two destroyers in thirty seconds. That's good shooting!"

Then her finger came up and she poked the lower, blue ribbon once more. "That's the Aeolian Combat Action Ribbon..." she said.

Rob nodded.

"And that one," said Phoebe, moving her finger to the topmost ribbon, "is the Star of Aronte. That can only be awarded by the Empress herself."

Rob nodded again.

"So, you met the Empress?"

"Many times," said Rob. "She presented me with these two ribbons, but I was also the assistant military attaché at our embassy for six months. I had quite a lot of interaction with her."

"What's she like?" asked Phoebe.

Rob perused her. "Actually, she looks a lot like you."

Phoebe grinned. "What are you planning to do on Earth?"

Rob thought. "Well, I had planned to go hiking down in Patagonia. Do you know where that is?"

"No," said Phoebe.

"It's down in South America. Ever heard of it?"

"No, sorry," said Phoebe.

"What are you going to do?" asked Rob.

"Well, I wanted to see all the great cities of Earth. Or as many as I can see in two weeks. You know, Athens, Istanbul, of course, near where my ancestors were abducted all those centuries ago. Then maybe London, Paris, New York, Beijing. Like that."

Rob nodded. "You'll have fun. I think, in two weeks, you should be able to see at least six cities, if you don't spend too much time in each one."

Phoebe looked at him strangely. "You said you spent six months in Aronte?"

"Yes," said Rob.

"Then you know that in Aeolian society, the women make the first move, right?"

Rob, puzzled, nodded.

Phoebe gently placed her hand on his leg.

"A guide would make this trip so much better," she said.

NEW GENEVA

I distrust those people who know so well what God wants them to do, because I notice it always coincides with their own desires.
- Susan B. Anthony

Kamilaroi - New Geneva
RimFed Parliament Building

<The ambassador from Sierra Nevada is here, Mum> said Bianchi's MEMSAI.

Carla Bianchi nodded. Confusing one's AI with head gestures was a typical Human trait, and hard to break. <Send him in>

The door opened, and a short, stout man entered, typical of third generation stock from a planet with 1.2 times Earth gravity. His hair was black and the scowl on his face matched. Nevertheless, Carla stood and greeted him with a smile and an outstretched hand.

"Good day, Ambassador. Please, make yourself comfortable. Would you like some tea?"

"No," growled Daryl Johnson, "I'm fine." Then, begrudgingly, "Thank you."

Carla sat behind her desk and cocked her head at him. "How can I help you today, Ambassador?"

Johnson shifted in his chair, adjusted his collar, then spoke. "The Ostracization of Hanover cannot continue. They, as all peoples, have the right to choose the government of their choice. Sierra Nevada, as the closest neighbor to Hanover, has protested this multiple times - yet no action has been taken. Today, I am here to provide a final warning. The people of Sierra Nevada and Hanover will not stand for this any longer. If RimFed does not remove the Ostracization of Hanover, then Sierra Nevada will withdraw from RimFed immediately. In addition, we will not be responsible for what some of our citizens may do."

Carla looked hard at Johnson. "That sounds suspiciously like a threat, Ambassador. As you know, RimFed does not respond very nicely to threats."

Johnson shook his head. "It is not a threat, Madame Secretary. It is merely fact. Sierra Nevada..."

Carla interrupted him with the slam of her hand flat on the desk. Shocked, his mouth froze in the "O" of surprise.

"Mr. Ambassador," she began icily. "First of all, it was Hanover's decision to overthrow their legitimate government and institute a reign of terror. They have killed over 60,000 people in the last four years in the name of 'God's Covenant'. The Ostracization will remain in effect."

"Secondly, you do not come into my office and threaten RimFed. If Sierra Nevada wants to withdraw from RimFed, you are more than welcome. However, if you do so, you will no longer be protected by the RDF. If you are attacked by the Bats or any other force, you will not be defended. You will not have access to FTL drives and you will not be permitted to use QE boxes for communication. Those are the rules, and we intend to enforce them. Now...if that is what the people of Sierra Nevada wish to do, have at it."

Johnson sneered, then waved a hand at Carla. "Just as I suspected; your female arrogance will not let you see the handwriting on the wall. This is what comes of letting women have roles in government!"

"And we are done, Mr. Ambassador. Sergeant Reed will show you out." Ambassador Johnson looked up to see a large Marine guard standing beside his chair, appearing as if by magic. Despite his short stature, Johnson was a heavy, well-muscled man. But the Marine beside him looked more than capable of picking him up and carrying him to the door if necessary.

With a snort, Johnson rose to his feet. "Remember - you had your chance!" he yelled at her. Waving his hands in disgust, he went out the door.

* * * * *

RimFed Prime Minister Sanada Yukimura considered the message from General Secretary Carla Bianchi. He didn't like it at all. He skimmed it to Home Secretary Adele Brodeur, sitting beside him at dinner. Adele perused it on her personal holo, then shook her head.

"I've got a bad feeling about this, San," she said.

"As do I," replied Yukimura. "Do you think they'll act?"

"I wouldn't be surprised."

"What do you think they might do?"

Brodeur pulled on her ear, thinking. "Maybe start a terrorist campaign, try to make our life difficult. Blow up some buildings, that kind of stuff. I wouldn't put it past that bunch of fascists."

Yukimura considered. "Where's Jake Hammett right now? I'd like to get him in on this."

"Unfortunately, he's on his way back from a conference in Aeolis. I think he's due back in a week or so. Do you want me to burst him a quick QE message on this?"

"No, I think it can wait until he gets back. But do me one favor," said Yukimura. "Talk to Captain Marchand at the Naval Attaché. Give him a copy of Carla's note. Tell him I said it might be a good idea for him to run through some anti-terrorist drills with his security team."

* * * * *

Daryl Johnson settled back in his seat on the transport sloop to Sierra Nevada and opened a book on his tablet. It was a long, three-day journey back to Sierra Nevada and the sloop had somewhat limited recreational facilities, but Daryl didn't mind. He had brought a selection of lurid novels to read, and in his large, expensive cabin two of his many wives waited.

Daryl thought about the ticking time bomb back in the basement of the building housing his embassy office. It was set to go off at 1930 hours on Sunday, February 19, 2189.

Daryl had made sure it was a big one. It would bring down not only the building housing his embassy office, but the buildings next to it as well. That should attract a lot of attention, he thought smugly. Enough to divert everyone's attention to that area. Far from the real attack.

PARIS, FRANCE

Arizona – *the first RDF battleship built, named after a venerated 20th century ocean-going ship of Earth. Laid down in March 2125 at Liberty Navy Yard,* Arizona *completed outfitting in March 2127 and was commissioned into the RDF in July 2127 with Captain Marien Howard commanding.* Arizona *served as the flagship of the RDF for 52 years, until 2179, then was assigned as flagship of the Reserve Fleet at Tolleson Base. In 2186,* Arizona *underwent a one-year modernization program at the New Athens Navy yard at Mitsikeli.*

- RimWiki, 2230 Edition

Earth - Paris, France
14 February 2189

Rob pushed the sheets away and, pulling his displaced pillow back under his head, looked down the length of the bed. He could see straight out the window - directly in front of him, maybe a half mile away, was the Eiffel Tower. It looked a bit piebald these days, as the French government worked steadily on replacing the old, weathered iron and steel components with new plasticized steel. About half the Tower was completed, mostly the bottom part, with a slightly different texture and color than the rest. But still, he thought, it looked beautiful.

Beside him, he felt a stir. He reached over and tapped Phoebe gently on the forehead. She wiggled her nose but did not open her eyes. Gently, he tapped again. Without opening her eyes, she said in a husky voice, "Do that again and you won't be able to walk for a week, sailor."

Rob grinned. "We have one last day in Paris, babe. Don't you want to get up and get moving?"

Phoebe groaned. "I think we did enough moving last night. And don't call me babe."

Rob persisted. "But that's a term of endearment, babe."

Phoebe rose up on one elbow. "Not in Aeolian. In our language, it just means 'baby', and I'm not a baby!"

"OK, OK," said Rob. "But at least I got you to move."

Sitting up, Phoebe's bead glowed as she accessed the net, her eyes defocused a bit.

"Crap, Rob! It's only 8 AM! Couldn't you let me sleep a bit longer?" spat Phoebe in Aeolian.

Rob replied in kind, "C'mon, Phoebe! This is our last day on Earth. Bright and early tomorrow, we have to head back to Kamilaroi. And we have so much to see!"

Phoebe crashed her body back down into the bed, and in English said, "Rob if you don't let me sleep for another hour, I'm going to cut off your...well, I don't remember the word in English, but you won't be able to have children in the future. Got it?"

Rob got it.

*****

Late next evening, the transfer sloop from MarsBase to Kamilaroi cruised quietly, as Rob and Phoebe slept, exhausted but happy, in their compartment in Officer Country. Their transfer at MarsBase had gone smoothly, and now they had a 36-hour journey back to Tolleson Base.

Plans for the annual kickoff of Strategy School were well underway. The Strat School Gala was an annual event, on the Sunday before Strat School started. Tolleson Great Hall had been cleaned and decorated. Tables were placed, with one side cleared for dancing. All the timetables and schedules had been checked and double-checked by Rob Walker before his departure and delegated to responsible officers to ensure their completion.

All Rob had to do upon his arrival was make final inspection of the venue and check up on any loose ends that might need his attention.

And come to grips with the fact that he was in love.

Tau Ceti - RDF Leeds Naval Base

The battleship *Taizong* lifted slowly out of orbit and took a vector for the 36 Ophiuchi system, some 28 light years away. With her screen of two cruisers, two frigates and two destroyers, it was an impressive sight to any intelligence that might have been watching.

Leading the way, two corvettes stayed ten million kilometers in front of the fleet, acting as scouts. The *Taizong*'s destroyers and frigates formed a rear guard, her cruisers running beside her and slightly in front. And in between, two home-built troopships from Hanover and Sierra Nevada carried 600 paramilitary troops - 300 for the assault on RDF Headquarters at Tolleson Base, and 300 for the RimFed coup at New Geneva.

Meanwhile, far away at Hanover, a signal was received in the QE boxes of the two destroyers there. Suddenly all tDrives, QE boxes, sensors and weapons were disabled. And a few minutes after that, six Hanoverian ships came out from behind the large Hanoverian moon and made a beeline for the crippled RDF warships.

And as Cobb's fleet made for the mass limit to sink out, the cruiser *Strasbourg*, packed with Marines and just arriving in the Hanoverian system to perform a rescue of the embattled destroyers, found her QE boxes and tDrives suddenly inoperative, and her sensors and weapons disabled.

In his day cabin, Cobb sat with a hologram of the 36 Ophiuchi system in front of him. The holographic captains of his now-rebel fleet were arranged around the table staring at it.

"OK, one last time. We arrive at Point Bravo above Kamilaroi at 1100 hours on the 19th. From there we have two hours of weapons and equipment checks. At 1300 hours, we split. TF1 goes directly to Tolleson Base. We arrive and start bombardment of the base at 1930. TF2 goes directly to New Geneva. You will arrive and start dropping troops at 1930 as well. Remember - it must be quick; it must be thorough. Don't leave any opposition alive who can hurt us later. I cannot emphasize to you enough - do NOT underestimate your opposition. This is the RDF you're talking about - basically, guys as good as us - or better. So, don't give them any chance at all. Hit them hard, keep hitting them until they're dead."

Cobb leaned back and folded his hands. "Any questions?"

VENUE

Injuries are revenged; crimes are avenged.
- Samuel Johnson

19 February 2189
Kamilaroi - Tolleson Base
1430 Hours

Rob walked to and fro across the entrance to the Great Hall in front of the hanging banner, checking the view as if he were a guest just arriving. After several excursions, he stopped in the middle and gestured to his assistant, Lieutenant Mika Matayoshi. "Looks good! I think we got it!"

Mika nodded and waved to the crew on ladders, giving them a thumbs-up. They waved back and started descending.

"Well, that should be it," said Rob. "I think we are ready."

Mika - nicknamed 'Mike' - nodded in agreement. "Yep, think so."

"OK," said Rob. "What's left?"

"Nothing, really," said Mike.

At that moment, Rob saw Marine Major Nick Rosser approaching. As he came to a stop in front of Rob, Nick saluted. Rob returned the salute then stuck out his hand. "Hey, Nick!"

"Hi, Rob," said Nick, shaking his hand. "How was your leave?"

"Pretty damn awesome," said Rob. "I'll tell you about it sometime. What's up?"

"You had ordered two dozen men for security tonight, and we're all here. Will that be enough?"

Rob nodded. "Sure. I don't expect any trouble. I'll have a couple of extra rifles put in the office, just for backup. That way, we can always get them if we need them."

"Sounds good," said Nick. "We'll have six men outside for guest arrival, twelve in the Great Hall around the perimeter, and me and the rest will rove. Should be plenty of coverage."

"Fantastic." Rob turned to Mika. "Mike, will you take care of getting some extra rifles in the office?"

"Will do," said Mika.

Rob turned back to Nick. "Let's walk the perimeter and see how things look."

Nick nodded and they took off for a stroll around the facility. Mika, in her typical efficient manner, sent a message to the Armory. Around them, the last workers departed, and the Great Hall stood ready for an evening of gala and fun.

19 February 2189
1905 Hours – Battleship RDF *Arizona*

"Sir, I've got a strange signal here," said Yeoman Carter.

Lieutenant Commander Vladimir Victorovitch Volotskoi, half asleep in the command chair, roused a bit and looked at the rating. "What?"

"I've got signatures of a half-dozen ships coming in on a common vector. They'll end up right behind us as we come around the planet. But nothing in the log for any arrivals like that."

Vlad yawned. "Not our problem. Kamilaroi Approach can handle it."

"Well, sir, I know. But...these look like RDF ships. But no IFF on any of them. And they're at max decel, like a combat approach."

Vlad waved at Carter with one hand. "Somebody screwed up somewhere. Don't worry about it."

Suddenly, a ping occurred from the Comm console. There was no rating there, as it was a weekend. The *Arizona* was in standby mode. Carter was covering both consoles.

Carter flipped over to the Comm console and read a short

message. Looking puzzled, he flipped his fingers to skim the message to Vladimir's personal holo.

"Look at that, sir...what do you make of it?"

Vladimir groaned, then raised up slightly and peered at his holo to read the message.

<Coming at you not friendly. Battle Stations or die>

"What bullshit is this?" croaked Vlad. "Somebody is playing a joke!"

Yeoman Carter looked nervous. In fact, his hands were shaking. "Sir, should we scan them for hot plates?"

Vladimir shook his head at first, then seemed to make up his mind. His initial negative head shake changed to a nod. "OK, fine, scan for hot plates. But a waste of time."

Carter switched back to the Tactical Console and moved his hands rapidly. In a dozen seconds, he looked up at Vladimir. His face was white. "They are weapons hot, sir. In fact, their grav plates just came online."

Vladimir froze, for a couple of seconds. "If this is a drill..." he mumbled. He thought hard. If this was a drill, and he sounded a false alarm....

But if this was not a drill...

Then the blue bead on his temple glowed fiercely as Vlad issued orders. The klaxon sounded for battle stations. All consoles on the Bridge came alive. The confused and short-handed crew of the *Arizona*, stumbling and cursing the idiot who called a drill on a Sunday evening, made their way to their assigned stations.

Only a third of the normal crew complement were on board - after all, it was a Sunday night, and the *Arizona* was powered down. Quickly Vlad sent additional orders to the ships Master AI, Buster:

<Buster, emergency start the Mains>
<emergency start all weapons>
<notify the Captain, XO, and Cheng dirtside of the status -

copy them on the sensor report and the message>

<Send to Admiralty and Kamilaroi Approach: Code Zulu Able Zulu - this is not a drill>

<get me some console techs for Comms and Tactical>

Those tasks done, Vlad turned to Carter.

"Carter, you're on Weapons. Make everything hot as soon as you have enough power."

Carter gulped and said rather shakily, "Aye, sir." He moved over to the Weapons console just as the Bridge door opened and two additional ratings ran in.

"Rogers! Tactical!" yelled Vlad. Yeoman Maria Rogers dived for the Tactical console and slid into place.

"Kawasaki! Comms!"

"Aye, sir!" yelled Yeoman Yuka Kawasaki.

Two armed Marines entered the Bridge, closing and sealing the hatch behind them. They were half-dressed in combat armor, carrying the remainder of their kit in their hands along with their rifles. Hastily they completed putting on their armor and took their positions beside the door.

"How long 'til Mains?" yelled Vlad.

Rogers queried her console and turned to Vlad. "20 minutes, sir."

"Crap!" said Vlad. "In 20 minutes, they'll be all over us."

Yeoman Rogers, somewhat shakily, asked, "Is this a drill, sir?"

Vlad shook his head. "I don't know, Rogers. If this is a drill, it's the most realistic one I've ever seen."

"But sir...we don't have enough crew onboard to operate!"

Vlad looked at her and smiled. "We will damn sure operate, Rogers, one way or another."

Rogers nodded, then smiled a bit nervously. "Aye, aye, sir."

19 February 2189
1927 Hours – near Kamilaroi

Cobb hated the RDF. Of course, that was ironic since he was a Commodore in the RDF. But he hated it nonetheless. Because they held him back. In his mind, he should have been a full Admiral by now. But they refused to promote him. They blocked him at every turn. Now he was even assigned as a jailer - a prison guard, to enforce the blockade at Hanover.

No more, he thought grimly. *The days of the RDF holding me back are over. In a matter of hours, I'll be the new Chief of Naval Operations for all of RimFed. And why should I stop there? Why not take over the entire government? Appoint myself as Prime Minister for Life?*

"Captain Schneider, are you ready?" he asked over the tactical ship-to-ship. The reply came quickly.

"Ready, just open the door," replied Captain Ernst Schneider, commanding the Hanoverian home-built troopship *Bismarck*, named in homage to a ship of the early 20th century on Earth. The *Bismarck* would drop the three hundred paramilitary troops on Tolleson Base to storm the Great Hall, and capture or kill all senior RDF officers present. By decapitating the RDF, it should be relatively easy to mop up the remaining staff at Tolleson Base and take over.

Cobb turned in his command chair to the Weapons officer. "Open fire when in range, Marty, and be sure to take out the *Arizona* first."

Lt. Commander Martin Eugen nodded. "Aye, sir."

Cobb turned to the Tactical Officer. "How's it looking?"

"Good, sir," said Lt. Voss. "Although it looks like the *Arizona* and a number of other ships are powering up."

"Well, I didn't expect them to be completely blind to us," said Cobb. "But too late for them, I think. It'll take at least 20 minutes for them to be powered up and ready for a fight."

Cobb's Navigation Officer, Lt. Foster Arnold, spoke up. "We'll be in position above and behind the *Arizona* in three minutes, sir. And we can open fire dirtside any time."

"Very good, Foster. Open fire dirtside now, and on the *Arizona* as soon as you have targeting. The rest of my screen can take care of the small fry."

*****

Rob had gotten the warning message at 1920 hours on his Comm. At first, he thought it was a joke. But he brought up a holo of the Kamilaroi system and saw the ships coming in. They were at high speed and max decel, typical of a combat approach. Their IFF transponders were turned off. Their weapons were hot, and their grav deflectors were up.

Surrounding him, the gala was in full swing, with hundreds of people having completed their meal. Now they were socializing, dancing, drinking, simply enjoying the party.

Across the hall, he saw Phoebe engaged in conversation with his boss, Ginger. But Ginger had received the same messages he had. She was looking at him across the mass of people, a question in her eyes. Rob looked askance at her, lifting his hands in uncertainty, not sure how to react.

He saw Phoebe's conversation come to a halt, as Phoebe realized Ginger wasn't paying attention. Phoebe turned and looked at him as well.

Rob wrestled with his thoughts for a long moment. This had to be a drill. It just had to be...

But another thought kept nagging at him. If you wanted to destroy the RDF senior officer corps, this is how you could do it. He couldn't get that thought out of his mind.

If he called for an evacuation, and was wrong, his career was probably over. But if he didn't, if this was a real attack, then hundreds could die.

Rob shook his head. Given the alternatives, one man's career didn't stack up to losing so many people. His comm bead glowed as he issued orders to his MEMSAI.

Suddenly, the fire alarm sounded. Hundreds of people, confused, stopped what they were doing. Rob stopped the alarm and made an announcement over the PA.

"Everyone, please remain calm. We have a security incident. Everyone move calmly and quietly to the basement stairs on the

south side and go down into the basement. Please remain calm. There is no cause for concern at this time. Please move quickly to the basement stairs and go down into the basement."

Rob issued several more orders via his MEMSAI:

<Nick, call for reinforcements, I don't care where you get them from. Anywhere. Bring everybody.>

<Casper, notify the Admiralty we are moving to the basement as a precaution>

<And notify Admiral Hammett of the situation>

His MEMSAI, Casper, replied quickly:

<All orders issued. Admiral Hammett is onboard the *Denali*, returning from Aeolis. I sent a QE burst>

<Good. And notify Captain Marchand on New Geneva>

Rob's comm was now overwhelmed with queries coming in. His prioritization ignored all but a few. He could see Nick, across the hall, looking at him.

<What's up, Rob?> queried Nick.

<I think we may have an attack coming, but not totally sure. Let's assume the worst>

<Wilco. Orbital or ground?>

<Assume both. Move your guys down the stairs to the first level of basement and prepare for a ground attack>

<Aye, sir>

Rob felt, rather than saw, Ginger and Phoebe come up behind him.

"What do you think, Rob?" asked Ginger.

Rob turned to her, but before he could respond, a tremendous explosion went off outside in the courtyard, blowing out every window in the Hall. Glass and bits of wood and plaster flew everywhere. Rob was cut on his hands and face, and he could see that Ginger had taken a few hits too. Phoebe had been mostly shielded behind them.

"Get to the basement!" he yelled at both. "Quick!"

They started running for the top of the wide staircase leading down to the basement. An almost continuous barrage of explosions could be heard across the base, some near and some far. A few seconds of screaming when the first explosion had occurred quickly faded, and people now focused on running for the basement.

Rob held back, trying to assess how many people were still topside. Most of the crowd had disappeared down the stairs; there were only twenty or so people still on the main floor, many of them bleeding from the flying debris.

Ginger pulled off to one side and tried to help some stragglers lying on the floor, several women with evening gowns covered in blood. Rob reached the top of the staircase and turned to Phoebe.

"Phoebe!" he said. "Get them all down to the bottom level, I think there may be a sub-basement down there somewhere. Get them as far down as possible. Then form them up for defense. I'll get you some help as soon as I can."

Phoebe nodded and was gone, helping people ahead of her down the stairs. At that moment, another huge explosion went off, knocking Rob down and tumbling him down the first few steps. Plaster, bits of wood and other shrapnel zipped over his head, making that particular singing sound unlike anything in the natural world. Ginger, landing almost on top of him, crouched below the level of the main floor with him.

"That was a big sucker," she said.

"Yep," said Rob. "My base comms are down now, but just before they disappeared the *Arizona* sent a gencom. They ID the attack as led by the *Taizong*."

"That rat bastard Cobb!" yelled Ginger in his ear. "I knew that sonofabitch was trouble!"

Rob nodded silently. Suddenly he saw his assistant Mika sprinting across the main hall through the rubble, carrying a half-dozen rifles in her arms. She jumped down the stairs and slid to a stop beside him, panting. "Here!" she shouted, handing a rifle to each of them. Rob took the rifle, checked it, noted it was fully charged. Mika handed them both a bandolier of extra charges.

"Damn, Mike, I told you to put a couple of extra rifles in the office, but wow...!"

Mika grinned. "No, you said to get some extra rifles. You didn't say how many."

"Good stuff, Mike," said Rob. "Take the rest down to the bottom floor, find Phoebe, and help her put together a defensive position. Put yourself on the Marine local loop to stay coordinated."

"Aye, sir." said Mika. "See ya!"

Mika scuttled off down the stairs. A second later, another tremendous explosion took out the far north wall of the hall, and most of the north ceiling came down, blocking the north entrance to the basement stairs. Rob ducked, then looked at Ginger.

"Let's go down another level, I think the rest of the roof might come down," he said.

"Agree," said Ginger. Together they moved off down the stairs.

Halfway down, the stairs reversed direction, turning to go the rest of the way down to the first basement level. At the bottom, a long hallway down the center of the basement had doors opening on both sides into additional ballrooms.

Nick's Marines were finishing up a makeshift barricade about halfway down the corridor. Another team of Marines worked at the far end of the corridor, creating a barricade at the top of the stairs leading down to the next lower level, which was the sub-basement storage area. Rob and Ginger came up to Nick and they huddled.

"Can we hold them here?" asked Ginger.

Nick shook his head. "I don't think so. If they're willing to bombard us, then they'll bring at least a couple of hundred, maybe more, to take the hall. We can delay them for a while, but we can't hold more than twenty, thirty minutes I think."

Rob looked at Ginger. "Do you have any comms?"

Ginger shook her head. "No. Everything went down when we were running for the stairs. I think they got the Base AI. All I have is the local loop with Nick's team."

Rob nodded. "Me too." He looked at them. "So, I read this as a bombardment for ten-fifteen minutes, then they'll land troops outside in the courtyard and we'll get the main assault on the Great Hall. How about you guys?"

Nick nodded. "That's how I read it."

"And we can't possibly hold for long here." Rob turned to Ginger. "Ginger, I recommend you go down to the bottom level with Phoebe and Mika and direct the defense down there. We'll hold them here as long as possible and try to buy you time for reinforcements to arrive."

Ginger nodded. "Take care of yourself, guys." Then she ran down the stairs to the next level.

Rob looked at Nick. "Bet you didn't expect this for your Sunday night activities."

Nick grinned. "Not hardly. But I think we can give them some surprises, what do you say?"

1929 Hours - *Arizona*

Vlad heard the Assistant Engineer, Constance Turner, come up on the command net.

"Vlad, what the hell is going on? The AI is doing an emergency start!"

"It's no joke, Connie. The *Taizong* is coming up our ass weapons hot and about to start shooting any second. If you don't get me Mains in the next thirty or forty seconds, I think we're toast."

"What the hell?" said Connie. "Why is the *Taizong* attacking us?"

"Connie, not now," said Vlad calmly. "Get me Mains or bend over and kiss your sweet ass goodbye."

"Thirty seconds, Vlad," said Connie. "This better not be a

joke."

Vlad turned back to the holotank. His MEMSAI pinged and the holotank updated with a sidebar message,

<Railgun 1 online and ready>

Rogers pointed at the *Taizong* in the display. "They'll be in firing position in thirty seconds, sir."

Vlad mulled it over. "It's going to be tight, guys. Here's what we're gonna do."

<Railgun 2 online and ready>

"Rogers, when I give you the word, give me max emergency burn on the station keeping thrusters. Burn 'em out, I don't care. Bring the nose up and around to face the *Taizong*. Try to stop the pitch-up with our grav deflectors to her and enough angle to shoot. Got it?"

"Aye, sir," yelled Maria.

"Carter, start shooting as soon as you are even close to acquisition. Don't wait for a good sight picture, we're trying to keep them off balance. I want them ducking their heads. I don't care if you miss 9 rounds out of 10, for the first 10 seconds I want you to just throw everything possible at them even if the WEPSAI still doesn't have a good lock. Got it?

"Got it, sir," said Carter, his voice a little less shaky now. The holotank side messages updated rapidly now:

<Railgun 3 online and ready>
<Railgun 4 online and ready>
<Beamer 4 online and ready>
<Beamer 2 online and ready>
<Grav Deflector online and ready>
<Frigate *Moscow* reports Mains and Weapons ready>

"Hot damn!" yelled Vlad. He assessed the holotank rapidly. The *Taizong* was coming in hot above and behind them, positioning for a perfect shot into their rear to take out their main engines. Cruisers screened each side of the *Taizong*, both bombarding the planet below with railguns. Behind the *Taizong*, the rebel frigate *John Paul Jones* was settling into orbit as a rear screen for the *Taizong*. The RDF frigate *Moscow*, following the *Arizona* in orbit, was almost directly below the *John Paul Jones*, just a little behind her.

<Direct *Moscow* to open fire on the *John Paul Jones* NOW!>

<*Moscow* requests confirmation on live fire against an RDF ship, sir>

Suddenly the *John Paul Jones* sent a flurry of railgun shots toward the planet below.

<*Moscow* says never mind>

In the tank, Vlad saw *Moscow* rotating to fire on the rebel frigate. The *Moscow* had a bad angle, as she was almost directly beneath the *John Paul Jones*, but she was rotating fast and within seconds got her guns elevated enough to start shooting. Her first shots caught the frigate by surprise, enough so that Vlad saw the *John Paul Jones* pitch up and away from her position behind the *Taizong*.

"Now, Rogers, now!" yelled Vlad. With a lurch that pushed Vlad down hard into his command chair, the *Arizona* started pitching, bringing her nose up and over to face the *Taizong*, which was just coming into shooting position above and behind her. Vlad heard the station keeping thrusters whining as Rogers pushed them into emergency. They passed through 45 degrees, then 90 degrees. Rogers reversed thrusters to start slowing the pitchup. As they neared face-on to the *Taizong*, both the *Arizona* and the *Taizong* opened fire simultaneously. Vlad felt and heard the *Arizona*'s railguns "thump" as they pumped out rounds. At the same time, he heard a tremendous "clang" as the *Taizong* got a round against their grav deflector, and then heard a distant explosion as a round penetrated the *Arizona* somewhere aft. On the holotank, Vlad saw a sidebar message:

<Compensator and Mains ready>

"Rogers, run us right past her, quick now!" yelled Vlad. Rogers slammed the throttle home and the *Arizona* shot forward like a stuck pig, passing by the *Taizong* in seconds. As they went by, Carter and the WEPSAI peppered the *Taizong* with a volley of shots from fore and aft railguns and beamers, leaving a trail of holes in the *Taizong* and, as they cleared her rear, knocking out at least one engine.

In two minutes, the *Arizona* was clear of the *Taizong* and out of functional range of her railguns. Vlad turned her around and headed back to the battle, but this time with an operational battleship. Within a minute, he had a perfect shot at the back of the frigate *John Paul Jones*, still weaving to avoid the *Moscow* shooting from below. A dozen beamer and railgun shots and the *John Paul Jones* exploded in a ball of fire, throwing debris in every direction.

Vlad grinned; a hunter's grin now that he had a fully operational ship. He saw the *Taizong* ahead, still throwing railgun shots down to the surface and shooting at the *Moscow*, which was taking terrible hits.

"Rogers, take us down that asshole's butt and let's welcome him to Kamilaroi!"

1940 Hours – Tolleson Hall

The bombardment had stopped a few minutes earlier. Nick and Rob moved a dozen men back upstairs to the ruins of the Great Hall. Pushing together as much debris and solid materials as they could, they put together a hasty barricade, facing out towards the main steps of the building. Then the Marines lay down behind the barricade, facing out toward the courtyard, rifles at the ready.

They had completed four more barricades between the main entrance and the sub-basement.

Their plan was to trigger a succession of ambushes, each

followed by a retreat to the next lower barricade.

This first ambush would be as the invaders attempted to make entrance to the building; as they came up the main steps, they would be met by quite a surprise.

Then the Marines would quickly retreat to the top of the South staircase, where a second barricade had been thrown together right at the top of the stairs. From there, a second ambush would unfold as the invaders came into the Great Hall.

On the next level down, half-way down the basement hallway, their third barricade stood, where they would ambush the enemy as they came down the final flight of stairs into the basement.

At the very end of that basement hallway, where the stairs started down to the sub-basement level, their fourth barricade waited.

And down in the sub-basement, where 200 terrified VIPs huddled, their fifth and last barricade was being assembled, their last-stand hope.

It wasn't much, but with the few troops they had, it was all they could put together.

"That bombardment didn't last as long as it should," said Nick. "I wish I knew what was going on."

"Yep," said Rob. "But maybe that was good news - maybe we got some ships moving and distracted them. How many troops do you think they'll bring?"

"Three or four hundred, I think," Nick answered. "If it were me, I could do it with a hundred, but they're not as good as me. They'll bring a lot more."

"So maybe ten, fifteen shuttles?"

"I think so. Maybe more, maybe less."

"And you're pretty sure they'll land right out in the courtyard?"

Nick nodded. "Time is not on their side. They know that reinforcements may come at any time. They'll take the quickest route."

Rob nodded silently. Nick turned to his team, speaking

loudly and clearly. "Guys, remember your ambush protocol. Five seconds of fire, concentrate on personnel, get the hell out of here and back to the next barricade. Don't lose your head and fire too long; if you do, you'll probably be dead."

A chorus of "Aye, aye, sir" came from the fire team. Nick looked at Lt. Jeff Abrams, his number two, and Gunny Sergeant Ron Cook, his senior NCO. "Guys, see you at the top of the stairs. We'll be waiting there and fold you in as you come down."

"Aye, sir," said both in unison.

The Marines behind the barricade made a strange sight. Because they had planned to be guarding a social event, each had originally been wearing dress blues; but they had long since discarded their heavy formal tunics. Glass and debris lay under them, some adhering to their clothes. Their blue trousers with red blood stripe down the sides were covered in plaster dust and, in some cases, blood. Each had a pulse rifle and a bandolier of charges.

Rob and Nick carefully moved back to the South staircase, and ran quickly down to the next level, then down the central hallway to the halfway point. Because the ballrooms were connected internally, they had realized they could set up a third barricade here and still have a path of retreat to the other, North staircase going down to the sub-basement.

As Rob approached the half-way point, he saw the muzzles of five rifles on each side of the hallway, behind barricades made of furniture and equipment. Rob started to duck behind one of the barricades, but Nick pulled on his shoulder.

"Let them do their job, Rob. We need you to stay with me."

Rob nodded, and they trotted to the end of the hall, where the North staircase went down to the sub-basement storage area below. The upward-going staircase at this end was blocked by the collapsed roof – dozens of huge concrete blocks and other debris closed it off completely - so they didn’t have to worry about an attack from the main floor at this end of the hall.

Here Ginger, Mika, and Phoebe, along with volunteers from the guests hiding below, were finishing up the fourth barricade.

Rob took a second to fold Phoebe into his arms, kissing her and then looking into her eyes.

Phoebe looked back at him and said, "I want to stay here with you."

Rob shook his head. "Phoebe, I need you downstairs with the guests. Please."

Tears showed in her eyes. "Rob, I... I can't...if something happens to you..."

Rob kissed the tears off her cheeks, then looked deep into her eyes.

"I will be fine, and so will you. Go down with Ginger and Mike, take care of our guests. That's our job, Phoebe."

Phoebe nodded, then kissed his cheek and turned to go. Ginger and Mika were ahead of her, heading back down the stairs toward the sub-basement. Phoebe's hand held on to Rob's until the last second as she walked away - then she was gone.

Rob and Nick turned quickly, went back up the hallway, and once more up the stairs to the top of the South stairwell, where the second barricade overlooked the litter and rubble of the main floor.

In front of them, they could see the Marines huddled behind the first barricade at the building entry, checking their weapons one last time.

They both heard shuttle engines at the same time. "Here they come," said Rob. He unlimbered his rifle from his back and checked the charge again, then looked at Nick.

"Good luck."

Nick grinned. "You too!"

1941 Hours – Tolleson Hall

Captain Armand of the Hanoverian Guard screamed at his troops as the back ramp of the shuttle fell away. "Go, go, go!" he yelled, following them out and down the ramp. As trained, they spread out quickly, forming a perimeter, taking cover behind the rubble and debris strewn around the plaza from the bombardment. Within seconds, all ten shuttles had disgorged their cargo. Three hundred paramilitary troops filled the plaza, some huddled behind cover, others kneeling, waiting for the order to advance. Noncoms yelled, and some order started to come out of the chaos. Captain Armand spoke into his comm.

"Sergeant Helmand, first platoon to the right and secure the South perimeter. Sergeant Gibbon, second platoon to the left and secure the North. Sergeant Wofford - take third and fourth platoons and advance into the hall. Any resistance, shoot first and ask questions later. But remember, try to capture senior officers alive, if possible."

"You bet, Cap!" shot back Sergeant Wofford. Over the tacnet, Captain Armand heard Wofford getting his troops organized. Soon he had two platoons - 160 men - advancing slowly toward the Great Hall. They advanced to the bottom of the wide stone steps, peering into the dim recesses of the building.

Suddenly gunfire erupted from the hall, a hail of pulses that decimated the troops. Dozens of men died instantly, dozens more screamed and fell wounded. Confused, the men didn't know whether to advance or retreat. Sergeant Wofford turned to yell at them but was cut down before he could speak. Immediately, his men turned to flee, running for their lives back toward the shuttles for cover.

Captain Armand yelled into the tacnet: "First and Second Platoons, covering fire, aim at the entrance to the Hall!" As he spoke the words, the hail of pulses from the top of the stairs halted. First and Second Platoons quickly turned from their perimeter defense role and aimed their weapons at the top of the stairs and sent a storm of fire up at the entrance to the hall. But shooting up as they were, they succeeded only in knocking chips off the remaining inside roof of the hall. There was no one there to hurt.

Angry, Armand stepped out from his cover, waving his pistol at the retreating troops coming back toward him. "Stop!" he yelled. "Stop or I'll fire!" He aimed his pistol at the nearest trooper running toward him and fired, killing the man instantly. "Stop, I said!"

Slowly, the troops lurched to a halt. Behind them, dead and dying littered the bottom of the steps. Armand looked at them grimly.

"Corporal Mueller!" he yelled, looking at a Corporal near to him. "You take Sergeant Wofford's place."

"Yes, sir," said Mueller.

"Reform the men and prepare to enter the Hall," Armand said.

"Yes, sir," said Corporal Mueller.

On the tacnet, Armand called Sergeants Helmand and Gibbon. "Bring your platoons back over here and form up behind the others. We'll go in as a group and overwhelm them."

Armand got replies from the two Sergeants and saw their platoons coming back in his direction. Soon he had them formed up behind the remnants of the 3rd and 4th Platoons.

"We'll let the cowards go first, in the place of honor," he said openly over the tacnet, so that every man could hear it.

"Mueller, you're going to charge that hall - and any man who turns to run will be cut down! Got it?"

"Yes, sir," said Corporal Mueller.

"And just to be clear," he added over the tacnet, "Helmand and Gibbon, for the remainder of this mission, any man that turns to run, shoot them. Got it?"

"Yes, sir," chorused the two Sergeants.

1943 Hours – Tolleson Hall

Marine Lieutenant Jeff Abrams lay prone at the second ambush spot, at the top of the South stairs down to the basement level, where the squad had retreated after their initial ambush. The remainder of the squad lay likewise, heads pulled down below the level of the main floor.

A low, rambling barricade of furniture and debris lay across the entrance to the stairs, arranged to be as innocuous as possible. Between two blocks of stone the team had pushed into place, Sergeant Cook peered through a peephole, watching.

"Here they come," he whispered, as the Hanoverian rebels rushed the entrance to the Great Hall, firing wildly. Pulses glanced off the partially collapsed roof and the battered walls, ricocheting in every direction. Some even came back and hit the rebels, as they swept over the empty first barricade where seconds before the fire team had ambushed them.

Finding no one there, they came to a stop, milling around, searching the dim hall for anyone. Abrams saw another platoon press forward behind the first one, pushing into the hall as they all scanned the darkness.

Abrams watched as a Corporal and two Sergeants - identified by the stripes on their shirts - came up behind the mass of men and consulted together. Then, evidently in response to a command on their tacnet, the men started to spread out and search the floor.

"Standby," Abrams whispered, raising his hand slightly. The fire team watched him closely. As the rebels moved across the floor in all directions, bewildered by the lack of RDF personnel or bodies, they clustered up in several groups. Coming toward them, a large group of thirty to forty rebels began moving toward the staircase, and Abrams dropped his hand.

"Now!" he yelled. The fire team popped their pulse rifles over the top of the barricade and opened up, hosing the floor of the Great Hall with fire. In front of them, rebels dropped by the dozens, as the concentrated fire of twelve Marines with pulse rifles on full auto raked them mercilessly. Screams and shouts covered the floor of the Great Hall as hundreds of men ran for cover, sometimes tripping over the bodies of the dead and wounded.

In five seconds, the firing stopped. The fire team turned and ran, hunched over, down the stairs to the next level basement.

Behind them, an angry mob fired hundreds of pulses over their heads, then charged the top of the stairs. The enemy arrived to find an empty barricade.

A few jumped over the barricade and started down the stairs.

Sergeant Helmand cried "Stop!" at the men running down the stairs.

Almost all of them did. Several, however, kept running, around the bend in the stairs and into view of the basement below. They were cut down instantly by a hail of fire from further down the hallway.

Helmand had no trouble getting the remainder of his men to halt and come back up to the ground floor.

NEW GENEVA

RDF Seal Team Seven – the RDF Seals were an unconventional warfare unit of the Rim Defense Force, named in homage to a similar group from 21st century Earth. Seal Team Seven was the unit stationed in New Geneva, home of the Rim Parliament and Cabinet.
- RimWiki, 2230 Edition

Kamilaroi - New Geneva - Seal Team Seven Barracks
19 February 2189
1930 Hours

Grayson Clarke woke up when he hit the floor. Confused, he lay in the dark for a second, listening to the thumps of explosions occurring nearby. He jumped to his feet and burst a query out to the OOD, while he threw himself into pants and jacket.

<What's happening?>

<Big bomb went off down the street, sir. Took down a couple of buildings. Then a dozen shuttles landed and there's an attack on the Parliament Building>

<Who?>

<No idea, sir. They landed in the street outside the building. They stormed the building and went inside. Lots of small explosions going off, I think hand grenades>

<Call a Code Zulu Able Zulu>

<Already done, sir. I got responses from eight of our team, they're on the way in. Marine Barracks responded, but they're being bombarded by rail gun from orbit, so couldn't give me a firm ETA for readiness. Nothing from Fleet. I see lots of explosions overhead, I think Fleet has their hands full. Oh, and

the main AI is down, so comms are pretty bad. I think they blew it up. So, we only have our local tacnet>

<How many do we have in the barracks?>

<I show sixteen in the barracks, sir>

<Roger that. See you in two>

Clarke grabbed his go-bag and ran out of the room and down the stairs to the second-floor armory. He slammed his hand against the door, and it opened, getting the auth code from his MEMSAI, Samwise. He grabbed a rack of pulse rifles and pulled the entire rack out into the hallway, then pulled a rack of bandoliers out of the room and placed them next to the rifle rack. Grabbing three bandoliers and a rifle, he slammed a charge into the rifle and checked it just as Master Chief Petty Officer Li Tran ran up, still pulling his clothes on.

"Chief, we've got sixteen in the barracks, eight on the way in. I'm going downstairs to see what the story is. Stay here, get everybody kitted up, then send them downstairs. Capisce?"

"Capisce, sir. See ya!" said the Chief.

Clarke, commander of Seal Team Seven, ran for the stairs, passing five more of his team headed to the armory to get kitted out. Clarke pounded down the stairs to the OOD office, where Lieutenant (j.g.) Roger Battersea was peering out the windows at the Parliament building across the street.

"Anything?" he asked.

"No sir. They landed, went in, lots of small hand grenade type explosions, some firing but not much. There shouldn't have been very many people in the building on a Sunday night. Why assault the building if there's nobody there?"

"Smokescreen - a diversion. They want to draw everybody here."

"I'll be damn," said Roger. "What's the plan, Skipper?"

Kamilaroi - New Geneva
19 February 2189
1930 Hours

Prime Minister Sanada Yukimura had watched a holo and dozed off in his chair. He woke up to find a gun in his face. A voice said quietly, "No sudden moves."

Sanada nodded, then answered, "Yes. No problem."

"Get up and get your coat."

"Yes. No problem." He saw three men holding pistols before him. There was no sign of his security detail.

Sanada turned and walked to the front of his Japanese-style house, where the mud room contained all the shoes, umbrellas, and coats required in a wet climate like that of New Geneva. He took his overcoat off the hook and struggled into it. The man behind him pushed him forward with the muzzle of the pistol, so he went out the door. Outside, a flitter was parked on the lawn, and the bodies of two of his security team lay bloody on the ground.

Sanada was pushed harshly into the flitter. The door closed, and the flitter lifted off. It took a tack directly into the city, toward the industrial district.

Sanada saw smoke rising from the west, toward the Parliament Building. Soon the flitter descended, slipping between two small buildings to arrive at the back dock of a warehouse. He was roughly pushed out and stumbled, falling to his knees before someone grabbed the back of his collar and jerked him up. He was rushed into the warehouse as the flitter departed behind him.

Down a flight of stairs, Sanada was pushed into a small room. Carla Bianchi stood there, looking at him as the door slammed behind him.

"Well, hello, San-san," she said.

Sanada grunted. "That never was very funny, you know."

"Sorry. Couldn't resist." Carla replied.

"Any idea what's going on?" asked Sanada.

"Hanover," said Carla. "And Sierra Nevada, I think. I got a Code Zulu-Able-Zulu just before they put a block on my comm. And they're hitting the Parliament Building, for some crazy reason."

"Diversion," said Sanada. "To pull everybody away from us."

"Damn," said Carla. "Didn't think about that."

The door opened, and Home Secretary Adele Brodeur was chucked into the room, falling, and cutting her knee open on the concrete floor. Carla rushed over to her, helping her up. She assisted her to the wooden bench by the side wall, where she deposited her carefully. Carla began working on the wound, tearing off a strip of cloth from her skirt for a makeshift bandage.

"Adele, what do you know? Any news?" asked Sanada.

"They took the Parliament Building and they brought the City AI back up in limited mode. It's broadcasting that the RDF Headquarters at Tolleson Base has been seized and Admiral James Cobb has been installed as the new CNO, you and the entire cabinet have been captured or killed, and the Covenant of God has taken over as the new government of RimFed."

"Lovely," said Sanada. "Seems like they've jumped the gun just a bit, though. I only see three of us. That's far from the entire cabinet. And I still hear an awful lot of firing and explosions off in the distance."

Carla grinned. "Leave it to the Saints to lead with their mouth."

Kamilaroi - New Geneva
19 February 2189
1945 Hours

"You don't want us on the Parliament Assault?" asked Clarke.

"No," replied Naval Attaché Captain Louis Marchand, "I agree with you that's a diversion. I think the Marines and the Guard can take care of it. I want you to go get the Prime Minister and Carla Bianchi."

"How do we find them?" asked Clarke.

Marchand, on the other end of their backup tacnet holo, gestured at a small device on the table in front of him.

"Several years ago, we simulated a similar scenario to this one. We wanted to implant a tracking device in each cabinet minister when they got elected, but the Prime Minister vetoed that suggestion. However, Carla Bianchi got one as an experiment. When we offered to take it out, she just laughed and said she would keep it. I had almost forgotten about it until today. I don't think anybody knows about it."

"Fantastic," said Clarke.

Marchand went on. "I've got a weak reading, but it should get stronger as you get closer. It shows her somewhere in the warehouse district. Pick up this homer on your way. Be careful; we want them back alive if possible."

"Aye, aye, sir," said Clarke. "Can do."

THE BASEMENT

It is well that war is so terrible, otherwise we should grow too fond of it.
- Robert E. Lee

Kamilaroi - Tolleson Base
19 February 2189
2015 Hours – Tolleson Great Hall

Cautiously, the rebels peeked around the staircase into the darkened basement hallway. They knew the Marines were there, but there was no other way to get to them.

They had tried. They had spent the last ten minutes looking for any other way to get around them and flank them, but there was nothing. The North stairway at the other end of the Great Hall was blocked by the collapsed roof.

There was nothing for it but an all-out assault straight down the hallway - or go home. Captain Armand conferred with his Sergeants and Corporal Mueller.

"You just have to hit them hard, keep going, don't stop for anything. There is no other way. And this time, I better not see anyone stop. Keep going, keep firing, kill them all. Then we can be done with this."

Sergeants Helmand and Gibbon nodded, as did Corporal Mueller.

Armand glared at them. "We've got 250 men left. They have maybe a dozen. Get this done!"

The noncoms nodded and moved out, back to their troops huddled all along the stairwell to the basement. Gibbon muttered quietly out of the side of his mouth to Helmand,

"...more like 150, I think..."

"Shut up," said Helmand.

Arriving at the top of the stairwell, Helmand issued orders over the tacnet. Soon he had organized the assault into three platoons. An initial group stood right at the cusp of the turn in the stairwell, only feet from a direct view into the basement. Their job was to charge into the first ballroom on the right, then out the back into the service hallway, and flank the Marines positioned at the middle barricade, halfway down the main hall.

Behind them, another platoon stood ready to go to the left, through the ballroom on that side, and through the service corridor into the next ballroom, flanking the Marines from the other side.

And finally, the third platoon, looking nervous, was positioned to charge straight down the main hallway at the middle barricade, after the two flanking platoons took the Marines under crossfire.

Helmand issued the orders and with a yell, the first group charged down the last half of the stairs and into the ballroom on the right side. A wave of shots took its toll on the attackers, leaving five more bodies on the stairs; but most of them got through.

Immediately behind, the second group charged down and went to the left, losing a half-dozen troopers, but making it into the ballroom and out of sight.

After a minute, sporadic fire from both platoons turned quickly into a full-on assault as they flanked in from both sides toward the Marine's third barricade, mid-way down the hallway. Then the third platoon charged, down the hallway toward the makeshift barricade halfway down the hallway. Shouting and screaming, they fired at full auto into the stacked furniture and debris.

Unfortunately, their comrades coming from the left and right were also still firing on full auto, reloading their rifles as fast as they could, screaming at the top of their lungs. By the time the carnage stopped, more than fifty troopers had died.

Only twenty were killed by the Marines, who had long since abandoned the decoy mid-hallway barricade and were firing from the very end of the hall, from the fourth barricade at the top of the North stairs.

The other thirty rebels were killed by their own troops in the crossfire.

And then all was quiet. Sergeant Helmand arrived at the makeshift barricade at the half-way point of the hall, looking in disgust at the dozens of bodies lying around. There were no Marine bodies behind the barricade.

Helmand cursed. "Devils! It was a sham! They knew this would happen!"

Gibbon stood beside him, looking down the long hallway at the fourth barricade at the end, leading down to the sub-basement level. There was no sign of activity. Nothing moved.

"I really hate these bastards now," he said.

Kamilaroi - New Geneva
19 February 2189
1945 Hours

Carla Bianchi paced the floor. Sanada looked up at her.

"Carla, I think you should sit down. Save your energy."

"Dammit, I don't want to save my energy. I want to kill somebody!"

Sanada laughed. "Be careful what you wish for. You may get the chance!"

The door slammed open, and they saw a big bear of a man standing there, in front of two guards with pulse rifles. He was wearing a uniform, with shoulder flashes and insignia like a general. He advanced into the room and stood in front of Sanada, ignoring the other two.

"I am General Ernst Wolff. I am now the Prime Minister of RimFed. You are no longer in charge here, Sanada."

Wolff produced a tablet. "You will sign this document."

Sanada grinned up at Wolff. "Actually, I won't."

Wolff slapped Sanada across the mouth, breaking his lip. The blood dripped down Sanada's hand as he held his lip.

Wolff shoved the tablet at Sanada. Sanada ignored it, his gaze challenging Wolff. Wolff hit him again, knocking him off the bench.

Carla ran at Wolff, but one of the guards behind her knocked her down before she could get to him.

Wolff bent over Sanada. "Last chance, chink. Sign or die."

Sanada looked up at him. "I can't believe you're so stupid you don't know the difference between Japanese and Chinese."

Wolff sneered at him and spun around, leaving the room. As the door closed, Carla crawled over to Sanada and wiped blood away from his eye where he had hit the floor.

Kamilaroi - New Geneva
19 February 2189
2015 Hours

Clarke and his team inserted into the warehouse district about ten blocks from the suspect warehouse. They did their equipment checks and then moved out cautiously, scanning for snipers, watchers, or other threats. They saw nothing until they were within a block of the warehouse. Then the Seal on point pumped his hand, and they froze. On the tacnet, the point whispered, "Snipers ahead, two each side of the street, top of the roof."

Clarke acknowledged. "Fire Team One, left side, up through the building beside us, take them out on my mark. Fire Team Two, right side, up through the building beside us, take them out on my mark."

Acknowledging, the two Fire Teams moved out. Clarke and Chief Tran took the other four Fire Teams and moved into the cover of the building beside them, waiting for Teams 1 and 2 to get into position. After several minutes of waiting, Clarke heard the acknowledgement over the tacnet.

"Team One, in position, ready."

Shortly after, he heard the other team's acknowledgment and called, "On my mark...3...2...1...mark!"

Up the street, seconds later, he heard a thud.

"All bogeys down, one went over the building, sorry about that," he heard from Team One.

"Shit happens," said Clarke. "How's it look?"

"All quiet so far."

"OK," Clarke said on the tacnet. "We're on the clock now, as soon as they poll the snipers and get no response, our surprise is gone. Teams Three through Six, with me, move forward fast to the edge of the target building. Teams One and Two, stay in place, cover our butts."

Acknowledgment came quickly, and Clarke moved out with the rest of his fire teams. They made good time to the edge of the warehouse.

Clarke leaned carefully around in the pitch dark and saw a dozen guards lounging in front of the warehouse door.

"Team Six, go around the back and see what's up."

Clarke waited for a minute, until Team Six called in.

"Four guards in back at the loading dock."

Clarke issued orders.

"Teams Three and Four, wait here. Teams Three and Four only, on my mark, wait five seconds then take out the guards in front. Be noisy about it. Then move through the building, making lots of noise. Remember, somewhere in here is the Prime Minister and at least one of his cabinet, so watch your targets. Team Five, with me."

Teams Three and Four acknowledged. Clarke reversed course and moved toward the back of the warehouse where Team Six waited. Getting to the back corner, he leaned out carefully and scanned the rear with his night goggles.

There were four guards, two standing and two sitting in chairs. Clarke withdrew and spoke softly over the tacnet.

"Team Six only - on my mark, take out the guards in back as quietly as possible. Teams Five and Six only - after the bogeys are down, move fast into the warehouse and secure a perimeter. Be as quiet as possible. All teams - remember watch your targets, we have good guys in there. Any questions?"

All teams acknowledged. Clarke took a deep breath.

"On my mark...3...2...1...mark!"

Team Six disappeared around the corner of the building, followed closely by Team Five. Clarke waited 5 seconds, then went around the corner of the building.

Four bodies lay on the ground by the loading dock, and the last of Team Five was entering the building. From in front, he heard noisy gunfire as Teams Three and Four attacked, intentionally making as much disruptive noise as possible.

Clarke followed Team Five into the building and scanned quickly. Three more bodies lay in the hallway. On the steps leading downstairs was one more body. Teams Five and Six were setting up in the rooms beside the hallway, covering both directions.

Clarke scanned with the homing device. He was close, but it was hard to tell where Carla Bianchi was with the device. It showed her right on top of him, but he couldn't get a direction.

Clarke thought for a moment. He looked at the lone body on the stairs leading down to the basement. He motioned to Chief Tran and they ran down the steps to the next lower level. Beside the first door they came to they found an empty chair.

Clarke looked at Tran and they stood on opposite sides of the door, raising their pistols for entry. Clarke tried the handle, but it was locked. He nodded at Tran, who placed a small charge on the door at the lock. They crossed the hallway to the opposite side and Tran sent a command via tacnet, then started counting.

"3...2...1..."

The blast was not large, but it was well-shaped. Clarke ran across the hallway and kicked the door, which flew open. He rushed inside, Tran behind him. He was immediately hit in the back of his neck by something, and stumbled, almost falling. Before he could react, he heard Tran yelling: "Stop! Seals! Navy Seals!"

Carla Bianchi held up the wooden leg of the bench, staring at

Clarke. He groaned, rubbing his neck. "Carla, it's me. Don't hit me again!"

Carla dropped the bench leg and grabbed him in a bear hug. Clarke tried to break free, finally getting her hands unwrapped from him. He broadcast over tacnet, "I have the good guys, basement level, first door, Team Five down here to escort. The rest of you, light 'em up!"

Immediately he heard a barrage of fire overhead as his teams cleaned out the remaining survivors of the erstwhile Hanoverian Guard.

DONE AND DONE

It is an unfortunate fact that we secure peace only by preparing for war.
- John F. Kennedy

Kamilaroi - Tolleson Base
19 February 2189
2019 Hours – Tolleson Great Hall

Below Basement Level One, Level Two consisted of a storage area. Rob and his Marines waited at their last barricade, behind a wall of furniture, tables, chairs, and cases of wine. Nick had groaned as they placed the cases of wine in the front of the barricade, butted up against the hard surface of banquet tables. "What a waste of good wine!" he said to Rob. Rob grinned and kept stacking.

Now they waited, crouched behind their makeshift defense, knowing this was their last stand. There was no way out of the storage area - except back up the way they came, right into the teeth of the enemy.

Behind them, the hundreds of Navy, Marine, and civilian VIPs lay on the floor, having dragged furniture in front of them to protect them from the coming onslaught. Mike had passed out the two extra rifles to a couple of VIPs who insisted on joining the fight. All of them together made twenty-eight people, counting Phoebe, Ginger, Mika and the two VIPs.

"How many do you think they got left?" asked one of the VIPs, a Marine Colonel.

"Roughly, I'd say about 150," said Nick. Rob nodded in agreement.

The Marine Colonel grinned. "Good, that makes a half-dozen for each of us."

Rob pointed to the back corners of the room. "Nick, what do you think about putting a couple of rifles in each of the corners? Get them in a crossfire..."

Nick shook his head. "We'd only have the element of surprise for one volley, then they'd be completely exposed. I'd keep everybody together."

Rob nodded. Just then, they heard noise up above, and pieces of their previous barricade came tumbling down the stairs. "Here they come," said Nick.

Around the corner of the staircase came a solid wall of men, firing madly in every direction into the sub-basement. As they had briefed beforehand, they held their fire until the staircase was completely full of packed men. "Fire," yelled Nick, and they opened up on full auto.

Rob fired until his gun went silent, out of charge. He yanked the old magazine out and slammed a new one in and fired that one dry. Still, they kept coming, now halfway across the floor to their barricade.

Rob fired his third magazine dry and prepared to fight hand-to-hand. But just then he saw the attackers falter. The wave of men stopped, then reversed, many of the enemy screaming in fear as they ran away, back up the staircase. The floor and the staircase were littered with bodies. In a moment, it was quiet again.

Nick looked over the barricade, counting.

"Looks like we took out about forty," he said. "That leaves them with about a hundred-ten and change, I think."

"Yeah, but I'm out of charge," said Rob.

"Me, too," said Phoebe and Ginger.

Nick canvassed the group quickly. Between them, they had only six magazines left. Six of their cohort were down, two dead and four with severe wounds. The survivors dragged the dead and wounded farther back, placing them in the care of some of the VIPs who had formed a makeshift aid station off to one side.

Coming back to the barricade, Nick looked at Rob grimly. “We can’t hold back another rush like that,” he said.

Rob looked around, trying to think of anything they could do to hold back the next attack. But there was nothing. “I guess we’ll go hand-to-hand at the end,” he said to the group. Everybody nodded, their eyes glinting with anticipation of death.

Suddenly, Rob heard a faint “ping” in his comm. It was the sound that usually meant his comm was going online to the Base AI. He saw from the faces of the others that their comms had done likewise.

<This is Commander Walker, anybody there?> he broadcast.

Immediately he got an answer. <Marine Company One, where are you, sir?>

<In the sub-basement, two levels down. The enemy is one level above us, preparing for another rush. We’re just about out of ammo. How soon can you be here?>

<Thirty seconds, sir> came the response.

Rob looked at Nick, who shook his head.

<We don’t have thirty seconds. Move faster!> Rob told them.

His words were prophetic, as within fifteen seconds the stairs suddenly filled with yelling, screaming Hanoverians firing wildly at them, charging down the stairs and across the basement floor. They rushed the barricade, shooting and screaming.

Rob’s team – those who had charge left – fired slower this time, trying to space out their shots to have something left at the end. But Rob heard the rifles go silent, one by one, as the Marines depleted their magazines.

Rob had earlier grabbed a fistful of butcher knives from one of the boxes around them and handed them out to the Marines. Now he prepared to stand up and fight to the end. But just before he stood, when the enemy was no more than fifteen meters from him, a fusillade of shots rang out behind the Hanoverians. There on the stairwell, Rob saw several dozen Marines taking careful aim, knocking down rebels by the bunch while trying not to hit the friendlies. Pulses whizzed over Rob’s head, and he hunkered down trying to dig a hole in the concrete floor, as was everyone else behind the barricade.

"We surrender! We surrender!" someone yelled. The firing stopped. Rob hesitantly peeked over the top of the barricade. 60 to 70 Hanoverians stood between him and the Marines on the stairwell, their hands in the air, their weapons tossed on the floor.

Rob looked at Nick, and cautiously they rose. Marines poured into the sub-basement from the stairwell, surrounding the Hanoverians quickly.

Rob and Nick moved out from behind the barricade, keeping an eye on the enemy. Half-way across the floor, they met the Captain of the Marine company. He handed them both full magazines and they checked and inserted the charges, their hands shaking with after-action jitters. Lieutenant Owens and Gunny Cook came up to join them.

"Gentlemen," Rob said, "I don't know about you, but I was composing my speech to St. Peter!"

Nick, Lt. Owens and Gunny Cook nodded. Together they turned off their pulse rifles and listened to them whine down as the Marines secured the prisoners.

*****

Vladimir Victorovitch Volotskoi, temporary commander of the battleship *Arizona*, watched with satisfaction as *Taizong* gave up the fight and pulled out, making for the outer system on two of her four engines. Behind her, the rest of Cobb's fleet followed, excepting the frigate *John Paul Jones* and the cruiser *Galileo*, which were both dissipating clouds of debris orbiting the planet.

Vlad almost giggled at the relief he felt as he realized he, and the rest of the crew of the *Arizona*, had survived. He looked across the holotank at Carter, who was simply catatonic, staring into space. Maria Rogers and Yuka Kawasaki were not much better; both just stared at him as if he were an apparition.

On the holo, damage messages blinked in red for nearly every major system, and Vlad was receiving updates from at least ten damage control teams hell-bent on saving the ship from fires and perforations to space.

But they were alive.

<Buster, priority message to Admiralty and Kamilaroi Approach, and gencom to all stations, *Taizong* departing with her tail between her legs> Vlad said to the ship's AI.

<Message sent> responded Buster.

Kamilaroi - Tolleson Base
26 February 2189

It had taken a week to get everything cleaned up and restored back to some semblance of normal. Jake Hammett had returned from his trip to the Aeolian Empire and now sat at his conference table with his staff. They waited patiently while he finished reading last-minute reports on the holo. Finally, he looked up.

"Where's Cobb now?" he asked.

"He ran for Earth," said Ginger. "He claimed political asylum and the North American Alliance gave it to him. The bastards. He's sitting in a bar in Denver right now, enjoying a cold beer, while we bury our dead."

"Not too surprised," said Jake. "Earth has always had leanings toward the Saints, especially the North Americans. Where's the *Taizong*?"

"Parked in orbit around Earth, along with all his other ships," said Ginger. "The North Americans are claiming it and refuse to give it back."

"Fine, let them keep it," said Jake. "I want to make sure he has a way to leave Earth, because someday he will, and when he does..."

"Roger that," said Ginger. "We'll light him up like a Roman candle if he ever sets foot off that planet again."

"He will," said Jake. "And we'll be waiting."

"I have a question," said Wei Lei, Jake's Chief of Logistics. "Where did that signal come from that alerted the *Arizona*? The one that said, '*Coming at you not friendly...*'"

Jake grinned. "You know where it came from. She's still puttering around our little neck of the woods, keeping an eye on us. Like an old mother hen..."

"*Pandora*," Ginger breathed.

PART THREE - DESTINY - 2205

ANDREA IONA

No man is so foolish as to desire war and not peace, for in peace children take their parents to the grave, in war it is the parents who take the children to the grave.
- Herodotus

Kamilaroi - Tolleson Base
4 February 2205 - 83 Years after Pandora

Lieutenant Commander Vitus kicked hard left rudder, and the A40 spun around, facing back the way it came. Running backwards, he fired two missiles at the pursuer, and watched as they both ran hot and true toward the Bat corvette chasing him.

The enemy corvette jinked to dodge the missiles, but it was hopeless. The corvette had maneuvered too close, and Vitus had it cold. With a flash, the missiles hit, and the corvette disintegrated.

Vitus' screens froze, and his canopy opened automatically as the simulation was ended by the training NCO.

"Not too bad, sir," said the Senior Chief running the simulator. "Remind me not to go up against you in one of these new birds."

Vitus grinned. The A40 was the latest attack craft in the RDF arsenal, and much improved over prior models. Vitus loved it. It was responsive, fast, and deadly. With two full-size shipkiller missiles, it could - in theory- take down a battleship if the missiles hit in just the right spot. Of course, that was the trick all right - getting the missiles to the right spot without getting killed on the way in.

Intelligence reports on the Bat Fleet stated their close-in

point defense weaponry was not as good as the RDF's - but even mediocre point defense could kill you.

Vitus stepped out of the simulator just as his MEMSAI pinged.

<Hey son>

<Hi, Dad>

<Will you be home for dinner tonight?>

<No, sorry. I'm going out with Eva again>

<Getting serious with her?>

<Absolutely. Talk later>

<OK, be safe out there>

* * * * *

Vitus stepped quickly to his quarters and changed, getting ready for his date with Eva, one of the young Daneki of his generation – a girl born just days after their arrival in the RDF, nineteen years before. She had recently graduated from Kamilaroi University as an engineer and started work in the Weapons Lab, where the entire Daneki contingent spent their time developing "skunk works" projects. There was no better group of engineers in the Rim – their prowess was legendary. At their fingertips had been born the A40 attack fighter, the shipkiller missiles that it carried, the sentient AI that now powered many of the RDF's point defense systems, and a host of other innovations – all of which crafted a Rim Defense Force of power much greater than thought possible just twenty years before.

And she was cute, thought Vitus. Very cute. They had been dating for two months now, and he had brought her home to meet his Dad, Captain Cassian, a few days before. And Cassian approved. With the small population of Daneki that had survived the Bat onslaught on their home planet and escaped to the Rim, there was an unspoken – but very real – pressure to re-populate the race as quickly as possible. And Vitus was all for that.

Leaving his cabin, he ran up the ladders to the long transit tube down the starboard side of the ship and, reaching for a grab handle as it went by, got himself on the fast slidewalk toward the stern of the *Enterprise*. In a few seconds, he jumped off at the shuttle bay doors and slapped his hand on the exit pad, getting the green light and beep that cleared him to leave the ship.

Jumping through the doors, he ran to the dirtside shuttle, which was just on the point of leaving. Slapping his hand once more on the pad at the shuttle entrance, he got the green light and beep and the guard nodded, checking his name off a tablet in his hand.

Vitus slammed himself into a seat just as the door closed behind him. He felt the shuttle pressure up as the door sealed, felt the grav plates energize, and with a bump and a thud, the shuttle was out the launch tube and on its way to Tolleson City.

Vitus thought about the last twenty years of his life. In those dark days after their escape from the Bats, struggling to find a place to survive, he could never have foreseen the events that led him to his current place – an officer in the RDF, living his dream, flying the best bird any pilot could ask for, in love with Eva. He still missed his parents - he never stopped thinking about them – but he knew they would be proud of what he and the other Daneki had accomplished.

Vitus was content, even more than content – he was happy. And soon, very soon, he was sure, it would be time to take the fight back to the killers of his family. He could feel it in his bones.

And it would never be soon enough.

With a slight lurch, the shuttle touched down and everyone started filing off, down a boarding tube into the terminal. Vitus followed, in no hurry, knowing that no matter how early he arrived at the restaurant, Eva would not be there. She was always late. If Eva said to meet at six pm, he arrived at six-thirty and then waited a half-hour for her. It never failed. It had become a standing joke between them.

Just outside the terminal, he caught a flitter to town and sat, looking out the window at the bright, neon-lit nightlife of

Tolleson City.

Beyond the city, just on the horizon, he could see a glow as the volcano Bombarri sent a small river of lava down its western slope.

Kamilaroi did not have a lot of habitable land area. There were only two major land areas in use - one holding Tolleson Base and Tolleson City, the town catering to the military - and on the other side of the planet, the slightly larger island area holding New Geneva, home of the Rim Parliament.

At Tolleson, the town surrounding the base was called the "ville" by the sailors from the base, a slang term that as near as Vitus could tell, dated back to the early 20th century on Earth, maybe even before that. Like most military towns, it had its share of problems, and a thriving business for the Shore Patrol on a Saturday night.

But tonight, Vitus was going uptown, to the high-toned end of the city, because he had a special question to ask Eva. He took the ring out of his pocket and looked at it again, smiling.

* * * * *

At the restaurant, Eva came in just as Vitus expected, more than forty-five minutes late. But he had arrived only fifteen minutes before, so he grinned. His timing remained intact. Once seated, Eva smiled at him, and apologized.

"Sorry, I got tied up working on a modification to the grav fluctuations we've seen on the new deflector. I lost track of time."

Vitus grinned. "No worries. How's it coming with that?"

Eva shrugged. "Pretty good. Can't talk much about it, you know, but we're getting there."

Vitus nodded. "Right, glad to hear that."

"How about you? Still killing Bats in the simulator?"

"But of course," grinned Vitus. "That's my life. I kill them by morning, I kill them by night."

Eva laughed. "Let's just hope, when the day comes, you can

maintain that record."

Vitus got serious for a minute. "Any idea when that day might come?"

Eva shook her head. "You would know better than me. You're Fleet, I'm just R&D."

Vitus grimaced. "I am getting damn tired of waiting. Sometimes I feel like I can't wait another day. I just want to jump in a ship and take off for Nest, start shooting things."

"I know, hon," said Eva. "But patience…it will come. Admiral Hammett says we must be absolutely ready before we take the initiative. And I agree with that."

Vitus sighed. "I know. But…"

Eva patted his hand across the table. "Patience, Vitus. It will come."

Vitus suddenly reached his hand in his pocket and pulled out the box containing the ring.

"I was going to wait until after dinner to ask this, but I just can't wait, Eva."

He slid out of his chair and knelt on his knee next to the table, holding the ring out at Eva. Amused diners all around them turned to look as the young Daneki opened the box and showed the contents to her.

"Eva," he began.

Eva squealed. "Yes," she screamed before he could say another word. She snatched the ring out of his hand and pulled him to her. "Yes!"

The restaurant broke out into applause around them as Vitus held her, tears in his eyes and his heart soaring.

* * * * *

The door slammed open at the back of the classroom and Jake Hammett marched in.

"Ten-shut!" someone yelled, and the assembled officers - mostly Commanders and Captains, a couple of newly-minted Admirals – rose to a loose attention.

"At ease," Jake said, his voice carrying across the room. He marched to the front of the classroom, turned at the podium and dropped his tablet down on it. He gazed around the room.

"Welcome to the 2205 session of the Command Officer Strategy School," said Jake. "Or as we like to call it here, 'Advanced Bat-Killing'."

A titter of laughter ran around the room.

"Now, one of the questions that we get over and over again, is – why hasn't the RDF made it known that we have a battle plan for meeting the threat of the Bats, and when do we expect to do that?"

"Any ideas on that, class?"

An Aeolian officer in the middle of the classroom stood up. Her holographic nametag, <Commander Derinoe>, appeared in front of her in Jake's vision.

"Because that could be giving away too much to the enemy, sir."

Jake grinned. "That is correct. Also, everyone, we won't be concerned with the formalities here. Please answer from your seats, and that will help us to focus on our objective - learning how to defend our worlds."

He stepped out from behind the podium, and paced slowly in front of the class, hands clasped behind his back.

"I am here to tell you today, that we do, indeed, have a battle plan for meeting the threat of the Bats. And a schedule."

A collective intake of breath sounded like a massive sigh around the room.

"Yes, I know. We have spent eighty-four years focused on colonization, development of technology, build out of the fleet, weapons research and design, forming the Alliance – and repeatedly, civilians - and of course RDF staff - have asked, 'When will you actually start letting us know about the end game?' "

Jake stopped and looked at the class. "Today is the day. I am here to tell you that, after eighty-four years, you - the officers in this room - will be there at that battle. You will execute the battle plan. And you will deliver to us the victory that will remove the

Bat threat from the Rim forever."

There was silence in the room.

"Captain..." Jake, gazing at the holographic nametags in front of each person in the audience, directed his question to a male RDF officer in the front row.

"...Achsasi. What is the most recent estimate of the discovery of the Rim by the Bats?"

Captain Achsasi started to rise, but Jake waved him down. "No formalities in the classroom, please."

"Nine more years, plus or minus five years, depending of course on their rate of expansion and scouting in this direction." said Captain Achsasi, returning to his seat.

"Correct." said Jake. Once again pacing, he directed himself to the entire class. "Prepare to input." he said. Pausing, he looked left and right across the class. "What strategy at this point would have the best chance of success to defeat the Bats? You have one minute."

Most students closed their eyes as they began communicating via their comm beads with their tablets, making note of the problem statement and formulating a response.

Jake stood at the podium. He looked at Aeolian Admiral Andrea Iona Satra, sitting to his left, concentrating on her tablet - but with her eyes open, looking back at him. Jake smiled and sent a silent message to her via his MEMSAI.

<The *Empress Hecate* is beautiful. Congratulations on getting her as your flagship>

Andrea smiled slightly as she continued work on the problem statement.

A minute later, Jake called time. He turned to the holographic screen behind him as the AI automatically correlated the answers and placed them on the screen, collected into categories pre-defined by Jake.

"Hmmm...fifteen responses are some form of 'conduct guerrilla warfare and attacks of attrition'." Jake nodded, looked at the class. "I like it. That is a very good answer. And part of the solution. But not the complete solution that I want today."

More silence pervaded the students. Jake turned back to the screen. "Twelve responses - 'attack the Bat's home fleet." Jake faced the class again.

"Not a terrible idea, but I would hate to go directly from no real experience fighting the Bats to an all-out, do-or-die attack on the center of their strength."

Jake grinned. "Although I do sympathize - we have waited for a long time, and it would be nice to get into some real action. But I don't want our first action to be a final battle that would decide the survival of the Rim instantly."

Turning back to the screen a final time, Jake continued. "And 3 responses - 'divide their Fleet by deception, defeat each component in detail.'"

Jake turned to the class. "I want each of the three people who provided this response to stand up, please."

In the front row, Captain Achsasi stood slowly. An Aeolian captain in the middle of the classroom stood – Captain Melousa. And finally, Andrea Iona stood, to Jake's left, a slight smile on her face.

"Everyone take a good look around. These three officers already have a pretty good idea how to kill Bats," stated Jake. "As a result, they will be your team leaders for the next week as we work on the strategy they have just formulated."

With a hand motion, Jake dismissed the hologram, and waved the standing officers to be seated. "There are thirty students in this class. We will divide into three teams, each team consisting of ten students. For the first week, the students who were just standing will act as team leaders. Each team will further sub-divide into three teams of three students each. Each sub-team will develop and publish part of the plan based on the last of the strategies we just discussed - divide the Bat's fleet by deception, attack them by surprise, and defeat them in detail before they can re-group. The team leaders will assign the sub-teams their part of the exercise. You will continue your classes with other instructors for the remainder of this week, and work on this project in your off-hours.

One week from today each team will publish their plans. Make sure they are published by next Monday, eight AM sharp. Your plans will be evaluated, and I will meet with you in this classroom at nine AM to critique them. Any questions?"

A mumble of negatives and head shakes ran around the room. Jake continued. "One more thing, the Team Leaders are responsible for ensuring that every team member participates, is engaged, and contributes value to the exercise. Rank - or branch of service - will be suspended and have no place in these exercises. If you give the Team Leaders any grief, you can expect to be on the next ship out of here and spend a long and boring life in Supply."

Laughter ran around the room. "Next Monday, at the end of our critique, I will ask another question, like the one I asked today. The best three answers will decide the team leaders for the last week of class. Oh - and the Team Leaders from this week will not be eligible."

Silence pervaded the room as Jake gazed coolly around. "Then get to it, folks. Class dismissed!"

FOURTH LIFE

By all means, marry. If you get a good wife, you'll become happy; if you get a bad one, you'll become a philosopher.
- Socrates

Kamilaroi - Tolleson Base
11 February 2205 - 83 Years after Pandora

The following Monday, Jake stood at the front of the class. They had gone over the various draft battle plans, and Jake was pleased. All three teams had developed a sound plan that closely matched the one Jake's team had already finalized. Of course, he couldn't tell them that. But now he was ready to move on.

"Today's question. Where do we fight?" he tossed out to the assembled students. "You have one minute to post your response."

From near the front of the class, Andrea Iona smiled at him. Jake had almost forgotten how beautiful she was, with her black hair, brown eyes, and tomboy build. Some Aeolians – including Andrea - were a bit darker than contemporary Europeans, he wasn't sure why. Sort of like a permanent suntan. Something about their genetics, frozen from the 8th century B.C. But he liked it.

Jake caught himself thinking about her age. She had been about twenty-five when he first met her, twenty years before. So... maybe about forty-five now, he thought. Biologically, Jake was still only 38, not really aging compared to the rest of Humanity. He pushed the thought away. His biological age didn't matter. Everyone knew his real age. Jake was pushing 123 now. It was silly to think about it.

* * * * *

Jake's AI pinged, then "Visitor Waiting" flashed into his upper peripheral vision.

Jake scowled. <I don't have any meetings scheduled now, Zoe>

<No, sir> said Zoe. <This is a drop-in. Admiral Andrea Iona Satra would like to speak to you>

<Ah> said Jake. <Send her in!>

Jake stood up and adjusted his uniform. The door opened, and Andrea Iona stood there, magnificent in her AEN dress uniform. She had her cap under her arm, in the RDF fashion. Jake couldn't help but smile.

"Andrea! Come in!" he came around the desk and held out his arms. Andrea walked into them, and the hug they executed was perhaps just a bit too long.

Jake finally pulled away, blushing slightly, and motioned her to a chair. Walking back around his desk, he grinned at her.

"You are kicking ass in the Strategy School, Andrea."

Andrea grinned back at him. "Well, remember what Hecate used to say - if you want something killed, send Andrea!"

Jake chuckled. "Yes, I remember! How is my granddaughter?"

"She's magnificent. Keeping a close eye on the shipbuilding and crew training, making sure we get our plan done on time. I just got a message from her this morning. She said to tell you hello."

"Fantastic," said Jake. "I miss her. I haven't seen her in, oh...maybe three years now. I wish I could see her more often."

"I know," said Andrea. "But you have a lot on your plate. And it's a long trip. Six weeks now, with the new drives in a fast corvette. Still, a bit of a hike."

Jake nodded. "How can I help you?"

Andrea leaned back in her chair, collecting her thoughts.

"You know that we Aeolians are fully committed to your plan of surprise attack against the Bats. Because of our Rebellion, we've fought in space long enough to know the pitfalls that can arise with such plans, but wc continue to believe that's our best chance for long-term success." She paused.

Jake nodded.

"We are concerned about these neo-fascists in the Rim Parliament - the ones you call 'Saints'. These proposed initiatives they are attempting to pass... This idea...this half-baked idea they have, of trying to approach the Bats and negotiate a peace treaty...this is crazy."

Jake nodded again and smiled. "Andrea, trust me. That idea is going nowhere. The Saints will not succeed in getting that passed through Parliament."

Andrea looked askance at Jake. "Are you sure? It certainly looks like they have a lot of public support. The latest polls are showing they have 49% of the votes in the lower house, and a good chance of passing the upper."

"Yes, but there's one thing you don't know. The Prime Minister will veto it, even if it passes."

Andrea looked puzzled. "Wouldn't that be the end of his career, if he vetoed a popular measure that had passed both houses?"

"Probably," Jake said. "In fact, almost certainly. But there are some things that are more important than career. Every time we go out into space, we risk our lives for the sake of the future. I know it seems impossible that a politician would do the same, but in this case, I can assure you that he will. He is a close friend of mine and will never let this bill go into law. Feel free to pass that on to Hecate as well."

Andrea smiled. "You're very perceptive. Of course, that was the nature of her message to me this morning. She was concerned."

"Tell her not to be concerned. It is handled." said Jake.

Andrea leaned forward and looked at Jake, biting her lip.

"There's one more item I'd like to discuss with you," she said. "But it's personal. Is that OK?"

"Sure," said Jake. "Anything."

"You say that now," said Andrea.

"No, seriously," said Jake. "Fire away."

"Well," said Andrea. Jake could see it was something hard for her to get out, which surprised him. The fiercest warrior in the AEN, unable to spit something out? This must be serious, he thought.

"I know you lost both of your original wives many years ago," said Andrea.

Jake stiffened.

"I don't mean to say anything to hurt you or bring you pain, Jake," said Andrea, rushing to finish before Jake took offense. "I know how much they meant to you. And Antiope, as well. I understand your grief, even after all these years."

Jake waited, his face like stone.

Andrea met his eyes. "Jake, I have had feelings for you since the first day I met you, twenty years ago. I think it's time you let go of the past and looked to the future again."

Jake stared at her. His mind blanked out. This was something he had not seen coming.

"Andrea," he began gently.

"And don't tell me how old you are," interrupted Andrea. "I don't care."

Jake stopped. She had read his mind. That was exactly what he was going to say.

A wry little smile managed to make its way to the corner of his mouth. "You say that now," he said. "But how about when I'm 125?"

Andrea grinned. "As long as you can still perform."

Jake was speechless. He blushed like a schoolboy.

Andrea rose. "I know that nothing can happen now, while Strategy School is still in session, because I know you won't do a damn thing while that is going on. But...next Friday, Strategy School is done..." Andrea leaned forward across Jake's desk, her scent overwhelming him - "On that day, Jake Hammett, I expect an answer from you. Don't let me down."

With that, and before Jake could un-track his brain and get it working again, she was gone.

Jake sat in stunned silence for many minutes before he was able to finally, with a chuckle and a smile, get back to his work.

* * * * *

A week later, the Strat School graduation ceremony was done. All the students had been dismissed. They had drifted out of the auditorium, but as Jake made to exit, Andrea was waiting for him in the hallway.

Before he could react, she clasped his arm in hers and began walking with him down the hallway.

"Well?" asked Andrea Iona.

Jake looked down at the floor as he walked.

"Andrea," he began. "In a few years, we'll be in the fight of our lives."

"All the more reason not to be alone right now," said Andrea.

Jake shook his head. "We'd never have time to ourselves. You know how my life is; yours will be just as bad. You'll spend most of your time on the *Empress*; we'd never see each other."

"You're making up reasons not to; why not think up a good reason to do it?" Andrea said.

Jake sighed. "You can do so much better, Andrea."

Andrea wiggled his arm. "No, I can't. I've already found what I want."

10 April 2205
Tolleson Base - Base Chapel

Vitus stood nervously, awaiting his bride. The chapel was quiet, with only the noise of the fans blowing air across the crowd. Behind him, a priest waited, and to one side, his father, Captain Cassian, stood with the ring, with several of Vitus' fellow pilots from the *Enterprise* lined up behind him. On the other side, Eva's bridesmaids stood ready, clutching their flowers.

The Daneki followed a religion that closely paralleled many

RimFed religions, based on a belief in a Creator behind the universe, one that was both loving and aloof, leaving creatures mostly to their own affairs. It had not taken much for them to adapt to the RimFed customs of marriage and family. Some had even converted to the more common Human religions. Vitus was one of those, considering himself a good Episcopalian.

Now the back door of the chapel opened, and Eva came through, escorted by her maid of honor. She looked beautiful in her long white gown, five and half feet tall – as tall as Vitus and Cassian. Most of the second generation Daneki had grown taller, due to changes in their lifestyle and nutrition. Her hair was done up in a classic Daneki marriage whirl, and flowers garlanded her in a ring of color, around her waist and down her back, an old Daneki tradition. In her hand, rather than flowers, she carried a small book – an old copy of the Daneki Holy Book, one of the few remaining survivors of the Great Escape they had made from Danek years earlier. To the traditional Human tune of "Here Comes the Bride" she started down the aisle.

Through the door behind her, a second bride came, in Aeolian Navy dress whites, showing the rank of Admiral on her shoulder boards. Following close behind Eva, Andrea Iona Satra and her own maid of honor, Commander Derinoe, also stepped down the aisle.

In the front of the church, Vitus turned to look at Jake Hammett, standing beside him and looking just as nervous as he. Jake managed to wink at him, though, then turned back to look at Andrea as she approached. Vitus stepped forward and took Eva's arm, turning to the priest in front of them. Seconds later, Jake stepped forward and took Andrea's arm, also turning to face the priest.

Minutes later, the priest finished reciting the Daneki marriage vows, and Vitus took the ring from Cassian, placing it on Eva's finger, following the Human tradition. Then the Daneki service was done, and the priest focused on Jake and Andrea. He quickly finished the initial part of the RDF ceremony, and Jake turned to Ginger, standing behind him, and took the ring from her, placing it on Andrea's finger.

The priest continued. "Do you, Jake Hammett, take this woman to be your wife?" asked Father Scipio Tolleson II.

Jake looked at the priest, grandson of his marriage with Teresa Tolleson.

"I do, Grandson," he said.

Scipio looked irritated but continued.

"And do you, Andrea Iona Satra, take this man to be your husband?"

Andrea looked at Jake, grinning. "I do," she said.

Scipio glanced down at the tablet in his hand.

"How long is this marriage contract to be?" he asked.

"Five years," said Andrea. Jake nodded.

Scipio looked at each of them in turn.

"Then by the power vested in me by the Holy Church and the RDF, I pronounce you man and wife for the period of five years per the marriage contract, subject to renewal upon mutual agreement at the end of that period, or automatic dissolution if no mutual agreement is formally logged. You may kiss the bride."

"Negative," said Andrea, "You forget I'm Aeolian. I'll kiss the groom."

And she did.

Fourteen Months Later...

"You're a father!!" said Ginger Barnett to Jake.

Jake smiled and handed her two cigars. "Yep...and twins!"

"What will you name them?" asked Ginger. "And please, not...Scipio or...Caesar or...whatever..."

"No, Andrea put her foot down on that one. She selected the names. The boy will be Alexander Orien, after her grandfather, and the girl will be Ligeia Antiope, after her grandmother."

"Alexander and Ligeia. Kinda fits," said Ginger.

"Kinda does," said Jake. "And they are both perfect, squalling so loud I thought I'd lose my hearing. Couldn't ask for a better

Valentine's Day present."

Ginger looked puzzled. "Valentine's Day? What's that...?"

"Never mind," said Jake. "Before your time. What's on the agenda for today?"

Ginger thought into her AI for a second, eyes focused on infinity.

"You have a meeting with Captain Cassian on the engine revisions for the A40 in ten minutes."

"OK, good," said Jake. "Give me five minutes to review notes and then if he's here, go ahead and send him in."

Ginger nodded and left the office. Outside, she looked at Lt. Commander Martina Garcia, Jake's office administrator. "What's Valentine's Day?" she asked.

"Beats me," said Martina. "Why?"

THE PLAY

All the world's a stage, and all the men and women merely players.
- William Shakespeare

Nest – Bat Home Planet
1 January 2207 - 85 Years after *Pandora*

Privend had been on Nest for fourteen years. He had come when he was sixteen - in Earth years. That was eighteen in Bat years. Bats lived a shorter, faster life than Humans. Maybe, he thought, that was why they bred so prolifically. And colonized so aggressively.

It had not been easy to get him and his team here. The RDF searched far and wide to find ideal candidates. They had to be thin - almost to the point of abnormality. They had to be long-faced, gangly, and dark - a shade that looked reasonable to a Bat. And they had to be highly intelligent, highly focused, and willing to put their lives on the line for Humanity.

They had found Privend - his name then Ingumba - in Kenya at the age of thirteen. He had been an orphan, living on the streets of Nairobi, working with a gang to steal, rob or extort enough food for one more day, and to find one more place to spend the night. The RDF had taken him. They never asked; they just took him one night, and he woke up on Mars the next day.

They trained him for three years. Bat culture - what little the RDF had learned of it from long-distance monitoring of the Bat's home planet, which the Bats called Nest. Bat language - via machine learning at night while he slept. And Bat education - preparing him to play the part of a well-educated, upper-class military brat.

Then there were the physical mods. The gene-splicing, to give him the ears and the fangs, the fur, the vestigial wings, the ability to hear frequencies much higher than Humans. The daily physical training, to provide the rock-hard muscles the Bats displayed. Combat training, hand-to-hand, small arms, explosives, knives, poisons, the gamut. His days were full.

They finally asked him, once. About the middle of his second year on Mars. He was brought into an office and placed in a chair.

He waited. Time stretched on, minute after minute, but Privend didn't mind. He had already adopted that Bat name, barely remembered his other. Privend waited patiently. Anything in this life was better than the old life, so he didn't mind waiting.

After a half hour, a man came in. He was huge - at least to Privend, he seemed that way - and dressed in a dark blue uniform. There was a lot of gold braid and ribbons. He walked around the desk, stood behind the chair, and looked at Privend.

His face was hard - the face of a warrior - but kindly. He smiled at Privend, then sat down. He placed his hands folded on the desk.

"You are Privend," he stated.

Privend nodded.

"I'm told that you are first in your class in almost every area."

"Yes, sir," answered Privend.

"Good. Very good," said the man.

Privend waited. He was good at waiting.

The man steepled his hands, then folded them and rested his chin on them. This brought his head down to Privend's level.

"Let me ask you a question," he said.

Privend nodded.

"You know what we want you to do?" asked the man.

"Yes, sir. You want me to go live with the Bats."

"And you know why this is important."

Privend nodded again. "There will be a war. We need to save Earth from the Bats. You need information."

"You'll be in danger almost every day."

Privend agreed, "Yes, sir. I'm not afraid."

"But..." the man paused. "But if you could go home today - leave all this behind - would you want to do that?"

Privend shook his head vigorously. "No, sir."

The man persisted. "I'm offering you that chance. We'll send you home. With what you've learned here, you should be able to survive, do better than before. You could have a good life."

Privend shook his head. "No, sir. I know what's coming. I'm ready. This is my life now."

The man smiled. He stood up and reached across the table. He shook Privend's hand.

"Thank you, Privend. Thank you for doing what I wish I could do."

The man left. Privend sat for a second, then whispered, "You're welcome, Admiral."

* * * * *

Now, fourteen years later, Commander Privend sat at his desk in Bat Empire Naval Intelligence, considering the day. He had sent his monthly QE burst of intel back to the RDF last night. And unusually, there had been a brief reply. It was a rare occurrence for them to contact him. He only received one, at most two, responses per year, these days. There was just not that much to discuss anymore. He sent them everything he knew, and that was it.

But last night they had sent back. The message was short.

"Begin Project Skyhook."

City of Aronte
14 January 2207

Andrea and Jake sat on the stone bench. In front of them, on a patch of green grass, a blanket held the twins Alexander and Ligeia, gurgling at each other. Empress Hecate sat on the blanket with them, trying to get Alexander to hold on to her pinkie. Hecate's daughter, Princess Asteria, lay beside the twins on her stomach, feet kicked up, trying to convince Ligeia to play with her fingers. Hecate looked up at Andrea and laughed.

"Oh, Andrea, thank you for entrusting them to me," she said, a smile in her eyes. "You know I'll treat them as my very own!"

Andrea nodded at her. "I know, Hecate. I know you will."

Andrea glanced at Jake and rose. "Let's walk."

Jake looked up at her, and then nodded. He got up and waited as she turned back to Hecate.

"We're going to walk for a bit."

Hecate nodded. "No worries. Have fun!"

Andrea started away, Jake following. They went down the path toward the Guard barracks that Jake remembered, from all those years ago. Past the barracks, they came to the semi-hidden gate that let out into the public street.

Jake paused and looked at Andrea, but without hesitation she pushed the gate open and walked out. Jake followed; a bit puzzled by Andrea's demeanor. Together they walked along the street, mixing with the townsfolk and the tourists staring at the Imperial Palace. Andrea walked with her head down, not looking at Jake.

"Just so you know, Jake...," she began, and paused.

Jake waited, well used to Andrea's moods. He knew this was a serious matter, so he did not interrupt. Andrea reached out and took his hand as they walked.

"Just so you know, I've updated my will," she finally got out. "If I don't come back from this war...well, the twins go to Hecate. I knew you would approve, but I'm sorry I didn't talk to you first."

Jake walked silently for a bit, then nodded. "That's the way I would want it," he said. "You did well."

Andrea walked, head still down, not looking at Jake, but holding his hand.

"It seems like yesterday, when I saw you on the *Paris*," she said.

"I know."

"And when we were at Strategy School."

Jake nodded silently.

"And when we got married."

Jake continued to walk beside Andrea, holding her hand, keeping his counsel.

"Jake, do you believe in the Creator?" Andrea asked.

Jake thought for a while. "Yes," he said. "Maybe not like the churches say, but I believe the universe was created. And that something - someone or something - created it."

Andrea nodded beside him. "So, what happens when we die?"

Jake considered. "I don't know, Andrea. I can only puzzle it out up to a certain point. Our lives leave an imprint on the universe. Maybe that imprint is good, or maybe that imprint is bad. It's not a very big imprint, when you stop and think about it. But it's up to us to make the best imprint we can. After that, it's up to the Creator."

Andrea thought for a while. Then she glanced over at Jake.

"I have tried to make you happy, Jake."

He looked back at her. "Andrea, you have made me totally, completely, utterly happy. Thank you for coming into my life."

They walked. They held hands for a while, silently.

Suddenly Jake realized they were at the riverbank, where he once docked his sailboat, so many years before. He had unconsciously led them there.

Andrea turned to him, backing off and staring at him.

"Jake, I know you. I know you better than you know yourself."

Jake nodded. "Probably..."

"If I don't come back, you'll shut down. You'll curl up and die. I know what happened to you when Kirsten and Teresa died."

Jake shook his head. "You'll come back, so why talk about it?"

"No," said Andrea. "You will not do that. Understand? If something happens to me, you keep living. Promise me."

Jake shook his head again. "No promises."

Andrea slapped him, hard, right across the face. Stinging, Jake looked at her and saw a person he had never seen before. The woman in front of him now was an Amazon warrior, battle-hardened, fierce, in fighting mode. Her eyes blazed.

"You will find something to live for. Say it."

Jake shook his head. "No promises."

Andrea slapped him again, hard. "Say it!"

Rubbing his cheek, Jake nodded slowly. "OK."

Andrea repeated. "If something happens to me, you will not curl up and die. You will find something to live for. You'll go on."

Jake nodded. "I promise. But you the same."

Andrea nodded. "I promise the same. For our children."

Jake opened his arms and gathered her in, holding her close. He felt her shudder as the adrenalin wore off and she came out of battle mode.

Holding her, he looked over her shoulder at the river moving slowly by, inexorable and unchanging. So many thoughts ran through his mind. His life had been extraordinary. In an incredibly long life, he had known great love, not once, not even twice, but four times.

He kept thinking about a quote from long before his birth, back in the 20th century – a quote he heard in a movie about the first flight of man to orbit the moon. The mission had been called Apollo 8; it had occurred one hundred fourteen years before his birth. One of the astronauts – Jim Lovell – spoke of the view of Earth from the Moon – the first time any Human had seen the distant Earth from space.

Lovell had said, "God has given mankind a stage, upon which to perform. How the play turns out is up to us."

Jake smiled. He held Andrea Iona, beside the flowing river, thinking about the play.

MAD DOG

Whoever said the pen is mightier than the sword obviously never encountered automatic weapons.
- Douglas MacArthur

Zeta Capricorni A – 386 Light Years from Earth
BEN Corvette *Ratkiller*
4 February 2207

Captain Nolot was frustrated. Scout duty was always dull, but lately even more so. Headquarters hadn't sent out a new colonization expedition in fourteen years. One was certainly due. Rumor was one was coming soon, and in this direction. He certainly hoped so.

In between colonizations, there just wasn't much to do. And this two-week swing around the Zeta Cap A system was about as painfully boring as possible.

Nolot reached forward on his desk and took his bottle, poured another drink into his glass, slugged it down, and sighed again. He debated bringing in another female from his crew, but as he had already had two females this week, he was feeling a bit run-down.

Nolot's AI pinged. *Something, at least,* he thought.

"What!"

"Sir," said his XO, Commander Tovor, "We have an unidentified ship following us."

"Bullshit," said Nolot. "There's nothing for a dozen light years in any direction. You're picking up a rock."

"It's a confirmed vessel, sir. We had a sensor ghost behind us. We reset the console, and it was still there. We dropped a passive buoy, and it confirmed a frigate-class ship, no IFF, about ten thousand km behind us, very stealthy, just barely detectable."

Nolot straightened in his chair. "Crazy Ivan! Now!" He jumped from his chair, grabbing his warsuit as he ran to the bridge door.

Around him, he felt a strong Coriolis force as the compensator could not quite handle the sudden, violent rotation of the ship spinning to face the opposite direction – the "Crazy Ivan" maneuver.

Holding on to a railing against the push, he burst into the bridge just as Tovor sounded Battle Stations. The klaxon was not particularly loud - but given that nobody had ever heard it except in training, it got everyone's attention.

Nolot saw the stars spinning outside come to a stop, as the corvette completed the Crazy Ivan maneuver. Sure enough, the somewhat better sensors on the front of the ship showed a very dim, almost invisible wedge-shaped outline, classified by the AI as frigate sized, and no IFF. Now, after their sudden reversal, directly in front of them.

"What the hell is that?" exclaimed Nolot, still climbing into his warsuit.

"Don't know, sir. Never seen anything like it. No record of it in the AI," said Tovor, also sliding on his suit, along with the rest of the bridge crew.

"AI, is that ship showing any weapons?" asked Nolot.

<*Unable to determine, sir*>

"And no match in the database for anything like that?"

<*No, sir, unknown type and origin*> responded the AI.

Nolot looked at Tovor. "We got ourselves a bogey," he grinned.

"Yes, sir," agreed Tovor.

Nolot stared at the holo for a second. He turned to the Comm Officer.

"Try to contact them, Comm."

"Aye, sir," answered the Comm Officer. He bent to his console.

Nolot turned to his slave, standing nearby. "Fath - hot drink."

"Aye, sir," said the slave, rushing out of the bridge toward the galley.

Nolot turned back to the Comm Officer. "Anything?"

"Nothing, sir," said the Comm Officer. "I've tried all normal frequencies and all frequencies we've ever encountered with other races. Nothing."

Nolot peered at the holo. "Send a warning shot down their beam," he ordered.

Tovor hesitated. "Sir, that's a damn big ship."

Nolot frowned. "Well, yes, now that you mention it, it is, Tovor. But what is our job out here?"

Tovor looked down. "Find out whatever there is to find out, sir."

"Exactly," said Nolot. "And I can't find out what that ship is doing out here just by looking at him. He won't talk to me, and he just keeps following us. He probably thinks we'll just let him. Let's see what he does when he knows we won't. Send it!"

"Aye, sir," said Tovor. He turned to the Weapons Officer. "Weps - send one railgun round, right down his beam, but make damn sure you don't hit him. Tac, make ready for return fire just in case."

"Aye, sir," replied the Weapons Officer and Tactical Officer, almost in unison. After a second, the Weapons Officer confirmed, "Round away."

Almost instantly, the Tac Officer yelled, "Incoming!"

"Helm, bounce!" yelled Nolot, but it was too late. A crash shook the corvette hard enough that dust fell from the ceiling fixtures. The overhead lights went out and the battle lanterns came on. The compensator went away momentarily, then returned, fluctuating, causing Nolot to falter and almost fall.

He saw on the holo that they were turning hard; he realized one of their engines was out.

"Helm, get us out of here," he yelled. He looked and saw the helmsman was already doing that. Their one remaining engine went to full power, and the helm adjusted to bring them back to a reasonably straight vector away from their attacker.

As they began to pull away, Nolot saw two things in the holo. He saw the ship behind them come out of stealth and got a good look at it. It was a black, wedge-shaped ship, unlike anything he had ever seen before. And he saw it take a vector away from them and pour on the coal, accelerating rapidly away from them toward the mass limit.

"Tac! Get a vector on that guy," yelled Nolot. "He's gonna sink out!"

"Aye, sir," yelled the Tactical Officer, clinging to his console with one hand as the g-forces jerked them around erratically due to compensator instability.

Nolot watched as the black ship sank out and disappeared.

"Got it, sir!" yelled the Tac Officer.

"Good! I think we'd better let HQ know we got some company out here!"

Tolleson Base
5 March 2207

Admiral Phoebe Walker stepped into the apartment, tossed her hat on the shelf by the door and hung her tunic on the hook. Inside the kitchen, Rob Walker yelled, "Dinner's ready in five minutes, babe!"

"Thanks, hon - and don't call me babe!" growled Phoebe, but with a grin on her face. After eighteen years of marriage, the joke never got old. She went to the dining room where Rob had already prepared the table and sat down, bringing up her personal holo in front of her face.

She had spent the afternoon in conference with Admiral Hammett and his staff. Now she studied the formal orders she had received, her mind whirling.

"TOP SECRET

Distribution: CNOStaff001, CNOStaff002, Admiral Phoebe Walker ONLY

To Vice Admiral Phoebe Walker, RDF, Commanding, Task

Force14.

You will form TF14 consisting of:
Battleships: *Vercingetorix, MacArthur, Agrippa*
Cruisers: *Kuznetsov, Raeder, Nimitz, Jellicoe*
Frigates: *Dallas, Moscow, Birmingham, Shenzhen*
Destroyer Squadrons: D02, D04, D05
Scout Squadrons: S10, S11

You will advance to the system designated as Zeta Capricorni A, taking care in all manner of operations that you are not detected by the enemy, to arrive not later than 15 May 2207.

While enroute you will prepare in all respects for a fleet action against the Bat Empire Naval Forces.

On 15 March 2207 enroute, open the date-activated sealed orders contained herein.

At a time and place as contained in the sealed orders, you will engage the Bats in the designated Fleet action.

These orders may be modified by QE burst at any time.

Do not fail in these orders at your peril.

<Signed>

CNO Jake Hammett, RDF, Commanding"

Phoebe sighed. At that moment, Rob came out of the kitchen, carrying a steaming dish with a savory smell. Noting her distraction, he quietly prepared her plate while she stared off into space. Placing it in front of her, he took a bottle of wine and filled her glass, then returned to his chair and prepared his own dinner. Filling his own wine glass, he clinked it with a fork until he had Phoebe's attention.

"Everything OK?" he asked.

Phoebe nodded. "Yes, everything's fine." She started eating, distracted, then stopped after a few seconds.

"I have to go do a thing," she said.

"A thing?" asked Rob.

"Yes. I'll be gone for a while, I think."

Rob ate slowly, contemplating. Then he asked, "Sort of a shooting thing?"

Phoebe nodded. "Sort of a shooting thing."

"Why can't I go with?" asked Rob.

Phoebe grinned. "Because that pig boat of yours is too damn slow."

Rob laughed. His fleet carrier, the *Enterprise*, was the largest ship in the RDF, and carried 242 A40 fighters.

"That pig boat of mine could take out any three of your battleships, my dear," he grinned.

"I'll spot you one battleship, then I'll blast you into the hereafter," said Phoebe, her spirits lifted. "Because your pig boat is just too damn slow!"

Rob turned serious for just a moment.

"But really…why can't I go along?"

Phoebe shook her head. "Jake's not willing to reveal the A40 to them. Not yet."

Rob looked depressed. "I really hate to sit this one out."

Phoebe grinned. "Be patient. We're in the end game now. You'll have plenty of missiles flying your way soon enough. Probably be crapping your pants on the bridge right in front of your crew."

Rob glared at her. "Not happening, babe."

"And don't call me babe…"

* * * * *

Later, in bed, Phoebe couldn't sleep. She kept thinking about the meeting with Admiral Hammett and his staff that afternoon. Jake had flicked on a holo and showed a system labelled 'Rome'. Phoebe had never heard of it.

"This system contains a planet, code name 'Rome', about 386 lights from us." he said. "We've scouted it before and know that it contains a Humanoid civilization on par with that of ancient Rome, hence the code name. By that I mean, they have metals, swords, and shields, that kind of thing. Draft animals, rowed galleys, all the trappings we would associate with Rome of the 1st or 2nd century A. D."

Phoebe had studied the holo. The system appeared to have five planets - two outer gas giants, a rocky world in the hab zone, and two smaller rocky planets in the hot zone by the star. The labels on the sidebar showed the inhabited planet remarkably similar to Earth, with an oxygen/nitrogen atmosphere near standard pressure, gravity at .95 Earth, and temperate climate. The sidebar showed a population of 500 million inhabitants.

Jake leaned back in his chair, with a steady gaze on Phoebe. "The Bats have made this their next target for colonization. We have intelligence they'll move out in roughly two months to destroy it."

Phoebe was silent only for a moment. "We have to stop them," she said quietly.

Jake grinned. "Luckily, I agree with you. We're going to defend this planet from the Bats."

Phoebe looked at Jake. "Of course, that violates your non-contact directive, to avoid all contact with the Bats until we're ready to take them on."

Jake nodded. "It does. And I've been very conflicted about this. But ultimately, I can't let another 500 million sentients die at the hands of the Bats. So, we're going to do this as a false-flag operation. You'll ambush the Bat colonization fleet as they approach Rome; then pretend to fall back towards another location called Farpoint, about 475 lights past Nest...right here..."

Hammett pointed out a system on the holo, well Coreward from the Bat home planet of Nest, in nearly the opposite direction of Earth and the Rim.

"Now the next thing I'm going to tell you is highly classified, and our entire future depends on it remaining that way."

ROME

War is common and justice is strife, and all things come into being and pass away through strife.
- Heraclitus

Kamilaroi – Aboard the *Enterprise*
2 April 2207

Vitus was leaving the *Enterprise's* A40 simulator when he got a comm.

<You are wanted in Captain Walker's office yesterday> said his AI.

<Roger, on the way>

Vitus stepped up his pace and as he came to the end of the passageway, he met his father, Captain Cassian, going the same way.

"You, too?" he asked the DCAG, or Deputy Commander, Attack Group. The title had been used with slight modification since the 1940's on Earth, so was one of the oldest in the RDF. The grizzled old Daneki had managed to hang on as an active officer of the RDF for the last twenty-two years, still hoping to get in his shots at the Bat Empire.

"Roj," said Cassian. "So, must be something going on."

Together they climbed the ladders to the Captain's day cabin, where they presented themselves to the Marine at the door, who knocked and let them in.

"Gentlemen, greetings," said Captain Rob Walker in perfect Daneki, showing off his skills. Cassian and Vitus couldn't help but grin as they presented themselves at attention. With the use of compressed learning, almost every officer in the RDF could speak at least four languages – usually English, Chinese, Aeolian and Daneki. But the quality of the learning still varied somewhat, person to person. Captain Walker's mastery of Daneki was near-perfect, and the quality of his Aeolian was legendary; undoubtedly helped by his marriage to Admiral Phoebe Walker, his Aeolian wife.

Gesturing to the conference table in the chart room, Captain Walker, CO of the RDF *Enterprise*, the largest attack carrier in the fleet, said, "At ease, guys, let's sit and talk. We have a mission order."

Vitus noted that several other officers were already sitting at the conference table, including the CAG, Captain Wayne; the Exec, Captain Davis; and the Tac, Commander Briggs; as well as several other department heads from Captain Walker's staff.

Quickly Vitus lowered himself into the junior chair, since as the Wing Intelligence Officer, he was the lowest ranking officer present.

Captain Walker sat at the head of the table and with a mental command to his bead, flicked on a holo. It showed the Sol system. Marked on the holo was a vector leaving Earth, headed directly for the Bat home world of Nest.

"We have a runner," said Captain Walker. "You remember that bastard James Cobb?"

Everyone around the table nodded.

"He's been sitting on his ass on Earth for the last eighteen years, hiding behind the skirts of the North American Alliance. Well, either he got tired of waiting, or the NAA kicked him out, not sure which. But he departed Earth yesterday on a direct vector to Nest with the *Taizong* and his remaining warships. Intel says he's going to sell us out in return for becoming viceroy of the remaining RimFed planets, after helping the Bats destroy Earth."

"Crap," escaped Vitus before he could stop himself. Walker laughed.

"Exactly. Crap. That's what their plan is, and we're not going to let it happen. We have orders to intercept him and make sure that doesn't happen. You've got twelve hours to prep your people, get everything loaded and be ready to go. Can do?"

At the other end of the table, Vitus saw Captain Davis form an evil grin. "Can do, Skipper."

"Hot damn!" said Captain Wayne, echoed by the other officers present. "Bout damn time!"

Cassian interrupted, "But I thought Admiral Hammett said no A40s in combat until we're ready to hit the Bats."

Walker nodded. "That is true. And he left us out of a mission just a few weeks ago for that very reason. And I can't tell you for sure that we will use them in this mission, either.

"But, in his call to me this morning, Admiral Hammett released us to use the A40s for this mission if we absolutely must, and the reason is simple – if Cobb gets through, the A40s will not matter. Cobb will spill his guts to the Bats about the A40s and everything else, and they'll come for us with everything they have. We must stop him at all costs. So, Jake – Admiral Hammett – released us to use them – but, only as a last resort. Only as a Plan B.

"Now, there are some other irons in the fire to stop Cobb, which I can't discuss with you yet. So, we may not use the A40s at all - or we may throw everything we have at Cobb. I wish I could tell you for certain one way or the other, but I can't."

Vitus nearly danced in his chair with excitement. The culmination of twenty years of R&D, applied engineering, flight testing, tactical training, and weapons development had gone into the A40 fighter. It was a work of art – and never used in combat, lest the Bats find out about it too early. But now...he grinned from ear to ear.

Walker leaned forward. "Captain Davis, make this ship ready in all respects for flight, with a scheduled departure for 2200 hours tonight, twelve hours from now, fully loaded for combat, all weapons loadouts checked and double checked, all fighters flight-ready, with supplies and stores for 180 days."

Davis nodded, his comm bead already flashing as he mentally issued orders.

Walker spoke again. “I need not say, this is classified beyond Top Secret, we cannot breathe a word of our mission or destination to anyone. Our official cover story will be that we are conducting an emergency sortie drill. Make sure that is the story you tell anyone who asks.”

Everyone nodded.

“Finally,” Walker continued, “as much as I hate to do this to you, you are forbidden to tell any of your loved ones about this. As far as they are concerned, this is just another drill and you’ll be back in a day or so. After we leave, Admiral Hammett will get the word to them that we’ve been re-directed on another mission of a few weeks’ duration. At some point, a few more weeks down the road, they’ll be told the mission was extended. I’m sorry, but you must realize that one QE burst to Cobb that we’re on his tail could mean disaster. And we all know there are spies on this base from the Saints, from the North Americans, from anyone who wishes to do us harm. We know who most of them are and feed them just the information we want. But there could always be one we don’t know about. So - keep that in mind and follow the plan.”

Vitus realized he would not be able to tell Eva what was happening. He thought about trying to get off the ship to see her, but quickly decided that would just make things worse. He would comm her the cover story and let the Navy take it from there. The meeting broke up and Vitus headed back to the simulator.

Vitus had a new sim to work on now.

Nest - Bat Home Planet
5 April 2207

Privend looked around the room. His team looked back at him. He raised his glass, and everyone raised theirs in turn. "To the beginning of the end," he toasted. They clinked the glasses together and drank.

Draining his glass, he placed it back on the table.

"Ravita - how are you doing with the Admiral?"

"He's eating out of my hand," replied a pretty female. "I can get him to do anything within reason - and some things that are not."

A titter of squeaks rang around the room, too high-pitched for Human ears. Privend bared his fangs in a smile. "Excellent. Just stay on his good side, give him what he wants, but don't let him get bored."

Ravita's own fangs came out in humor. "He won't get bored."

Privend turned to the next member of his team. Praxend was his second in command. "How are you doing with the remote sensing team?"

"It's a battle to stay ahead of them," Praxend replied. "The early twentieth century transmissions from Earth are only about fifty lights beyond the Bat Scout Station at Kaus Media now. All it would take is one of their scout ships taking the wrong vector and they'd pick up Earth EMF. So... it's definitely time. I'll put the Skyhook signals into the mix starting tonight. They'll be very faint at first and buried in noise. I'll give them a few days to detect them. If they don't, then I'll bring up the gain just a touch. Eventually they'll detect them. And when they do...well, I think all hell will break loose."

"Excellent," said Privend. "I'll send a QE to RDF HQ again warning them about the Scout Station at Kaus Media. I've told them before but seems like now they really need to do something about it."

Privend paused for a moment, in thought.

"When they detect the Skyhook signals, won't they spend a considerable amount of time checking their gear – repeater buoy, antennae and such - to make sure it's a valid external signal?"

Praxend grinned. "Yes, they will. And it will show valid. They won't find anything wrong with it."

"Good," said Privend. "Good." He gazed around the room. "All of you are doing well. I'm proud of this team, and proud of what you've done so far. But the best is in front of us now. We must sell them on Skyhook now. And we will."

*****

Commander Privend stood before the room, pointer in hand, and held up his hand. As the hubbub died down, he commanded his AI silently, and the holotank at the front of the room flicked on.

Privend pointed to the icon of a destroyer, labeled *Waspeater*. Behind it, very faint, could be seen the shadow of another ship, shimmering in the holo with some kind of stealth technology.

Chief of Naval Operations Makvil and his staff sat along both sides of the conference table. CNO Makvil was a tall, gray Bat, one of the oldest that Privend had ever known. Bats did not live as long as Humans, only about 60 years on average. Makvil had to be pushing 80, though. Yet, Privend knew him to be as sharp mentally as any young staffer. Nobody put anything past the CNO.

Privend spoke softly but clearly, pointing to the features in the holo as he recounted the events of a few days prior.

"As you have undoubtedly heard, during recent scouting operations at Pi Sag A, one of our destroyers detected a stealthed ship following behind as it came in-system. As you know from earlier reports, this is the second instance of an unknown ship following one of our scouts. A few weeks ago, another of our corvettes on routine patrol at Zeta Cap A was also followed by such a ship and was fired upon and damaged."

"In this more recent case, when the *Waspeater* realized it was being followed, and knowing what happened to the corvette, they did a Crazy Ivan and got a good read on the ship behind them. However, before they could take any action, the ship vectored away at high speed."

In the holo, the destroyer made a sudden 180-degree turn, coming around quickly to face the shadow of the other ship. The holo showed the unknown ship coming out of stealth, and for an instant, there was a clear picture of a black, wedge-shaped ship, frigate sized, turning to a new heading, and accelerating away.

"The destroyer gave chase, but they had too much of a head start. When it reached the mass limit and sank out, we did get a good vector, though," said Privend. "We sent a destroyer and corvette after them, but they were unable to find anything."

The holo displayed a vector of the alien ship leaving the system. Privend compressed the holo display with a silent AI command and froze it. He turned to face the assembled officers.

"Now, hold that thought in your mind momentarily while I give you a second item of intelligence."

Privend opened a second holo, floating silently above and to the right of the first one. In the second holo was the Nest system. At a considerable distance from Nest appeared a red dot, blinking.

"Recently, one of our remote sensing teams monitoring a QE repeater buoy detected some EMF - very faint - but they were able to isolate it from the background noise. It appears to come from a star-faring civilization with FTL, in this direction." Privend pointed.

The officers around the table nodded but sat up a little straighter. The first item Privend had discussed was not news to them - they knew all about the unidentified black ships, mostly via scuttlebutt. But this was new.

"As you know, in the last 300 years or so, we've detected a half-dozen civilizations with electronic communications. All of them have been tracked and their planets reduced for our colonization efforts. None of them, however, had more than rudimentary FTL capabilities. The Daneki came close - they had the beginnings of a small Space Navy - but we destroyed that in short order."

"However, this new civilization appears to have a significant starship presence and - if our understanding of the limited communications we’ve received is accurate - they are a very aggressive, expanding star nation."

Privend turned back toward the holo. "The blinking red dot shows our best estimate of the location of this space nation, based on the weak communications we have received – a planet called 'Earth'."

Now Privend, with a thought to his AI, caused the two holo displays to move together and merge into one.

As the two displays moved together, the vector in the first holo - the black ship leaving the Pi Sag A system - pointed directly at the red blinking dot in the second holo labelled 'Earth'.

Privend turned to the assembled officers.

"We definitely have company," he said.

Kaus Media – 348 Light Years from Earth
Bat Scout Station Fourteen
10 April 2206

The RDF frigates *Beijing*, *New Delhi,* and *Osaka* – also known as the 4th Asia Assault Squadron – came out of stealth 1,000 kilometers off the Bat Scout Station at Kaus Media and immediately opened fire with railguns and beamers. The station was a small base on one of the moons of a cold rocky planet just outward of the stars habitable zone – a moon similar to Phobos in the Sol System. The base was small, as its only function was to serve as a listening post and supply stop for scout ships working in the sector.

The Asia Squadron had waited patiently for several days until both small Bat corvettes assigned to the base were docked, taking some R&R time. This was to catch them uncrewed, if possible, or at least with minimal crew on board - and with any luck at all, to destroy both before they could send a QE blip back to Nest.

Their first thirty railgun shots had a hit ratio of 90%, meaning each corvette received nine railgun rounds and the base itself received another nine.

The net impact left nothing but an extremely large hole in the ground, surrounded by clouds of drifting dust and debris. No QE comms were sent.

Pulling off target, the Asia Squadron vectored back toward the mass limit to start their next mission. There was no need to check for survivors.

* * * * *

A Bat resupply convoy - protected with four destroyers and two cruisers - surfaced at the mass limit at the planet Danek and cautiously made their way in, keeping a sharp lookout for the mysterious Black Ships. About a quarter of the way on their run in to the planet, they were jumped by two of the wedge-shaped frigates. The two Black Ships managed to damage a merchantman before they realized they were outgunned and turned to flee.

Unfortunately, before they could make it out of the system, the Bat warships pounded them into scrap metal.

One of the Black Ships blew up during the fight and was of little use to the Bat Intelligence Office; but the other was mostly intact after the battle. It was immediately towed back to Nest for a painstaking examination.

It was a setup. The two frigates were purely AI-controlled - there were no living Humans on board. The Human bodies placed on the ships were inanimate clones, with brains completely lacking useful information. They looked very real, of course. Every detail of their bodies, their clothing, their quarters, and the remainder of the ship looked exactly as the RDF desired it to look - realistic and believable.

Even the AIs driving the ship were only partially functional. They were non-sentient, limited in capability, and contained exactly the information the RDF wanted placed there.

And most telling of all, the weapons and engines of the ship were intentionally de-rated to reflect a false story of their capabilities...

* * * * *

Privend stood at the observation window, gazing at the

wrecked Black Ship outside in the spacedock. Beside him stood his immediate boss, Captain Hakor, and Hakor's boss, the Chief of Naval Intelligence, Admiral Laksid, with his aide next to him.

The Black Ship was holed in a half-dozen places, and one entire quarter of the rear was missing. The engines and weapons had been removed and taken away for analysis. The remaining hull looked like the derelict it was.

"Definitely a frigate class," said Captain Hakor. "Three railguns, three beamers, six missile tubes. We found 120 bodies inside. We estimate about half the crew was ejected into space during the battle, so we're guessing a total crew of about 240."

"That seems a little light for a frigate," said Admiral Laksid. "Our frigates have, what? About 300 crew?"

"Yes, sir," said Captain Hakor. "That's true. But our frigates have four beamers and four railguns, so that's two additional gun crews and all the support required for them. So, not surprising this one has a smaller crew."

Hakor pulled up a personal holo in front of them, showing them the body of one of the crew members from the black frigate. “We are calling them ‘Apes’, because their body plan looks like the big monkeys we have in the Southern Jungle,” he said.

Laksid laughed. “Very appropriate. How about their weapons?"

Hakor nodded. "We managed to get one beamer functional again. About 80% of the power of ours, slightly different pulse train, but nothing special. Same with their railguns - about the same size and throw weight as ours, although as near as we can tell, it would have nearly twice the cycle time."

"Pitiful," said Laksid. "And you say the ship was a little slower than ours during the battle...?"

"Yes, sir. By the time they realized they were outmatched, we had already damaged one and it was down to one engine. They both turned and tried to make it to the mass limit, but our cruisers were able to run them down. Our lead cruiser put two missiles into the crippled one and it blew up instantly. This second one almost made it to the mass limit - but they were only pulling 155g, while our frigates can pull 205. We caught them just before they could sink out."

"So, their technology is nowhere near as good as ours," said Laksid. "It sure seems stupid for them to start this kind of trouble with us when our technology is clearly superior."

"Yes, sir. I agree. But we don't really know their motivation. Or their intentions. That's where Commander Privend comes in. He's been monitoring their communications since we discovered them."

Admiral Laksid glanced across at Privend.

"Yes, I've been reading the daily briefings. Seems like mostly it's just a boring mishmash of trashy game shows that you're intercepting, Privend. Anything new?"

"Well, maybe." said Privend. "We sent a fast scout to place QE repeater buoys closer to their system. We're now getting near real time intercepts. We haven't gotten anything definite - their military communications are encrypted, and we haven't been able to break them - but their newscasts do contain a few gems of information."

"Such as?" asked Laksid.

"Well, recently, we've found a news radio channel which seems to be politically oriented. As you know, the signals we receive are very noisy, coming via QE compression, and we don't have the bandwidth for video. But this radio news channel shows tremendous internal dissension among their political parties. It seems there is a hawk party which wants to attack us and wipe us out, and a dove party which wants to approach us and negotiate a treaty. Their government appears to be fragmented between those two parties, as well as some others which factor into the mix. Overall, I'd say they have no coherent plan of action at all."

"So why raid us?" asked Laksid.

Privend paused.

"Sir, I can only suppose that their military is very much in the hawk camp. I suspect their Navy is doing these raids on their own, without the full knowledge of their central government. But I can't be sure of that, with the limited intel we've got so far. We're working on obtaining better insight into that part of the equation."

"OK, keep working that angle." said Laksid. "And keep those daily reports coming my way. I want a better feel for why they are raiding us, especially since their technology doesn't seem very good. Now, Hakor, how about this ship? Anything else?"

"Quite a lot, actually. We were able to partially re-activate the AI. It's light years behind ours, an antique by our standards. Very little war fighting ability - it appears that the crew fights the ship manually, with only minimal assist from the AI."

"My stars," said Laksid. "That's primitive. How do these creatures think they have any hope of attacking us?"

Hakor shook his head, his ears pointed in agreement. “I think they are completely out of control, sir. Their government appears to be fragmented and their military appears to be driving the boat. I suspect they have no actual strategic plan at all. Just picking at us because they can."

Laksid shook his head. "It will be the end of them."

Laksid took one last look at the battered frigate, then turned to go. He gave one final look at Hakor.

"Find out everything you can about this ship, Hakor, because we're going to be fighting these Apes soon."

Hakor saluted, as did Privend. Laksid returned the salute casually and stalked away, his aide beside him. Hakor turned to Privend and looked at him sternly.

"Find out what they're up to, Privend."

"Aye, aye, sir," said Privend. He saluted and watched Captain Hakor walk away.

His face was a calm mask, with no sign of the tension within.

THE SHARP END

All warfare is based on deception.
- Sun Tzu, The Art of War, Earth, 6th Century B. C.

Zeta Capricorni A – 386 Light Years from Earth
Planet 'Rome'
7 May 2207

Phoebe's task force sat in stealth halfway between the Zeta Cap A system primary and the mass limit. Coming towards them, a huge convoy of Bat ships headed for the planet code-named 'Rome' – home of 500 million primitive sentient creatures, about to be destroyed.

The Bat colonization convoy was led by a battleship, leading two cruisers, two frigates and a half-dozen destroyers and corvettes.

Following well behind were transports carrying half a million young Bats - ready to form the core of a new colony for the Bat Empire once the warships had reduced the planet to rubble and stacked the bodies of the inhabitants into the reefers for food.

Phoebe sat in her chair on the flag bridge of the *Vercingetorix*, watching the tactical, biding her time. The Bat convoy came on, slowing rapidly as they approached the planet.

Below her elevated podium still called the 'Flag Bridge', even though it was not a separate bridge, Phoebe saw her Flag Captain, Selena Field, making the final preparations for the attack.

"Everybody stay cool," said Selena. "Stay patient, stay focused."

"Aye, Mum," came a chorus from the *Vercingetorix'* bridge crew.

Weapons Officer Benjamin Stafford, sitting strapped tightly into his chair, raised one finger. "Thirty-five seconds...."

"OK, Guns," said Selena. "Alert 1."

Benjamin nodded. "Alert 1 sent."

The alert signal propagated to the other ships in the fleet. In every ship, an alarm bell loudly clanged three times - the warning to the gun crews that firing would commence in thirty seconds. Throughout the fleet, gun crews re-checked their configurations one last time - even though they had been checked and re-checked a half dozen times already.

In the Beamer Two gun pit of the frigate *Birmingham*, the gun crew fastened their helmets and went on internal oxygen.

The gun boss slapped one youngster on the back of his head, as the boy was slow getting his helmet in place.

"You looking to die today, Matthews?" yelled the Chief.

"No, Chief!" cried the young man.

"Then get that damn helmet secured, son!" said the Chief.

"Aye, Chief! It's secured now!" said Matthews.

"OK," said Chief Myers. "Everybody stay cool, stay calm, keep your materials in your hand, be ready to go."

"Aye, Chief," came a chorus from the ten-man gun crew. They had no role in the actual firing of the beamer - that was automatic and controlled by the Weapons AI and the bridge. Their job was to repair the beamer if it became damaged or quit firing - or, as a last resort, if the bridge or WepsAI was so damaged they could no longer control the gun, the gun crew would fire it manually from the gun pit consoles.

Sweat glistened on their brows as the seconds ticked down.

Back on the bridge, the tension was just as high, and the sweat just as pronounced.

"Open fire, Guns." said Selena quietly. Instantly, Stafford hit the red button in front of him. Across all ships in the fleet, stealth dropped, and Phoebe's fleet opened up with missiles and railguns on the passing Bat convoy. Shortly after, the beamers also started firing as the range grew shorter.

Phoebe's flagship, the *Vercingetorix*, along with her two other battleships, the *Agrippa* and the *MacArthur*, took on the Bat battleship directly, while the rest of her fleet went after the remainder of the convoy.

Caught by surprise, the Bats were slow to react. The *Vercingetorix* put a half-dozen missiles and railgun slugs into the battleship's engines before she finally began evasive maneuvers, turning back toward the mass limit in a futile attempt to escape. But it was far too late. As she twisted away from the *Vercingetorix*, it only brought her into the crossfire of the *Agrippa* and the *MacArthur*. Within another thirty seconds, the Bat battleship was out of control, engines dead, at the mercy of the attackers. The three RDF battleships stood off at a relatively safe distance and put missile after missile into her, pounding her into junk.

Meanwhile, under mostly AI control, the remainder of the RDF fleet raked down the line of ships, tearing pieces off one after another. One Bat cruiser quickly took a hit in an engine, and a huge explosion destroyed the entire vessel in a heartbeat. Soon after, another exploded in a ball of flame, quickly snuffed by the vacuum of space, leaving incendiary trails in all directions as munitions cooked off.

Ripping right down the passing convoy, the cruisers and frigates of Phoebe's task force blasted ship after ship, easily destroying most of them within ten minutes.

At the ten-minute mark, all the RDF ships stopped firing and boosted for the mass limit, making their escape. Behind them they left more than two dozen hulks drifting in the void.

Nest - Bat Home Planet
8 May 2207

Privend sat quietly at a corner of the conference room table, listening to the raging officers yelling at each other.

Half of them wanted to send Home Fleet out to destroy Earth

immediately - today, if possible. The other half wanted to wait until a proper plan was developed. Privend was too junior in rank to join this discussion, so he simply sat, ready in case any question came his way.

Finally, after minutes of wrangling and disagreement, the door opened and CNO Makvil walked into the room. Instantly, the noise stopped, and everyone rose to a loose attention. Makvil took the chair at the head of the table and looked around the room.

"Latest estimates are we lost roughly half a million young Bats," he stated.

The hubbub started again. Many officers were too shocked to speak, but others made up for it with their vociferous yells of "Kill the Apes!"

There were many pointed exclamations to launch the Home Fleet and wipe out the enemy. Makvil waited patiently for ten seconds, then held up his hands for quiet.

“Let me hear your thoughts,” said Makvil.

Senior Admiral Bruntel grunted. "We sit here like mice! They are insects buzzing around our ears! To let them keep sniping at us, is beyond stupid, it's dereliction of duty! You've seen the reports on their ships - slow, weak armaments, no AI fire control. We go, we kill them, we come home! End of story!"

Privend sighed, but silently. Bruntel was a force to be reckoned with. Privend’s boss, Hakor, spoke up. "Sir, we do not know for certain the full magnitude of the force at their home world. All we have are scouting reports, compiled from a distance. And we don't know for certain there aren't bigger, better ships there."

Bruntel sneered. "I have seen these Apes, Hakor. Trust me, they are mere insects, grown to think they are Bats. They won't stand for ten minutes against us!"

"Please, gentlemen," cried CNO Makvil. He tapped on the conference table with his pipe, knocking ash onto the table. "Let's try to control our emotions."

Bruntel shook his head and sank back into his chair as Hakor gestured to Privend.

Privend ordered his notes and collected his thoughts. He was playing a dangerous game here. Too much resistance, and he might actually talk the High Staff out of sending the expedition to Earth. Too little, and they might not take enough of the Home Fleet with them. He was walking a fine line. Hakor nodded at him, and he stood and spoke.

"Granted, Admiral, that taking a portion of the Home Fleet might be sufficient, there is still the issue of leaving Nest unprotected for the three months that it would take to go there, reduce the enemy, and return," said Privend.

Bruntel bared his fangs in a smile. "There is no other enemy within a thousand light years of Nest, Privend. And even if there were, half of Home Fleet could defeat any fleet ten times its size, and we both know there is no such fleet in existence."

Privend nodded reluctantly. "Yes, sir, I know that is your position. But it's my job in Intelligence to cover all the bases. That's all I'm trying to do."

"And we appreciate it, Commander Privend," said CNO Makvil. "Truly, we do."

Makvil turned to Bruntel, effectively dismissing Privend. "How many would you take, if we approve this?"

Bruntel showed his fangs, sensing victory. "Half the Home Fleet should be more than enough. With that, I could blow away two hundred Ape frigates!"

Privend held his breath. CNO Makvil pondered for a moment. Then he nodded.

"Present a plan to my staff, Bruntel, and if they approve it, so will I. Then you can go off to Earth and destroy these annoying Apes."

Bruntel squeaked in victory, his ears pointing up hard and his fangs bared.

Privend found it hard to resist doing the same.

61,252,000 km from Nest - Asteroid 1.0105-4605
1 June 2207

"I hope this works," said Walker, strapped into his chair on the bridge of the *Enterprise*.

"You and me both," said Captain Davis, his XO. "Cobb's no fool. He'll be expecting us."

"This is our only chance, Jim. Otherwise, he gets inside of us, and we'll never catch him." said Walker.

"Yep," said Davis. "But God, when we were planning this, I didn't anticipate the hairs standing on up the back of my neck like this. We are so damn close to Nest."

Walker grinned. "Closer than any Rim ship has ever been, and we're the biggest ship in the RDF. With the entire Bat Fleet in orbit just sixty million kilometers away. If that doesn't make the hairs on your neck stand up, you're not Human."

Davis shuffled nervously, staring at the large tactical holo in the center of the bridge, hoping for any kind of detection that would show where Cobb might be entering the Nest system. He turned away from Walker and walked over to the Comm console, leaning over the yeoman's shoulder.

"Anything?" he asked.

"No, sir," said the yeoman. "Just normal check-ins."

Davis muttered, looking back at the holo. It showed the Bat home system, with sixteen groups of A40 attack craft spread out at 6 AU from the planet Nest, like the tips of the spokes of a wheel.

Each group contained eleven A40's, powered down and waiting quietly.

On the perimeter of the system just at the mass limit, sixteen additional A40s – each one spaced 1/16 of the way around Nest – also waited, their QE boxes ready to spit a burst to the *Enterprise* at the first sign of contact with Cobb's renegade task force.

Between each of the outer birds and the next were a dozen QE repeater buoys, laid by a small fleet of scout ships over the last few days.

And one anomalous lone group of twenty-four A40's rested quietly, seven AU from Nest, at 120 degrees away from the line pointing back toward Earth, thirty-five degrees down from the Nest system ecliptic.

Finally, there was the Enterprise, latched like a big flea on the backside of the asteroid, hiding.

"Got him, sir!" yelled the yeoman at the Comm console, turning excitedly toward Captain Walker. "Ten AU out, 135 degrees, twenty-two down – unbelievable, sir, almost right where you said!"

Davis threw his hands in the air and looked at Walker. "How in the hell do you do that?"

"Just playing the odds, Jim. Just playing the odds. Don't forget that bottle of scotch when this is done, though."

Davis just shook his head. "It'll be there. Remind me never to bet with you again."

* * * * *

At the seven AU point, Vitus sat in his A40, studying the holo. Captain Walker had predicted that Cobb would circle around the Nest system, come in from the backside somewhere around 120 degrees from the line to Earth – from the direction of the Galactic Core - and from somewhat below the galactic plane.

Vitus understood Walker's reasoning – Cobb's biggest bargaining chip was the true location of Earth, and he would not do anything to make it easy for the Bats to discern that vector.

Then Walker had said something about how lazy Cobb was - so he wouldn't spend any more time disguising his vector than necessary. Just enough.

That was how Walker came up with his prediction of 120 degrees from Earth, and thirty-five degrees down from the Nest system ecliptic – the minimum he felt Cobb would do to disguise his back vector.

But now Vitus was here – his squadron inside the vector of this traitor, a man who would betray the Rim, a man who would allow the Bats to destroy Earth and its eleven billion Humans.

In the background of his comm, he heard the CAG issuing

orders, directing all the other A40 squadrons to thrust quietly away toward a rendezvous point in the outer Kuiper belt, and await pickup by the *Enterprise* – they were too far away to join the action. Their part was done.

Vitus issued orders to his squadron and felt the gentle tug of acceleration as his ship, and all the others in his squadron, turned and started boosting toward a point that would intercept Cobb in seven hours, at five AU from Nest – too close for comfort, but there was no other choice.

However, his squadrons were not moving under their own power. They were mounted, temporarily, on a huge frame of plastisteel, with a core of large system engines in back pushing them on their way. Their own engines were powered down.

The entire assemblage was a kludge – a construct hastily assembled while the *Enterprise* was on its way to Nest. From any kind of distance, the conglomeration looked like a Bat merchant ship. And it had a valid Bat merchant ship ID – where that had come from, Vitus had no idea.

But it was starting to look suspiciously like the RDF had assets on Nest, thought Vitus. *How had they managed that?*

At the Bat merchant ship standard in-system acceleration of 100g, the kludge headed for their appointment with Cobb's task force.

But now Vitus understood the complete plan – he would not get to fight this day. He was the backstop – the last ditch, fallback position to stop Cobb if Plan A didn't work. And Plan A was a pretty damn good plan, he had to admit. Admiral Hammett had put it together eighteen years ago, as a contingency for this day.

Vitus stood in awe of the foresight required to predict this event eighteen years in the past. But it had been done, and now Plan A would be executed. Only if it failed would Vitus and his squadrons enter the battle.

*****

On the *Taizong*, Cobb sat loosely in his command chair,

studying the holo. Because he had no access to any of the QE detection buoys in the system, he was entirely dependent on lightspeed sensors – light detection, radar and lidar. Thus, his information on the configuration of ships at Nest was eighty minutes old.

The Bat Home Fleet showed in orbital anchorage around Nest and parked at the LaGrange points nearby Nest and its moon. Various merchant ships vectored here and there throughout the system, most coming or going on a direct line from the outer system mass limit. Nothing was close to him. All looked normal. He didn't buy it, though.

"They're here somewhere," he said to Flag Captain Oleg, pointing toward the tactical holo. "We just have to find them."

Oleg grunted. "I don't see a damn thing. Maybe we beat them here."

"Not a chance," said Cobb. "They're hiding here somewhere. Just keep your eyes peeled."

Cobb turned to his Tac Officer, Commander Maxim Reznikovich. "Rez, anything?"

"Nothing, sir," replied Reznikovich. "Just a bunch of Bats going about their business."

Cobb nodded. "OK, start boosting in-system. Comm, prepare to start the broadcast."

Cobb looked down at the script on his tablet. The broadcast he was preparing to send was simple. It had been translated to the Bat language and recorded. All the Comm officer had to do was send it on a known Bat Naval comm channel.

"To the Bat Empire Navy: I am Admiral Cobb of the Human Federation. I am here to make you an attractive offer. In exchange for certain considerations, I can offer you all the information you want about the capabilities of the Federation Navy – their locations, armaments, tactics, capabilities, and plans. Please respond via this frequency if you understand my offer and have an interest. If I do not hear from you in three hours, I will reverse course and exit the system, never to be seen again. So please do not delay."

Inside the Bat Home System
1 June 2207

Cobb settled into his seat, getting comfortable in order to watch the broadcast go out. At that moment, all the lights on the bridge blinked, and every console re-booted. The tac holo blinked out, then came back on, slowly re-painting the environment from sensors. Cobb jumped out of his chair.

"What the hell?" he yelled.

"Don't know, sir," yelled Reznikovich. "I think the AI just re-booted."

"Crap!" yelled Cobb. "What is this shit?"

The Comm officer looked over at Cobb, face white. "Sir – all ships reporting that their AI has just re-booted. Same as ours."

Oleg looked up from the Tac Console, his face grim. "We just had an AI core swap. It re-booted from backup media. Absolutely no clue why."

Cobb swore. "I know why. Those bastards at the RDF. They put a back door in our system."

Suddenly the holo blinked, and all the system information disappeared. In its place stood a large image of Jake Hammett. He stared directly at Cobb, as if he could see him. Then the image spoke.

"Did you really think I would sit idly by for eighteen years, you son of a bitch, and never prepare for this moment? Welcome to hell, Cobb. The next few hours are going to be your introduction to it – soon followed by your real entry there. You killed thousands of people, you bastard, and now I'm going to kill you. Not directly, you stupid shit. I'm going to let the Bats kill you. And thanks for the opportunity to fox them even more. At least you can die knowing that you helped the RDF defeat them. Goodbye, Cobb. Enjoy it!"

Suddenly the *Taizong* began boosting at 155g, directly toward Nest. All the other ships of Cobb's task force did the same. At the same time, the Comm console lit up.

"Sir!" yelled the Comm officer. "There's a broadcast going out!"

"Put it on," snapped Cobb. The Comm officer pressed his console and James Cobb's own voice came through their comms.

"...Admiral James Cobb to the Bat Navy. We are tired of your aggressive colonization and wanton destruction. This will be a warning to you that we will no longer tolerate it. We are willing to do whatever it takes to stop you. Prepare yourself for justice!"

Cobb chilled to the bone. "Stop that transmission!" he yelled at the Comm officer.

"I can't, sir!" yelled the Comm officer. "The AI has taken over the console! I can't do anything!"

Oleg looked up from the Tac Console grimly. "We're headed directly for Nest, at 155g. We can't control the ship."

"Shut off the AI!" yelled Cobb.

"We've tried, sir," said Oleg. "No joy. We're completely locked out. The AI has sealed itself and the engines as well, using the boarding defense protocol."

Cobb sank into his command chair, pounding his fist on the armrest in frustration. "Keep trying!" he yelled at the bridge crew, as they frantically worked to regain control of the *Taizong*. "Tell Engineering to disconnect the AI! Tell them to manually shut down the engines!"

But in his heart, Cobb knew. He knew that the RDF had spent the last eighteen years secretly modifying his ship, and the other ships in his task force.

Why he hadn't thought of that, he couldn't say. But it had never crossed his mind that Hammett would be that patient, have that much foresight. They must have infiltrated the maintenance crews over the years, slowly building up their presence, carefully putting in place the pieces to do this.

And now – Cobb knew. He knew in his heart it was too late.

Hammett had him.

*****

Eleven hours later, the Bat battleship *Warmonger* – the second of that name – approached Cobb's fleet, just about halfway between Cobb's initial entry point and Nest.

Around it, four other BEN battleships and their associated screening cruisers and frigates were under flank decel, to maximize the engagement window.

Cobb's fleet had also gone to decel about halfway to them, but had otherwise never wavered since their initial broadcast, and no other communications had been forthcoming. They did not respond to any messages from the *Warmonger*.

Onboard, Bat Commodore Rashtal studied the holotank, shaking his head.

"I've seen stupid before," he commented to his XO, Caltel. "But this takes the cake. They're committing pure suicide."

Caltel nodded. "I can't even imagine what they hope to accomplish by this."

Rashtal grunted. "I call this a weapons test for our fleet."

Caltel grinned. "Not even a very good one."

A console pinged, indicating they were in range.

"Open fire, Caltel." Said Rashtal.

Caltel nodded. The *Warmonger*, and the rest of Rashtal's fleet, sent a massive wave of missiles toward Cobb's puny task force.

*****

"Anything?" Cobb grunted, talking to Oleg. Oleg just looked back at him passively.

"We've tried everything. The manual controls in Engineering are all disconnected. We can't shut down the engines. We can't change course. We cut our way into the AI core and found out it had been distributed all over the ship, into dozens of locations. We found one in the back of a reefer in the galley, disguised as a refrigerant motor. But every time we shut one down, another one somewhere else takes over. We have no control over any of the consoles. And all the weapons are powering up."

Cobb pounded his command chair in frustration. Tears came into his eyes as he heard all his weapons start firing at the Bat task force in front of him. Oleg looked at Cobb with disgust.

"Thanks for killing us all, you stupid son of a bitch," he said.

*****

1/2 AU behind Cobb's task force, and off to one side, Vitus and his squadron stood by, just coasting along. Their recorders ran at full speed as the scene played out in front of them. Their primary task – acting as a backup in case anything went wrong with Plan A – was done. Cobb's task force was a field of debris now, the more so because as each of his ships took even the slightest hit, they exploded, so that nothing was left – no survivors, no AI core to be examined, nothing. One by one, the ships had detonated, leaving behind only clouds of debris.

When the last one was gone, and the Bat task force had halted, sifting through the wreckage, Vitus and his squadron stopped their recorders and slowly, carefully boosted back out of the system, still squawking their Bat ID code, looking to all the universe like just another Bat merchant ship on its way to a distant port.

In the Kuiper belt, they rendezvoused with the *Enterprise*, which carefully sank out of the system, heading for its next stop.

Bat Home System – Kuiper Belt
15 June 2207

It looked like an asteroid. It moved like an asteroid, in a nice, semi-stable orbit in the Kuiper belt of the Bat Home System, far from any perturbing influences that might be caused by inner planets. Nothing about the frozen, icy rock looked abnormal.

Inside, a central hall ran down the center of the heavily disguised RDF Scout Ship *Polaris*. Crew quarters, a kitchen, an entertainment area, a gym, storage areas and life support centers came off the main hallway at intervals. At the rear, a propulsion unit rested cold and silent, retracted inside the ship and covered by a thick, rock-covered hatch.

On the bridge at the center of *Polaris*, Captain Richard Eidson of the RDF Scout Service squinted at the console. His XO, Commander Rachel Aubrey, stood beside him, shaking her head.

“They're still moving away from us," said Rachel. "At least 1 AU out. I think we're good."

Richard nodded. “Fine, but it was damn strange that as soon as we shut down the reactor, that Bat scout showed up making a sweep through the belt. Makes me damn uncomfortable sitting here with no power. How’s Commander Aiken coming on the reactor repair?”

"About another twenty-four hours," she reported.

"And tracking?"

"Passive sensor tracking is good," said Rachel. "We're not seeing anything other than the one scout ship there, and it's no threat at the present."

Richard grunted. "OK. Keep a close eye on things.

Rachel nodded. "Aye, sir."

Richard turned and headed towards the stairwell down to crew quarters. "I'm going to get some shuteye. If anything so much as twitches in our direction, I want to know it yesterday."

* * * * *

His MEMSAI was screaming in his head. Richard woke up with that instant attention that comes with years of military service.

<Richard, wake up!> yelled his MEMSAI again. <Bat frigate on fast approach!>

Richard jumped out of bed and ran for the bridge. He burst into the bridge just in time to see Rachel turn toward him, her face grim.

"We've got a Bat frigate coming straight up our ass on a combat approach, he came out of nowhere. He clearly knows we're here."

"Crap, crap, crap," said Richard. "How did they find us?"

As the remainder of the bridge crew slammed their butts into the chairs around them, Rachel shook her head. "There's too much coincidence between our shutting down the reactor and the scout ship appearing, and now a frigate. I think the reactor must have shunted some stray RF through the hull when we shut it down. There's no other way they could know we're here."

"Well, they know now. And we still have no power?"

"No, sir. Commander Aiken says even with an emergency startup, he can't get the reactor back for at least an hour."

Richard nodded slowly. "So - no guns, no power to move, nothing."

Rachel's face was white. "That's about the size of it."

Richard looked around the room at the scared faces surrounding him. Grimly, he turned back to Rachel.

"I'm sorry, Rachel," he said.

Rachel nodded. "I know," she whispered.

Kamilaroi – Tolleson Base
16 June 2207

Jake hit the conference table with his closed fist, just one time, but hard. He bowed his head.

Those assembled around the table waited silently. Those closest to him, at his end of the table, saw the moisture in the corners of his eyes.

In a few seconds, he raised his head and morphed back to normal, his face like stone.

"Ginger, please work on a memorial service for the crew and let's make sure it's a damn good one," he said. "Put Richard and Rachel in for the Medal of Honor, my personal nomination. Navy Cross for the rest of the crew."

Ginger nodded, her bead glowing once to show she had communicated notes to her AI. A tear moved slowly down one cheek.

Jake straightened in his chair and looked at his Chief of Intelligence, Admiral Bert Welby.

"You're absolutely sure they swapped cores?" he asked.

"Yes, sir." Welby responded in his quirky Yorkshire accent, “We got a nice, clean QE squirt and it confirmed the AI swapped the dummy core in before the self-destruct went off."

"And the dead-man drones?"

"Dead-man drones confirmed the destruct and confirmed the *Polaris* took the Bat frigate with her when she blew; it had already latched on for boarding. The dead-man drones monitored for twenty-four hours to confirm no residual EMF transmissions from either wreck, then did their own standard destruct."

Nobody said anything for a while.

Finally, Jake sighed, a long one.

"Let's get on to business, folks. That's what Richard and his crew would want us to do. My concern is that, in spite of the self-destruct, there could be some kind of debris floating around out there that might give the Bats a clue to the location of Earth. Something that a crewmember smuggled on board; any kind of contraband that could help their intelligence staff get a line on our location."

"There is always that possibility," said Welby. "We drill the Scout crews incessantly about not taking anything on board that could offer up a clue to our location, but people are people. All it would take would be one idiot with a chip of old Earth movies showing our solar system and they'd have us, if it survived the nuke."

Admiral Maxence Baptiste, Chief of Naval Ordnance, shook his head. "Nothing survived that nuke," he growled. "I promise you, any contraband on that ship was vaporized."

"Still, it makes me nervous," said Jake. "After eighty-six years of planning, for this to happen. Here we are, almost to the end..."

Baptiste looked sideways at Jake. "The plan never survives contact with the enemy, Jake. You know that."

Jake smiled slowly. "I know that. But I want it to be their plan that doesn't survive the contact."

Jake leaned back, placed both hands flat on the table, and

looked around the room. He included not only the senior officers sitting at the table, but their staff members seated in the second and third rows behind.

Jake turned to the table. "You all know we've had Intelligence resources on Nest for a number of years now. Resource Fourteen has been taking great risks to give us reports almost daily for the last couple of weeks, as we approach the end of this great effort. From his reports, we've learned that a BEN Task Force is likely to receive clearance to detach and attack the 'Apes' within the next month."

The intake of breath around the table was audible as Jake paused, then continued. "So - Andrea's First Fleet is not actually on an extended training mission as was announced when they departed two months ago. They are at Nest, staged for the attack on the Bat Home Fleet. Likewise, Second Fleet is not departing on its own extended training mission next week as announced. It will be leaving for Orinoco to stage for its part of the attack."

Although Jake's senior staff already knew of this, some of the staffers in the back of the room were stunned.

Jake continued. "The actual attack clock is not D-Day minus 405 as is commonly thought and bandied about by loose gossip." Jake grinned. "It is D-Day minus 50. Today, in view of the loss of the *Polaris*, I want to advance the attack clock to D-day minus 30. Give me your thoughts."

The room was silent. Then Ginger spoke first.

"Absolutely," she said. "Let's give these bastards the hell they deserve!"

Welby was more cautious. "If they don't split their fleet, we have to wait. Andrea would be going up against their full Home Fleet," he posited. "Her nine capital ships against their twenty-four. She'd be decimated."

Jake shook his head. "I think you underestimate Andrea. She'll be in and out of that fleet like a knife through butter. She'll tear them to pieces."

Welby shook his head again. "But with their detection of *Polaris*, they'll go on heightened alert. I'd rather wait another seven full weeks, ensure they really do split up their fleet and send a Task Force. I think the risk that they pull any useful intel out of the wreck of the *Polaris* is negligible."

Jake nodded. "Objections noted and they are good ones."

"Wei?" said Jake, glancing at his G4 Chief, Admiral Wei Li.

Wei Li leaned forward. "Risk either way, but I say go for it. Andrea can handle them. The thirty days will give them time to settle down after the *Polaris*. If they don't detect anything else for a week, they should calm down and go back to their normal routine."

Jake focused on his Chief of Planning, Kanako Matsumoto.

"Kanako? How about G5? Can we advance the clock for Orinoco without major glitches?"

"Yes," replied Matsumoto. "We'll make it work."

Jake continued his sweep around the room. "Does anyone have any additional objections to advancement of the attack clock to D-Day minus 30, implemented immediately? I would like to hear it if you do. Or as always you can communicate with me directly if you want to make your concerns known outside of this room."

No one spoke. Their beads glowed fiercely as orders were issued.

MASKIROVKA

Don't take a knife to a gunfight.
- Old Texas Proverb, Earth, 20th Century

Nest Home System - 1 Light Year Above the Ecliptic
1 July 2207

Andrea yawned. It was past midnight ship time, and she had given up trying to sleep. Of course, that didn't help her not be sleepy - she could hardly keep her eyes open. But every time she put her head down on the pillow, her mind clicked into high gear again.

She saw the battle plan in her head. She thought of the thousand things that needed doing before a battle - even though most of them would be done by her Chief of Staff, Commander Derinoe, or by her Flag Captain, Captain Melousa.

And she missed her children. The twins - Alexander and Ligeia - were safe at home on Aeolis, nestled in the arms of their godmother, Empress Hecate. Today, she had watched one of the vids received as they were shoving off from Tolleson Station more than two months ago, showing Hecate - the Empress of a powerful empire - tucking them into bed. She smiled at the memory of it.

And she missed Jake. But Jake was 400 lights away near the Orinoco system, also waiting. Waiting for Andrea to lead the Bats to him.

And when? When would it begin?

Andrea hated the waiting. She understood the need for it...they absolutely had to sit tight, be patient, wait for the attack clock to wind down, hoping all the while that the Bats would take the bait and split their Home Fleet...but by the Stars, it was not her nature!

They had been sitting here in the middle of nowhere, hidden one light year above the ecliptic of the Bat's home system, for ten weeks now!

Incommunicado except for the occasional incoming QE message, running silent, sensors on passive, life-support minimal - cold and alone, just another few rocks out here where no ships passed by.

The crews were getting stir-crazy, that she was sure of - she certainly was!

Suddenly her MEMSAI beeped with Commander Derinoe's unique "Come Quick" sound. Andrea leaped to her feet, threw on her robe and ran out to the Flag Bridge, directly outside her suite. Derinoe was there, huddled over her repeater holotank along with Captain Melousa. Both turned to her and smiled.

"They're moving," said Melousa. "Just picked it up on the QE repeater."

Andrea Iona stared at the plot with relief. "Finally," she said.

Derinoe echoed her feelings. "Thank the Stars. I thought they'd never leave."

In the holo, it was clear that a portion of the Bat Fleet was pulling out. Their vector seemed to be right where the RDF had predicted – they were leaving to attack the 'Apes'. The Bat Expeditionary Fleet was headed directly toward Farpoint – 473 light years from Nest, but to Coreward – the wrong way.

"How many?" asked Andrea.

"CIC thinks just about half the Home Fleet. Just as we had hoped," said Melousa.

"Thank the Stars, thank the Stars," said Andrea. "OK, let's designate the departing ships as the 'Detached Fleet' in the holo." She turned to Derinoe.

"Pass a message to the Stealth Girls, Derinoe. Tell them to stay with them, but not too close. We absolutely cannot tip our hand now. It would be better to lose them and try to re-acquire, than to get too close and let them get a detection."

"Aye, Mum," said Derinoe. Her bead glowed and her eyes defocused a bit as she passed the message on.

Andrea got up from her command chair. "OK, tomorrow we'll start pulling this circus together. I'm going to go try for some sleep. It's...let's see, 0030 hours...set a meeting for tomorrow morning at 0900. We'll put the final touches on the plan then."

"Aye, Mum," said Derinoe, a huge grin on her face. "Sleep well."

Andrea smiled. "I will now."

* * * * *

On the slightly recessed bridge below, the XO of the *Empress*, Commander Duspera, sitting quietly in the command chair, grinned hugely as she heard the Captain and Admiral talking on the other side of the Flag Bridge partition. Her Tactical Officer, Lt. Commander Anaxo, stared at the main holotank and looked puzzled.

"Why are the Bats heading in the wrong direction?" she asked. "I thought they were planning to go out and attack Earth."

Duspera laughed. "Ah, now, I can finally tell you. Admiral Hammett started an operation over eighty years ago called Project Guano. He planted QE buoys at a system called Farpoint, 473 light years Coreward of Nest, and started them broadcasting recorded EMF from Earth, making it look like Earth was in a completely different place.

So, for the last eighty-plus years, a continuous broadcast of carefully screened radio, TV and comm signals from Earth has been patched through to Farpoint and then re-broadcast back toward Nest. And on Farpoint, he's built fake cities, roads, there's always dozens of AI spaceships buzzing about, looking for all the world like Earth.

And all the hit-and-run decoy raids that have been going on for the last six months – the ships always depart towards Farpoint. So that's where the Bats are going. They've been foxed by the Master."

"My Stars," said Anaxo. "How could anyone think more than eighty-six years in advance? No wonder *Pandora* picked him for his job."

Duspera grinned. "Remember what *Pandora* said, back in 2121? That she picked him because he could see 'all three sides of the coin'? She wasn't kidding!"

Anaxo frowned. "But...as I think about it...that wouldn't completely work. If he started re-broadcasting in 2121 from Farpoint, and it's 473 lights from Nest, then the Bats could figure out that there's a block of history missing from around 1910 through about 2121. So, they would know it's a deception."

Duspera grinned even wider. "So how would you fix that problem?"

Anaxo thought for a while. "Well...I guess you could put another QE repeater buoy about...let's see...about 210 lights out from Farpoint toward Nest...and have it broadcast EMF from the missing period, from 1910 up to 2121. Until the 2121 signals caught up to it. Then have it shut down."

"You're on the right track," said Duspera. "But it was five QE repeater buoys, spaced about sixty-five lights apart, providing complete coverage. In a spread array, repeating every forty-five degrees around the Farpoint system. Each of the outer ones shut down and self-destructed as soon as the signal arrived from the next innermost one. So once 65 years had passed, there was a complete signal stream for 325 lights, all the way from Farpoint toward Nest, with only the innermost repeater buoy still in operation."

Anaxo objected again. "But even so, the signal would still be...what...only 325 lights from Farpoint, and Nest is 473 lights."

"Well," said Duspera, "Let's just say the Bats had a little help detecting it. Maybe someone put one of their remote QE detection buoys in just the right place. After all, you can't make it too hard for them."

Anaxo shook her head. "How could anyone think of

something so sneaky?"

Duspera continued her grin. "I guess you have to be an Admiral."

2 July 2207 - 1200 hours

Andrea tapped on the table. The small talk died, and her officers looked at her. Derinoe was to her right, Melousa to her left. Down the table were arrayed the captains of her other four battleships. In the holo were the commanding officers of the rest of her fleet - four cruisers, eight frigates and ten destroyers. Her flag staff stood against the wall surrounding the conference table.

Andrea began. "This will be your last warning order. We will advance upon the enemy today at 1600 hours. It will take us twelve hours to come into effective combat range, so we should make contact at roughly 0400 hours tomorrow morning. That will be about 0200, Bat time. A nice wake-up call for them."

Grins went around the table.

"We all know the plan, and there are no changes at this time. Execute your orders as precisely as possible but improvise and adapt as necessary to assure the success of this attack."

The assembled officers nodded.

"I know I have said this repeatedly, but I'm going to say it again, especially for those of you new to combat. This is a hit-and-run. Do NOT get caught up in the heat of battle and try to kill just one more ship, get in just one more hit. I fought in a half-dozen battles during the Aeolian Rebellion, and I will tell you, it's easy to get your blood boiling and lose track of the overall objective. Stay focused. I want to inflict maximum damage on their Home Fleet, but WITHOUT losing a ship, if possible.

"So. Remember the number one objective. Pass through their fleet, shoot everything you can, sling around the planet and get the hell out. Do NOT slow down for anything. Get in, get out and keep going like your tail was on fire. Because it just may be."

Chuckles went around the table.

Andrea stood, and everyone snapped to attention.

"Good hunting and good luck. See you later in the tac. Dismissed."

The holo flicked off, and the assembled officers turned and filed out.

Andrea watched them go and wondered. How many would still be alive tomorrow?

Would this gamble work? So much turned on the success of this attack; if she failed, then the Bats might have enough strength left in their Home Fleet to run her down and destroy her.

Or even if she succeeded and got away clean, the Bat's Detached Fleet might not turn and follow her; might, in fact, simply return to Nest, regroup, and start hunting for Earth in earnest.

Or even if they did follow her, as planned, they might catch her before she got to Jake at Orinoco.

Andrea sighed. There's no point in thinking about the what-ifs at this point, she knew. The odds seemed to be in their favor. The die was cast. It was up to her and her Fleet to strike the first blow of the end game.

Andrea turned and retired to her cabin. It was in the hands of the Creator, she thought. She would do her best.

* * * * *

Sensor Officer Caltrun was half-asleep. The graveyard shift on the Bat Home Fleet Flagship *High Echo* was always difficult. But he could not sleep; the penalty for sleeping on duty was severe.

So, Caltrun managed - just barely - to stay awake. He decided to get up and walk around the bridge, to jostle his dull brain back into action. Moving around the various sensor stations, he looked over the shoulders of the technicians, pretending to gaze at their screens, but really checking to see if they were awake.

He completed his circle of the room and was nearly back

to his seat when the "ping" of a sensor was followed almost immediately by the soft "warble, warble" of an unidentified ship alarm.

Caltrun sighed. Another damn merchantman who forgot to set his IFF. He reversed course and went back to the long range holo tank. The technician was twisting the holo controls, looking puzzled.

"What's up?" asked Caltrun.

The technician shook his head. "I'm not sure, sir. There's a detection straight out the north planetary pole, about 100 k-klicks out. Moving way too fast to be a merchantman, if it's real."

"Crap," said Caltrun. "Maybe an incoming asteroid?"

The technician adjusted the holo tank again. "Possible, sir, but the vector is a bit strange for an asteroid. It's...wait, let me project the track...See? It's...not a typical asteroid orbit. It looks more like a ship coming in. In fact," he peered at the holo "...it's coming right at us...decelerating hard..."

Caltrun shook his head. "Nothing on the manifest, and no IFF."

"Ping!" Another blip appeared in the holo. Almost immediately, two more followed. "Ping! Ping!"

Then a concert of pings as an entire fleet of ships came into view, moving fast, straight at the various locations where Home Fleet warships orbited.

For several seconds, Caltrun stood frozen, his mind blank.

Then he shuddered and ran to his desk.

*****

"Open fire, open fire, open fire," intoned Captain Melousa. Immediately the *Empress Hecate* vibrated as railguns and missiles started firing simultaneously. In a loose formation covering orbits around the planet Nest and its LaGrange points, the other ships of Andrea's First Fleet went to work as well, targeting every major Bat warship near the planet.

Results were immediate - within seconds, two enemy

frigates exploded, an enemy cruiser had a hole punched completely through her midships, and a battleship vented from a large hole near her engines.

From their sensors, the Bats had received about ten minutes warning before the strike - enough to know they were under attack, but clearly not enough to fully prepare for action.

Andrea sat in her Flag Officer's chair raised on a dais behind Captain Melousa and his bridge staff. A plastic partition between her Flag Bridge and the bridge of the *Empress Hecate* served as a symbolic division between the officer commanding the ship – Melousa - and Andrea, the officer commanding the entire fleet.

Andrea watched in her own separate holo repeater as her hit-and-run fleet, at max decel, began to knock holes in the Bat fleet. They would remain on max decel through the end of the attack; then perform a slingshot around the planet, escaping on their vector toward Orinoco.

The *Empress Hecate* shuddered in a different way as an enemy ship got a hit on them, but the size of the round was too small to do any real damage - probably a destroyer, she thought.

Things were going well. Perhaps it was that thought of Andrea’s that jinxed it; for at that very moment the Bat Fleet got their legs under them, and fire began to sprout from all quarters.

"Wiggle and Wobble, Helm!" shouted the *Hecate's* XO from the main deck of the bridge, although it was clear from the way they were being jerked around in their harnesses that the Helm was doing just that. Andrea's inertial harness and helmet damped those excursions somewhat, but they still hurt like hell. The crew would be sore tomorrow - then Andrea grinned wryly.

Better sore than dead.

The *Hecate* sang a new song as the beamers came online, having a shorter range than the railguns and missiles. Another round hit them somewhere aft, and this one was bigger - maybe a cruiser, thought Andrea. Immediately an even larger round smacked into the nose, barely shunted by the grav dampers, heaving them up and to the side before the Helm caught it and returned them to attitude.

"Battleship," said Andrea.

"Right-o," agreed Derinoe.

"Half-way point!" yelled the Tactical Officer - they were halfway through their gun run.

At that precise moment, the ship clanged like a bell and the lights dimmed, then went out. The battery-powered lights came on immediately. The holotank flickered, went out, then came back on under battery power. The acrid smell of something burning came from the vents.

Andrea did nothing. It was not her place to fight the ship - that, and damage control, were up to Captain Melousa. She merely peered at the holotank to see if it was updating. It was – the Bat fleet passed steadily to their rear, any number of them now shedding pieces, burning, or simply vanished.

But her own fleet was not unscathed - she saw one of her cruisers spinning helplessly in space, burning as it went. Behind that, another ship - smaller, a frigate - also rotated end-over-end, venting gases.

The firing continued, but the range was quickly increasing. The hits became fewer; finally, Captain Melousa gave the order, "Cease fire, cease fire, cease fire!"

Immediately, as the warships achieved perigee on their swing around the planet, they went to max accel to slingshot around Nest. Within minutes, their outbound vectors had stabilized on a direct track to Orinoco, 398 light years back toward Zeta Capricorni.

Twelve hours later, they crossed the mass limit and sank out. Their vectors did not change as they did so, which was duly noted by the BEN Intelligence Office and the small BEN scout ships trailing them.

* * * * *

Bruntel roared. "Apes! Crap-eating, fly-infested jungle apes did this? I will crush them to jelly, I will smash them to paste! I will stack them like cordwood in the reefers!"

Before him, the Comm Officer remained in a low bow, afraid to move. He had just delivered the message to Bruntel that the Apes had attacked Home Fleet in their absence. The losses were significant; half the Home Fleet was no longer functional.

Bruntel kicked the stanchion before him, knocking his a'kaff cup and tablet onto the floor. He turned back to the shivering Comm Officer and drew back his leg to kick him, but finally thought better of it.

"Do we have a scout following them?"

"Yes, sir," said the relieved Comm Officer. "Two scouts right behind them, dogging their trail."

"Then," roared Bruntel, "Turn this damn task force around and get after them!"

OPEN GROUND

Victorious warriors win first and then go to war, while defeated warriors go to war first and seek to win.
- Sun Tzu, The Art of War, Earth, 6th Century B. C.

First Fleet, enroute to Orinoco
4 July 2207

Andrea stood in the docking bay of the *Empress Hecate*, her formal dress uniform gleaming in the overhead lights. Behind her stood Captain Melousa, Commander Derinoe, and Commander Duspera, along with the rest of her flag staff.

The docking bay - not as large as a carrier's, but large enough - contained most of the crew of the battleship. In front of her, holo cameras hovered to carry her image to the rest of the ships in her fleet. Andrea looked over the crowd and smiled grimly.

"Yesterday, we were given the honor of striking the first blow against a terrible enemy. We succeeded in our mission - in fact, we excelled. Our Stealth Girls have verified the following: seven destroyers killed..." - a cheer erupted from the crew - "five frigates out of action..." - another cheer went up from the crew - "three cruisers down..." - Andrea looked up and smiled broadly - "...and three battleships shot to hell and dead in space!"

A final cheer, the largest yet, went up from the assembled crew, and Angela let them go. It was the beginning of a war; best to let them celebrate while they could. She well knew this war was far from done.

After a few moments, the cheering and congratulations died down.

Andrea spoke again. "That was the good news, people. Now

for the bad news."

"From our fleet, we lost the cruisers *Prince Adrian* and the *Nimitz*; two frigates, the *Golden Mare* and the *Sao Paulo;* and destroyers *Desert Wind, Keen Wind* and *Whitney*." Andrea paused to look over the crew, many of whom had grim faces.

"I know that many of you had friends on those ships," she said. "There were, in fact, 4,268 people on those ships. Every one of them..." and here Andrea raised her voice - "...EVERY ONE OF THEM...died a hero to the people of our Alliance - and to Aeolis!"

There was dead quiet on the deck. Andrea looked around at the hundreds of people standing before her. Her heart pounded, not from excitement or fear, but from the depths of her emotion as she looked at this crew, this wonderful crew.

"In three weeks, we go into battle again at Orinoco. Here on the *Hecate*, and in the other ships of this fleet, are the best warriors the Rim has. The best of the best. We are no longer Earthers, or Aeolians, or Daneki...we are the Rim. We are one."

Andrea paused and quite publicly wiped a tear from the corner of her eye.

"When we fight again days from now, remember those who died at Nest. Remember what they fought for, and what we fight for - a future for our Homeland, a future for our children. Safe from fear; safe from danger. And in memory of those who died yesterday.

“I don't have to tell you more. I know you. I know what you can do. And I know what you will do when next we meet the monsters who seek to kill us."

Andrea paused. She looked around the room. There was dead silence. Slowly, silently, she raised her hand to the Aeolian salute position and held it. As one, so synchronized that it made a single sound, the assembled crew snapped to attention. Their hands went to their left shoulder in the formal hand salute.

Andrea dropped her hand and nodded. Then she spun on her heel and left.

* * * * *

Back in her conference room, Angela took her seat at the head of the table, handing her hat off to Gasperdy, her valet. As her officers filed into the room, she sat unconsciously drumming her fingers on the wood. When they had all reached their seats, she looked at Commander Derinoe. "What have we got?" she asked.

"Good news," smiled Derinoe. "Stealth Girls report the outbound BEN Detached Fleet has turned around and they're on a vector straight at us, so clearly they are hoping to intercept us before we get too far away. Evidently, they read our outbound vector accurately, and it seems they also went for the 'inadvertent' failure to erase our AI cores on the destroyed ships back at Nest."

"Good," nodded Andrea. "Although I would have much preferred not to lose any ships."

"Yes," said Derinoe. "But given they were lost; the rest of the plan seems to have worked."

Andrea sighed. "A lot of good people gone."

Silence reigned in the room for a few seconds, then Andrea slapped the table.

"OK!" she said. "We have a battle to plan. Let's be about it! Where are the Bats now, Derinoe?"

"They've made good time...they're only fifty lights behind us and making up the distance pretty much as we expected. They'll be on our tail right about twenty-five AU behind us when they surface at Orinoco. We'll be just ahead of them all the way into the primary, losing ground rapidly. I don't see how they can resist the temptation."

Andrea grinned an evil grin. "Let's make sure they don't - when those bastards surface behind us at Orinoco, I want to be looking as bedraggled and panicky as possible. Let's make sure."

Derinoe grinned back, her own evil grin a close second to Andrea's. "Oh, we will!"

Orinoco

25 July 2207

As they surfaced at the Orinoco system, the RDF ships dispersed into a ragged formation, some speeding up slightly and pulling ahead, some lagging behind. Several began venting volatiles to look damaged.

Twenty hours after their arrival, as they rode straight in toward the primary at 155g, the Bat fleet surfaced behind them and began pursuit. With their greater acceleration, the Bats reduced the distance, making up ground at a steady pace.

The Bat Detached Fleet had been joined by surviving remnants of their Home Fleet, including two battleships, two cruisers and three frigates. This now created a Bat Armada of fourteen battleships, fourteen cruisers, eighteen frigates and sixteen destroyers. As the RDF fleet approached the primary, the Bats were only six hours behind them.

Onboard the Bat flagship *Pride of Nest*, Admiral Bruntel paced, periodically cursing at the slow pace of the intercept. In frustration, he turned and slashed his baton across the face of his nearest slave. “Three damn weeks,” he cursed. “Chasing these crap-eating Apes for three weeks!”

"Sir!" cried the Tac Officer.

Admiral Bruntel grunted. "What?"

"Their fleet is...dispersing into some kind of random formation, sir!"

Bruntel - son of the famous Field Marshal Brunt who had conquered many planets in a previous generation - looked at the holo tank. He backspaced a bit and ran the tank forward again. He saw the Earthers were slowly dispersing into an even more ragged, staggered formation. He nodded. "The Apes are preparing to run in all directions," he said. "Cowards that they are!"

The Tac Officer nodded, addressing both the Admiral and the Flag Captain who stood nearby. "I think so, Sirs. They'll slingshot around the star and come out in random directions. To chase them all down, we'll have to split up."

"We can't hit them before their perihelion?"

"No, sir. We're short by just over three hours. They'll get around the star before we can intercept on the inbound. We can only intercept on the outbound, and we'll need to follow them around the star to have the speed."

"Damn," said Bruntel. He looked at the holo tank. "Alright, Captain Naptar, issue orders to the fleet: all battleships to designate one of the enemy capital ships and follow it around the star. Follow and destroy - without fail! Those who don't come back with a destroyed capital ship in their sensorium will pay the price!"

Captain Naptar nodded vigorously. "Aye, sir!"

"Frigates to join on their assigned battleship and stick with them for the nonce. Destroyers - ah, give them free rein. Tell them to just go hunting!"

The Flag Captain grinned, his fangs showing. "Aye sir - they'll like that!"

Slowly, over the next hour, the two fleets approached the small G9V primary, the BEN fleet gaining slowly on the RDF - but not quickly enough to intercept before the Earthers could sling around the star and disperse. Bruntel grew increasingly frustrated as they drew closer.

"Captain!" he yelled. "More speed!"

"Trying, sir. But if we are to stay together and maintain formation, this..."

"Damn the formation! Let the fastest ships go ahead!"

Captain Naptar grimaced, his ears erect from stress. "Sir, that is dangerous..."

In his anger, Bruntel spit as he angrily replied. "Dangerous? Dangerous? Chasing these Apes? Run up the engines, Captain! Now!"

The Captain nodded. "Aye, sir. Helm - increase engines to 110%. Comms - notify all ships to break formation as necessary and make max speed to intercept!"

Within a couple of hours, the Bat destroyer squadrons were streaking far ahead of the main fleet. Newer, faster battleships

- including the *Pride of Nest* - had pulled out well ahead of the older, slower ones.

Admiral Bruntel paced the bridge, shaking his head periodically at the slow pace of the intercept.

Suddenly the Tac Officer stared at the holo tank. With a puzzled expression, he backspaced and ran the tank forward again. Suddenly he yelled, "Captain! Something strange...!"

"What?" cried Captain Naptar.

The Tac Officer screeched in his excitement. "They are very slowly moving into new courses as they approach the star. I think this new arrangement does not disperse them...they will stay together!"

Admiral Bruntel shouldered his way to the holotank. Quickly he backspaced and ran the tank forward.

Only an hour prior, the projection of the enemy ships as they came out from behind the star had been random, shooting off in all directions. But now their outbound courses were subtly coming into parallel - and, he realized, if they had sufficient delta v available, they could come arcing back towards the Bat Fleet. Even as he watched, the holotank adjusted the courses slightly as the sensors got new data from the ships in front of them. Clearly, the projected outbound courses were starting to line up.

Captain Naptar said it first. "It's an ambush, Admiral!"

Admiral Bruntel grinned. "Perfect. We'll smash them!"

"But, Admiral," spoke Captain Naptar. "They could have more ships behind us, coming up our rear. We should re-group and get back into formation."

Bruntel grunted. "No way these slimy pirates have more ships."

Naptar persisted. "But sir. We are dispersed. We broke formation to allow the faster ships to go ahead. Now we've lost the interlocking fields of fire.

“Sir. Let's reverse, or at least slow down, to put ourselves back in formation."

Bruntel mused for a few moments, then sighed. "Very well, Naptar. We can just as easily smash them a few hours later.

Order the fleet to re-form."

Twenty minutes later, at flank deceleration, the *Pride of Nest* had started to move back toward the main fleet, along with the other fast burners who had jumped out in front. Admiral Bruntel and Captain Naptar huddled over the holotank, watching for any sign of ships coming up behind them. But it was not ships behind them that they saw.

"Sirs," said the Tac Officer. "I'm getting some kind of fuzzy signal from around us...very faint...possibly small craft, Sirs."

"What?" Naptar looked at him in puzzlement.

"Definitely there, sir. Small craft, or possibly shuttles. Now...now I see more, sir. They're coming fast."

"What do you think, Naptar? Could they be corvettes?"

With a "ping", the first of the unknown signals registered in the holotank. Naptar bent forward and looked at the estimated size and speed displayed next to the symbol.

"My Stars, Admiral! It's tiny...but it's coming fast!"

Suddenly the holotank erupted into a cacophony of "pings" as first several, then dozens, then hundreds of the unknown craft were detected by the external sensors.

"That's an attack, sir," said Captain Naptar. "I don't know what they are, but they're definitely attacking."

*****

"Cassian to First Wing, engage, engage, engage. Give 'em hell, guys!" Cassian called over the intership. Around him in a huge enveloping mass surrounding the line of Bat ships, 726 A40 fighters firewalled their throttles. Ahead of them, the BEN Fleet was well dispersed, scattered in a long, ragged line for two hundred thousand klicks.

With their targets pre-selected by their coupled AI, the attack craft raced toward the Bat battlewagons and their screening ships. The Bat destroyers, well ahead and desperately trying to reverse course, would not be a factor in this action. They were too far ahead. Cassian nodded, just once, before buckling down to his task. "Today, son of Brunt, murderer of my people, today feel the flame we felt all those years ago," he said quietly.

In seconds, Cassian came into range of the flagship - he knew it was the flagship, because it was the foremost battleship, and no Bat admiral would let another battleship precede him into a fight.

A few sporadic guns opened up on his squadron. But it was nothing like the full firepower that could be brought by a Bat battleship, and at that moment, Cassian knew he had caught them napping.

With a war cry, Cassian released his missiles and watched them run hot and true toward the flagship's engines. Following the missiles in, the old Daneki never wavered from his course. While all around him the remainder of his squadron peeled off after missile release and powered away, Cassian's A40 simply kept accelerating, on a direct course toward the well-protected bridge of the battlewagon.

Cassian knew it would take a lot of energy to get all the way through the armor, and the A40's impact probably wouldn't make it through. But...Cassian smiled as the wall of the huge ship loomed closer and closer.

He was content. He had fought the good fight. He could go home now.

*****

With a tremendous "clang", the lights went out. Admiral Bruntel found himself on his hands and knees on the floor of the bridge, in the dark. It took some seconds for the backup lighting to come on.

As it did, he looked around, stunned. Almost every officer was on the floor. Captain Naptar was face down next to him, unconscious. Blood oozed from his ears. Bruntel pulled himself up to a squatting position.

His AI interface was dead. He looked for the holotank. It was out.

"Tac!"

"Yes, sir," came a pained response from behind him. He turned and saw the Tac Officer on elbow and one knee, trying to get his feet under him.

"Give me a status! What's happening?" Admiral Bruntel struggled to his chair.

"Yes, sir," said the Tac Officer. He fumbled to his feet and stumbled over to his console. It was black, unresponsive. Grabbing his backup comm, he called Engineering.

"Engineering, Bridge. What's the status?"

There was a mumbled response which Bruntel couldn't quite make out. The Tac Officer turned to him. "Engineering reports all engines down, all reactors scrammed, sir."

Admiral Bruntel shook his head. "How? How could they hit us so hard?"

"I don't know, sir," said the Tac Officer. "They were so fast. And tiny. I've never seen anything like that before."

"Tell them to get Comms and Consoles back up ASAP."

"Aye, sir," nodded the Tac Officer. He relayed the message to Engineering. He listened for a few seconds, then responded to the Admiral.

"They're estimating fifteen minutes to Comms and Consoles, sir."

Bruntel cursed. "We could all be dead in fifteen minutes! Is there any other backup we can use to get a picture of the situation?"

It was his last thought. A tremendous explosion went through the ship, and everyone on the bridge was smashed to pulp.

* * * * *

Ten thousand kilometers behind the flagship, on the Bat battleship *Warmonger*, Commodore Rashtal stared at his holotank.

"Anything from the flagship yet?" he managed to grunt.

"No, sir," said his XO, gasping from the g-forces. "Nothing. She's still not talking to us."

"Very well," said Rashtal, turning to the officer. "Notify the fleet I'm taking command until we hear from the flagship."

"Aye, sir."

Rashtal turned back to the holotank. His ship was now in emergency decel, causing the g-forces to exceed the limit of the compensator by 6g. Even breathing was difficult.

But he had to rally the fleet. He was senior now.

Between him and the star stood chaos. Ten thousand kilometers ahead, the flagship *Pride of Nest* rotated slowly end over end, spewing volatiles and chunks of debris.

Five million kilometers beyond, the Ape fleet came at them head-on, a bit more than one hour from intercept.

Between the two fleets, the destroyer squadrons, in panic and disarray, desperately tried to reverse their vectors and come back to the main fleet before the Apes caught up to them.

They would not make it, he saw.

Rashtal sighed. "The destroyers are gone," he said to his XO, in harness near him. "The Apes will chew them up without even slowing down."

He saw the Ape fleet starting to decel also. He grunted, both at the scenario and the g-forces.

"They want to maximize their engagement window, Caltel," he said painfully. "Suddenly they don't seem so timid anymore."

The XO managed to gasp out a laugh. "No, sir."

Rashtal squinted further at the display. Behind his ship streamed the rest of the Bat fleet, in disarray. Besides the *Pride of Nest*, two additional battleships showed the red "X" of destroyed/out of action. At least five cruisers also showed non-combat ready. And eight frigates were in similar states - or missing from the display.

"We have...eleven battlewagons left," said Rashtal. "Looks like...nine cruisers...ten frigates."

He rotated the display slightly and expanded the range to

seventy-five million kilometers.

"And there..." he grunted. "There comes another Ape fleet up our ass. A truly good trap they have played."

The young Tac Officer, worry and fear in his voice, asked, "What shall we do, sir?"

Rashtal looked at him. "We fight."

FIGHT OR DIE

A good plan violently executed now is better than a perfect plan executed next week.
- General George S. Patton, 20th Century Earth

Orinoco System
25 July 2207

Five million kilometers in front of the Bat Armada, watching the scrambling Bat destroyer squadrons vectoring madly in front of her, Andrea Iona sat in the Admiral's chair on the Flag Bridge of the *Empress Hecate*, racing towards the battle. She gazed at the holotank in pleasure.

"Those fighters did a hell of a job, Jake," she said. "What a punch!"

Jake's voice sounded quite gratified on the scratchy QE box transmission. "Sure as hell they did. Cassian gets a medal for executing his attack."

Andrea's voice dropped a bit. "Cassian didn't make it, Jake."

There was a silence. Finally, Jake came back. "Well. He let them know he was here, though."

Andrea nodded silently. Then...

“The Bats are reversing course. They’ve obviously decided to take you on first.”

“Yep, I see that. I guess they see that as a better tactic. It gives them a little more time for repairs, and to think about their tactics.”

"Any last minute changes?"

"Negative," said Jake. "Work the plan. Continue your decel to sync with my arrival and we'll have them between us. Hit 'em hard and don't stop until you're out of ammunition - or targets."

"Wilco, Admiral."

"And Andrea..."

There was a silence once again. Then Andrea responded with a lilt in her voice.

"I know, Jake. I'll be careful. See you after."

* * * * *

As Andrea's fleet streaked past the madly vectoring Bat destroyers, she engaged in what was virtually target practice, wreaking havoc with battleship and cruiser grade beamers and railgun rounds that flashed through their thin hulls, sometimes passing all the way through and out the other side. Andrea didn't care to waste missiles on them; she was saving those for bigger game.

It took them only thirty seconds to pass in and out of engagement range of the panicked destroyer squadrons; but that was enough. They left behind them a sea of fragmented, burning Bat ships, with debris and bodies floating in the void.

Only five destroyers survived the encounter, those sheltered on the outside of the formation where they were somewhat protected by other ships.

Fifty-three minutes later, the Bats had gotten their fleet turned around and were charging back at Jake's Second Fleet.

Andrea's First Fleet then vectored out sideways a bit, putting fifteen thousand klicks lateral distance between her path and the one taken by the Bat Fleet she was now overtaking from behind.

The results of thousands of battle simulations over the years had shown that the optimal way to fight the Bats was to turn sideways and face them as you went by. Flying sideways, nose-on to the enemy, put the strongest part of the grav deflectors – the wedge at the front of the ship – facing the enemy, allowed all your weapons to bear directly, and placed your vulnerable engines to the rear. It also minimized the risk of friendly fire accidents.

However, it had the disadvantage that you had to stop your main engines at the last second as you turned to face the enemy - so you had to be damn good at predicting what the enemy would do and where you needed to be.

In this case, it was clear the Bats thought Jake's larger Second Fleet, coming up from behind them, was the bigger threat. They had reversed onto a direct course to engage Jake's fleet first.

Andrea was certain the Bats would attempt to pitch out laterally at the last moment, getting outside Jake's task force, putting Jake between themselves and Andrea. She would then have to shoot through Jake's fleet to hit a Bat ship, putting her at a disadvantage in targeting.

They had agreed in advance this was the most likely scenario; thus Jake now pitched out fifteen thousand klicks to the other side of the Bats' path. This forced them to choose between two hard alternatives.

Either they went between Andrea and Jake at the critical moment, or they would have to start overboosting hard, right now, to get outside Jake.

But during the entire engagement since entering the system, both Andrea and Jake had held their acceleration down to 155 g, the spurious value that they had "sold" to the Bats in all previous encounters.

At this critical moment, Jake jumped his accel up to his true maximum military thrust of 200g.

This had the effect of bringing the three fleets together much sooner than the Bats anticipated. The Bats no longer had enough time to pitch outside Jake without exposing their engines to Andrea.

They had no choice but to go right down the center of the crossfire.

Once they were committed, Jake started a new decel pattern at 200g, reducing his speed to maximize his engagement window.

As the Bat Armada approached firing range, onboard his

flagship the *Wellington*, Jake raised his hand slightly to his Flag Captain, Chris Rathburn, and gestured slightly. "Whenever you're ready, Chris."

"I'm damn sure ready, sir," grinned Chris, gesturing to his own Tac Officer.

Over the QE box, the Tac Officer spoke, "All units, Fire Plan Alpha-six. Fire Plan Alpha-six. Open fire, open fire, open fire!"

Jake grinned. Although the actual launches were AI-controlled, it seemed to do Humans a world of good to yell out the words, just in case somebody forgot.

In seconds, a stream of missiles erupted from Jake's Second Fleet. Four battleships spit out thirty-two missiles each, while four cruisers sent another sixty-four missiles on their way. Nine frigates sent an additional flight of seventy-two missiles. Twelve destroyers sent four missiles each. In total, 312 missiles left the tubes of Jake's ships.

Meanwhile, 20,000 km away, on the other side of the Bat Fleet, Andrea Iona's First Fleet let loose a similar hell of missiles, adding another 252 ship-killers to the mix.

Overall, 564 ship-killing missiles left the tubes of the two RDF fleets as the warships converged.

* * * * *

Captain Rashtal gazed silently at the holotank as it indexed the incoming missiles into groups and put the icons in place. As the numbers ramped up, he sighed.

Turning to Caltel beside him, he directed, "Open fire, Caltel."

Caltel turned to the Weapons officer and nodded. "Open fire."

In seconds, the Bat Fleet loosed their own version of hell. Thirty missiles from each of the eleven remaining battlewagons. Sixteen missiles each from the nine operational cruisers. Ten missiles each from the ten remaining frigates.

With no intact Bat destroyers left in range to fire, 574 Bat missiles answered the RDF barrage of 564 inbound ship-killers. Rashtal had ordered that sixty percent of his missiles be directed at the larger fleet, with only forty percent directed at Andrea's smaller First Fleet.

Accelerating at 4,000g at a range of 10,000 km, the three flocks of missiles screamed past each other at over 625 kps each, with a flight time of only 32 seconds. But as they approached their targets, they weaved, juked, decelerated, accelerated, seeking a path past the point defense system of the enemy to get in closer.

And in seconds, a glaring difference became apparent between the Bat military philosophy and that of the RDF. For generation after generation, the Bats had been the aggressors in every battle. They stood off from a helpless planet and smashed it to pieces. Never had they faced a fleet even close to their capabilities.

Defenses - especially missile defenses - had taken short shrift with the Bats.

Although hundreds of missiles were deflected by their non-sentient AI point defense systems, dozens got through. Missile after missile slammed into the Bat ships. In seconds, eleven of their ships were smashed, outgassing flames and smoke, burning from the inside out, including four more battleships.

On the RDF side, the fleet had spent eighty years honing defensive technology in anticipation of this day. Dozens, then hundreds, of the Bat missiles were foxed by ECM into chasing vectors for false targets and went streaming off to empty space. Missiles that got by the ECM were picked off in droves by the sentient AI point defenses of the RDF ships. Jake watched as nearly the entire missile cloud from the Bat ships was deflected or destroyed.

But no system was perfect. Jake groaned as he watched first one, then a second of his battleships take hits and lose way. A destroyer nearby - one of his screen - was obliterated in a direct hit, exploding so close that the hull of the *Wellington* rang like a bell from debris. A cruiser close by just disappeared, there one minute, gone the next in a huge fireball. He saw several of his frigates burning, rotating end over end, their engines flickering fitfully in their dying throes.

And in seconds, the first salvo was done. Jake glanced quickly at the Flag Bridge holotank to assess. Below him, on the Main Bridge, he heard Captain Rathburn encouraging reloading to proceed faster. Soon he heard the order, "Second salvo, fire, fire, fire!" as the *Wellington* completed reloads.

By now, the Bat ships were turning, as were Jake and Andrea's fleets, to keep their noses pointed at the rapidly departing enemy. Within twelve seconds of the first salvo going out, another 204 missiles were on their way from Jake's task force to the rapidly receding Bat fleet. At nearly the same instant as the *Wellington* fired, Jake saw First Fleet sending their second volley toward the remaining Bat Armada, containing 160 missiles.

It was then that Jake noticed it. His heart jumped to his throat. He couldn't breathe. He sat down hard in the command chair.

Ginger rushed over to him. "Sir? Are you OK?"

Jake could not speak. He shook his head, then put his head in his hands. Ginger glanced at the holotank. At first, she didn't see it.

Then it registered on her.

20,000 km away, the *Empress Hecate* was marked with a large red 'X'.

Orinoco System
25 July 2207

The *Enterprise*, standing off from the axis of battle by 25,000 km, had finally finished collecting up its surviving A40 fighters after their missile runs.

On the bridge holotank, Rob Walker saw the second salvo of missiles from the Bat Armada smash into Jake's Second Fleet in front of him. One of Jake's battleships, one of his cruisers, five of his frigates and four destroyers were hit hard, one of the cruisers exploding in fiery trails of debris that looked like fireworks going off. The battleship and the remaining vessels that were struck remained intact but were out of action, their engines down and their weapons offline.

Jake and Andrea's two fleets were in heavy decel, slowing to prepare to re-engage the Bat Fleet for the final showdown. The Bat Fleet was also in heavy decel now to get back into range. Rob knew this would be the final event. Whoever survived this next pass walked away with everything.

But there was no intention of letting Jake and Andrea fight this last round alone. It would take them over an hour to arrest their vectors and start back the other way, and the same was true of the Bat fleet. Thus, it would be well over two hours before they were back in range of each other again.

And Rob knew that what had started as a gun fight would then devolve into an eye-gouging, knee-breaking up-close battle of railguns and beamers. Neither side had any missiles left.

In that strange aspect of space warfare caused when a fleet was at max decel and a fellow ship lost power, the damaged and wrecked ships of Jake and Andrea's fleets appeared to be accelerating away from their task forces.

Some appeared to be moving back toward the primary star, some in the other direction. Of course, they weren't accelerating; it just looked that way on the holo. It was an optical illusion. In reality, they were now coasting, out of action, while the other ships under heavy decel moved counter to them. So, Rob watched as dozens of wrecked and disabled ships, both Bat and RDF, appeared to depart their fleets in the holo tank.

Rob shook his head. He had seen this in the simulator many times, but seeing it live was a strange feeling.

He realized that the RDF wrecks from Andrea's First Fleet would pass directly through the Bat Fleet as the Bats came back into the battlefield. He wondered if the Bats would finish them off as they went by.

He knew the RDF would not fire on a disabled Bat ship if it came back through the RDF fleet; Jake had made that principle clear in the pre-battle briefings. As Jake had noted, the winner could decide what to do with the survivors, and he intended for the RDF to be the winner.

Rob turned to his right, noting his CAG, Captain Wayne, just coming onto the bridge, still wearing his flight suit from the first sortie against the Bat battleships. His XO Jim Davis was staring at his tablet.

"How we doin', Jim?"

Davis looked up from his tablet and nodded. "We'll be reloaded in a half-hour, Skip. We've got 167 functional birds left. We'll be ready to launch in 60 minutes."

Rob grimaced. "That's going to be cutting it close. How about the *Yorktown* and *Midway*?"

Davis glanced down at his tablet again. "*Yorktown* has 176 functional birds, *Midway* has 171. They're on schedule. We can all launch on time."

"OK," replied Rob. He stared at the holo. "Still looks good for Plan Charlie to me, what do you think?"

Wayne and Davis stared at the holo. "I think so," said Wayne. Davis nodded agreement.

Rob looked at Captain Wayne. "How are your guys holding up in the face of these kinds of losses, CAG?"

Wayne shook his head and frowned. "We knew it would be rough, but not this rough. But they're holding up OK. They'll be good to go."

Rob nodded. Wayne gestured to the holo. "How's Phoebe doing?"

Rob glanced at the holo, where the *Vercingetorix* had taken over as flagship of First Fleet, his wife Phoebe now CO of that fleet.

"It's hard to tell from the holo, but she's still moving with the rest of the fleet, so at least she's got good engines. The sidebar reports her as heavy damage but still combat-capable." Rob shook his head. "Back to business, guys. Phoebe can take care of herself."

*****

Onboard the *Warmonger*, Captain Rashtal also studied the holo plot, trying to out-guess the Apes. His fleet, under heavy decel, was soon to turn around and head back toward the Apes. At the same time, the two Ape fleets were also under heavy decel, to join together and meet him as he returned.

"I don't think there's much to plan for on this one," he said to his XO. "We all come together, and we all start shooting. The time for strategy and tactics is over."

"Agreed," said his XO, Caltel. "Now it's just firepower."

Rashtal couldn't help but smile at his XO.

"That it is, Caltel. That it is."

*****

First Fleet – now under the command of Phoebe Walker on the *Vercingetorix* - had vectored downward from the battle axis slightly after the first pass, just enough to keep from following directly behind the Bat Fleet as it decelerated.

They were coming out of ten minutes of max emergency decel now, pulling 207g – 7g more than the compensator could offset – with the crews strapped in tight and grunting with pain. Phoebe knew they had to open some space between themselves and the Bats in order to get back to Jake before the Bats did.

Finally, she decided they had enough spatial separation and ordered a reduction back to 200g decel, the max standard thrust the ships could take and still have full compensation. With sighs of relief, the crews gulped air back into their lungs, rubbed their aching arms and legs, and returned to their duties.

The three fleet carriers *Enterprise*, *Yorktown* and *Midway* were at three points of an equilateral triangle, each 25,000 klicks from the axis of battle, which ran directly toward the primary star.

They were not quite even, each one a little staggered from the other, in terms of distance from the primary. Thus, their distance to the projected point of convergence of the three fleets varied slightly. This facilitated them launching their A40 squadrons for placement in a row, one directly behind the other, facing the Bat fleet.

After an hour, all three fleets – First Fleet, Second Fleet, and the Bat Armada - had reversed their directions and were now accelerating back toward each other. Rob could now project the point of convergence – the place where all three fleets would come together for the last time. Phoebe and First Fleet were now under 160g accel back toward Jake, while Jake was at 200g accel, to ensure he could rejoin with Phoebe before the Bats arrived.

But it was going to be close. The Bats were at 208g, trying to get back before Phoebe and Jake could rejoin. Briefly, Phoebe went to 207g again, crushing her crews back into their seats, but after another ten minutes it was clear the Bats could not get to them in time; and she dropped back down to 180 g.

At one hour before the projected rejoin and the renewal of the battle, all the ships in the three fleets went to hard decel, with the intention of moving much slower when at last they converged.

This was a final battle; this was three gunmen walking down a dark alley toward each other, ready for a fight.

At forty-five minutes before convergence, Rob ordered the launch of all birds from all three carriers. 514 A40's, fully loaded with two ship-killer missiles each, departed the three carriers and headed for their initial points – all that remained of the 726 birds that had started the battle.

Thirty-five minutes later, the Bats and the RDF fleets coasted toward each other, nose to nose, engines idling, weapons armed, knowing only one fleet could walk away.

WELLINGTON ALONE

Come and take them.
- Leonidas, Spartan King

Orinoco System
25 July 2207

Ginger squatted at Jake's side, trying to convince him. "Let the doc give you something, Jake," she said for the second time.

Jake just looked at her. "Nope. Not gonna happen, Ginger. I've waited eighty-six years to kill these bastards and I'm going to be sitting right here when we do."

Ginger sighed. "Jake…"

"Let's get to business, Ginger," Jake said. "We'll mourn the dead later."

Sadly, Ginger nodded, got up and went back to her command chair.

In the holo, Jake could see that the remaining Bat fleet had decelerated down to almost nothing, relative to them. In another ten minutes, they'd be in railgun range. It was going to be a slugfest.

He did some quick mental math in his head. By his estimate, and the notes on the holo sidebar, the survivors of First and Second Fleets – now joined together – had fifteen ships remaining, not counting the three carriers – four battleships, two cruisers, three frigates, and six destroyers.

With that remnant of his fleet, Jake estimated he could throw 832 railgun slugs per minute.

There appeared to be sixteen Bat ships left – four battleships, six cruisers, six frigates. His best intelligence estimates said they would throw 1,104 railgun slugs per minute. So, he was at a distinct disadvantage in throw weight.

The RDF had estimated that their railgun accuracy was somewhat better than the Bats, on average, mostly due to more training and better AI control.

He was about to find out.

"One minute, Admiral," came the call from the Bridge below. Jake nodded, knowing that his Flag Captain would take care of what had to be done. All the plans were laid, all the weapons were charged, all that was left to do was execute.

A klaxon rang, the singsong of the excess g warning. Across the RDF fleet, every member of the crew pulled their straps tighter, or laid down on the floor to endure what was coming.

With a bang, the entire fleet, synchronized by the AI system, ramped up to 207 g in a matter of eight seconds, charging toward the slow-moving Bat Fleet. They were roughly 2,000 km apart; it took only twenty-five seconds for the RDF ships to be in the middle of the Bats, firing every railgun and beamer they had as they passed through.

The Bats were ready, though – a maze of beams and railgun rounds came back at the Humans as they went through, knocking chunks off every RDF ship.

Jake saw a Bat battleship and two Bat cruisers lose way and stop firing. He screamed "Yes!" - as did almost every other person on the bridge.

Two Bat frigates also went silent, one of them losing way and the other remaining with the Bat fleet, but no longer firing.

Jake felt a huge clang as the *Wellington* took a railgun round somewhere aft; he noted the acceleration drop dramatically as the *Wellington* lost way, and on the holo sidebar he could see that two of their four engines had gone offline.

The remainder of the RDF fleet, following strict orders, pulled quickly away from them, leaving them limping along behind, able to muster only a bit over 100 g. His four screening destroyers stayed with him, though, following close behind, trying to screen his vulnerable rear.

Quickly, they passed out of range of the Bats; but at only 100g, he knew it would not take long for the enemy to run him down.

And indeed, even as he watched, the Bat Fleet began to turn, vectoring back toward him, their engines running up to full power to come after him.

*****

Vitus was drained. In the first round of battle, his squadron had attacked a Bat cruiser - which was one of the few ready for them in every way. Taking fire all the way in on their attack run, Vitus had taken shrapnel in his port engine from a close burst - one which also holed his canopy in several places. But he continued his run, holding right rudder as hard as he could to keep the A40 on target, sucking oxygen from the emergency supply as his suit inflated to pressurize his body.

Just as he released his missiles, another hit took out his electronics, powering down his instrument panel and all his navigation gear. He had managed to navigate back to the carrier using a handheld backup beacon, but it took him twice as long as everyone else.

By the time he made it back to the Enterprise, everyone thought he had bought the farm - until he came limping into the rear recovery area reserved for damaged ships and crashed into the barrier.

His right leg was numb from holding the rudder down to control the ship; as he sat wearily in the cockpit waiting for the space suited emergency crew to remove him and take him out of the unpressurized deck, he realized he was also losing pressure in his suit.

He could hear a slight hissing in his helmet now that the engines were off. Reaching up his hand to the right side of his helmet, he found two small holes, one in front and one in back, just at his right ear. His hand came away red with blood.

He realized a tiny piece of shrapnel had gone through the

helmet front to back, just catching his ear but missing his head. Quickly he grabbed a patch and slapped it over the two holes, sealing them, as the canopy was opened by the crew outside.

Manhandling him out of the cockpit, they laid him on a small power cart and rushed him through the airlock to the pressurized medical bay on the other side of the wall.

And then he found out about his father. As the corpsman attended to his ear, the CAG, Captain Wayne, walked into the room and quietly explained what had happened to Captain Cassian.

Vitus had taken it silently. He had known it was coming. He had always known that Cassian would not come back from this battle.

They had hugged each other fiercely, this morning as they prepared to board their fighters. And he had known then. He had pulled back and looked at his father, and Cassian had looked back at him. Then Cassian had said quietly, "You were the best son any Daneki could ask for. I will be proud of you forever."

And Vitus had known that he would never see him again.

*****

Now Vitus squinted at the holo in the A40. They had patched his ear and assigned him to a new bird, and he had launched again from the Enterprise, leading the Wing as temporary DCAG for this final pass at the Bats. He was exhausted, but so were all the other pilots.

This morning, they had waited for the Bat Fleet in their cramped cockpits for six hours, hidden in place with engines powered down, until the Bats finally showed up and passed right down the kill zone, oblivious to their presence.

Then the attack, and his difficult return to the ship, had taken another hour. He had spent an hour in the dispensary, conferring with the CAG on the final attack plan, and getting his new ship assignment, and another half-hour thrusting toward the position he now occupied with his Wing, 10,000 km behind the Bat Fleet, as the Bats reversed course to chase down the crippled *Wellington* and the rest of the RDF Fleet.

Vitus knew that the sudden thrust the RDF Fleet had made through the Bats was no accident – it was part of the plan. But having the *Wellington* crippled was not part of that plan.

Now the *Wellington* limped along, able to pull only 100g, screened by four flimsy destroyers, with the Bat Armada – what was left of it - turning to engage from the rear.

She didn't have a chance. The Bats still had three battleships left, four cruisers, and four frigates. It would be a massacre when they caught up to the *Wellington*.

Unless his Wing could do something about it.

Orinoco System
25 July 2207

Onboard the *Warmonger*, Rashtal stared at the holo. He was not oblivious to the three carriers sitting 25,000 km off his vector, and he knew exactly when they launched their fighters. He had watched the tiny ships form up behind him as he reversed course.

But right in front of him was the crippled Ape battleship, and he knew – he just knew – it had to be the flagship. Because the four destroyers screening it from behind had never wavered, covering the vulnerable engines as best they could, even as they were peppered with railgun rounds and beamers in the last pass, leaving them cut to pieces. Because two of the Ape battleships had come from the first group, the fleet they had chased all the way from Nest, and he was sure the flagship would not be one of those. It would be with the larger, second group that came in later – as this one did.

And because he just knew.

Turning to Caltel, he shook his head. "What we *should* do is break off and go back to Nest, and come after these Apes later, after we've re-grouped. But I suspect they won't let us do that. I think that's what the little ships are for – to prevent us escaping to the mass limit."

Caltel frowned. "But we still have them outgunned; why would we try to escape?"

Rashtal smiled. "Because if we don't, those little ships are going to come right up our ass."

Rashtal saw the shadow pass across Caltel's face as he realized they were still in a trap, just a different kind of trap.

"So, if we run, they stay right behind us all the way to the mass limit, and probably take out half of what's left of our fleet."

Rashtal nodded. "And if we don't run, they stay right behind us here, and probably take out half of what's left." He turned back to the holo. "We're not running. So at least let's take out that crippled battleship and as many of the rest of them as we can, Caltel."

"Aye, sir," called Caltel.

Rashtal turned back to the holo. "Full speed ahead at that crippled battlewagon, Caltel. Let's kill that one first."

* * * * *

Watching the Bat Fleet on his holo, Vitus saw that the Bat commander had made his decision. The Bats accelerated at 200g toward the *Wellington*, now close to 80,000 km ahead, limping along at 100g. Vitus slapped his comm button and called out, "First Wing, after them! Don't let them open separation on us!" Immediately his remaining fighters, the one hundred and sixty-seven that remained from the *Enterprise* squadrons, boosted to 206g, chasing down the Bats.

* * * * *

On the *Vercingetorix*, now nearly 80,000 km ahead of the *Wellington*, Phoebe Walker looked over the Flag Bridge partition at Selena Field, her Flag Captain, and pointed toward the holo. "Selena, reverse course and take us back to the *Wellington*."

Selena nodded, but felt compelled to add, "Admiral, that is contrary to Admiral Hammett's orders. The orders were not to turn back for any disabled ships."

"Noted and logged, Selena. You won't bear any responsibility for this."

Selena grinned. "Oh, but I want to, Admiral. If you hadn't said it, I was!"

Selena turned to her Comm officer and said, "To all ships, come about and return to defend the *Wellington*. Now, now, now!"

Phoebe heard the main engines stop and felt the Coriolis force that could never be completely damped out as the *Vercingetorix* started coming about. It took her about two minutes to reverse course, in which time she gained another 10,000 km on the *Wellington*.

Then her mains fired again, and the singsong of the excess g alarm sounded once more. Phoebe tightened her straps and placed her hands flat on the arms of her command chair, hearing the countdown to excess g over the comms.

The Comm Officer lifted his head. "Admiral, comm from Admiral Hammett on the *Wellington*."

Phoebe, knowing what it would be, smiled. "Read it to me, Comms."

The Comm Officer looked flustered. "Uh…out loud, Mum?"

"Yes, out loud, Comms."

The Comm Officer gulped and started reading from his screen.

"Phoebe get your ass turned around and get back on plan, or I swear I'll bust you down to Midshipman."

Phoebe smiled at Selena, shaking her head. "Ignore it, Comms. I can't hear up here for some reason right now. Must be the klaxon."

* * * * *

On board the *Enterprise*, Rob had a front row seat as events played out before him. He saw the Bats reverse course to chase down the *Wellington*. He saw the A40 wings boost at Max

Emergency Power to catch them up, per the battle plan. He saw the remainder of the RDF fleet turn back towards the *Wellington*, ignoring the battle plan - which was to keep the Bat Fleet chasing them as long as possible, so the fighters could do their dirty work.

He knew it was Phoebe making that decision. He couldn't help but grin, knowing he would have done the same.

Studying the plot a bit more, he realized that Phoebe would not get back in time. She would almost make it; but not quite. The Bats would have the *Wellington* well before Phoebe would be in range.

"Damn it!"

Rob looked at the plot some more. The Bats had just completed their course reversal 95,000 km behind the *Wellington* and were accelerating at 200g. They would be in range in five and a half minutes. Phoebe was about 100,000 km in front of the *Wellington*, but she had reversed course at a much higher speed and had a lot of delta-v to bleed off before she would come back their way.

And Rob was just 85,000 km from the *Wellington*.

"Mr. Davis, please set a vector for 40,000 km in front of the *Wellington*'s current position and boost at Max Emergency Power."

Davis looked at him. "Rob? Are you thinking about what you are doing?

Rob looked at his XO. "Objection noted, Mr. Davis. Please carry out the order."

*****

As his Wing approached the Bat Fleet from behind, Vitus realized that his fighters would engage the Bat Fleet just about thirty seconds before they caught up to the *Wellington*. Vitus flipped a switch and armed his missiles, checking his board to make sure all his squadrons did the same.

The last few seconds ticked down quicker than he expected –

suddenly they were in range. Missiles started to fly by him, first a few, then a flock, thicker and thicker as the hundreds of fighters following him fired off their ordnance under coordinated AI control. The AI selected the targets and fired the missiles, but only after the pilot confirmed the selections and authorized the release.

But Vitus did not fire. His authorization light was blinking madly, the AI waiting for permission to release the missiles. But his screen showed the AI had selected a cruiser, the nearest one to him on his vector.

The cruiser, along with the rest of the Bat supporting ships, completely blocked the battleships leading the pack. The battleships would not be scratched in this initial attack.

And the Second Wing, coming along behind, would not arrive in time to save the *Wellington*. Vitus felt it in his bones.

"To hell with this," snarled Vitus. He flipped a switch and turned off the automatic AI firing mode. Flipping a second override switch, he firewalled his throttle, and the A40 jumped, knocking him back against his head restraint as he exceeded the compensator's ability to manage the g forces by a full 12g.

Flattened against the seat, he pulled back on the stick, feeling the g-forces rise as the AI limiter prevented him from crushing himself into jelly – but not from feeling the full effects of 12g on his body.

Grunting under the pressure, Vitus rose to 500 km over the Bat Fleet in a few seconds, the AI jerking him around crazily as the Bat screening ships' point defense systems threw hundreds of rounds at him.

He heard a "chink" as shrapnel pattered off the aft part of the bird. Another round knocked chunks off his front fuselage, leaving a gaping hole through which he could see into the innards of his ship.

Finally, he was past the cruisers and frigates and could see the battleships, three monsters side-by-side, nose on to the *Wellington* which was just coming into their range.

*****

On the *Warmonger*, Rashtal studied the holo. The *Wellington* was coming into range of his ship, and he nodded to Caltel. "Open fire, Caltel."

Immediately the *Warmonger* began shooting, railgun rounds for now as they were not in range yet for the beamers. The *Wellington* was firing back and juking for all she was worth. Rashtal heard his own ship taking hits, but he no longer cared. This was a death match now. Both parties knew it.

For several seconds, the *Wellington* was lucky – taking hits, but nothing that seemed to hurt her too much. Then Rashtal saw a large chuck of ship come off her right side, and she spun, out of control, as another of her main engines quit. Instantly the other working engine shut down, to prevent the ship tearing herself apart.

The *Wellington* was now dead in space, spinning rapidly due to the imbalance from the uneven engine shutdowns. In the holo it caused the optical allusion that she was charging back at them as the distance suddenly lessened.

"Decel, Decel!" yelled Caltrun, and the *Warmonger* ceased her acceleration and started braking hard, to keep from overrunning the *Wellington*. Beside her, the other two battleships also dropped accel, their AI systems reacting to Caltel's command via the links between them.

Rashtal watched as his rounds now tore the RDF battleship apart, piece by piece. More large chunks of ship broke away as the railgun slugs tore into her. No more than 100 km from her now, their slugs traveled the distance in less than fifteen seconds.

"She can't hold together much longer," said Caltel beside him.

Suddenly the Tac Officer yelled. "Sir! We've got that big-ass carrier coming in between us!"

In the holo, Rashtal saw one of the Ape carriers decelerating madly as it interposed itself between the *Warmonger* and the

Wellington. On the front of the huge carrier, four small railgun cannons fired, throwing slugs at the *Warmonger*, along with all her point defense cannon, which were mere popguns to the *Warmonger*.

Rashtal shook his head. "Suicide." He nodded to Caltel. "Retarget the carrier, take her out, and then get back to the battleship."

*****

On the bridge of the *Enterprise*, Rob Walker placed a hand on Davis's back, encouraging him. Davis glanced at him, grim. "They'll tear us apart, Rob. We've got no business here."

Rob shook his head. "I won't let them take *Wellington* as long as we have a shell left, XO. Keep firing, keep juking, keep praying."

With a clang, the *Enterprise* rebounded from a direct hit somewhere aft, and it was all the Helm could do to keep her straight. An alarm rang as fire was reported somewhere in the ship. Davis looked at Rob, shaking his head.

Another round came through the ship somewhere behind them, in and out, somewhere in the crew quarters, leaving two gaping holes that rapidly bled out pressure.

"Rob, you dumbass, get the hell out of there!" came over Rob's comm, on the direct channel back to Phoebe and the *Vercingetorix*. "Let us handle this!"

Rob grinned. "I'll be more than happy to leave, Admiral, just as soon as you get here."

With a sound like a train wreck, something exploded next to the bridge, and all went dark.

*****

Behind the *Warmonger*, Vitus's A40 was also coming apart. A half-dozen point defense rounds had hit her now; she was just one small step above junk.

But her engines still worked, and he still had two good

missiles attached to the hardpoints. At least, he hoped they were good – the missile status console had gone dark.

Vitus sighted on the engines of the *Warmonger* and let the A40 run. For ten seconds he held his base vector, juking madly; it was near suicide, because by holding his base course, he became predictable. Point defense shrapnel rattled off the bird like rain.

Finally, five seconds out from the huge battleship, he switched the AI fire control back on, hitting the permission switch. Both missiles fired, and he pulled as hard on the stick as he could, nearly tearing it off its mount.

The AI, limiting the g forces allowable, still crushed him into the seat so hard he felt a rib break. He missed the huge engines of the *Warmonger* by no more than fifty meters as he flew by. In the tactical holo, he saw behind him a huge explosion coming up from the tail end of the battleship.

Then all was black.

*****

Phoebe watched in the holo as the leading Bat battleship blew up in front of them, sending chunks in every direction. The *Wellington* continued to spin rapidly in front of her fleet, and just on the other side of it, the *Enterprise* also spun, more slowly, but clearly out of action.

Then they were in range, and her fleet opened up with everything they had on the remaining Bat fleet. She saw another hundred-odd A40 fighters come over the top of the last of the Bat cruisers and frigates, firing their missiles into the engines of the Bat battleships. A third wave of fighters pulled in behind the Bat cruisers and frigates and sent a wave of missiles into them. A cruiser and a frigate lost way, their engines knocked out.

The Bat fleet suddenly vectored away, out of the battle line, running for the mass limit, chased by the remaining RDF fighters.

Many of the fighters were out of missiles – but some were not, and even as Phoebe watched, one of the Bat battleships lost an engine and her acceleration fell, her path turning slightly before she got things under control, just in time to watch the rest of her fleet leave her behind.

Phoebe issued orders for her frigates and destroyers to locate and rescue any A40 pilots still alive in the battle area, and then sent the rest of her fleet to pursue the escaping Bats. She knew they could not catch all of them - but they had a good chance of knocking out another three or four ships before they escaped.

Then she went to the shuttle deck where the rescue shuttles were going out to help the *Wellington* and the *Enterprise*. There she waited for news of her husband and her comrades in arms.

DEDITIO

You have talked with me about fighting.
...and I have told you of the time long ago.
All that is past.
- Cheyenne Chief Two Moons, describing the Battle of the Little Big Horn, 1898

Nest - Bat Home Planet
Raditel Spaceport
20 August 2207 - 86 Years after Pandora

Jake Hammett sat quietly in his cabin on the old corvette *Denali*, still his favorite after all these years, his hands folded in front of him. His uniform was immaculate. His eyes were closed. A gentle knock came at the door, and he sighed.

"Come!", he said, rising to his feet and reaching for his dress cap on the desk beside him.

Ginger stuck her head in the door. "They're ready."

Jake acknowledged with a nod and fitted his cap on his head. Then he took a cane, smiled at Ginger, and headed toward the door, leaning hard on the cane and limping as he went.

Walking down the corridor to the hatch, Jake held a grim expression. Ginger carefully remained silent. At the exit hatch, Jake walked off the ship and onto a large stage specially built beside the docked corvette.

A cover over the stage shielded the party from the dimmer sun of Nest, which still threw a good heat at noontime. On the far end of the stage, the Bat delegation waited quietly. Most of them wore Bat Empire Naval uniforms; but the one in front,

Emperor Lecator, was dressed in resplendent, flowing robes, trimmed in red and gold. He wore a tall mitre.

Jake thought he looked like a large rat dressed like the Pope.

Surrounding the stage were hundreds of reporters, holo techs and drones, capturing the historic event for the masses. Jake ignored them. Limping across the stage, he stopped at the table in the center and waited.

After some slight delay and a brief, muttered conversation, the Emperor and his aide advanced slowly to the table. The Emperor stopped opposite Jake and, slightly confused, turned to his aide. The aide spoke quietly and pointed to the documents on the table in front of the Emperor.

The Emperor turned back to Jake and, without expression, leaned forward and grasped the old-style ink pen placed there. For a moment, he looked at it - then leaned forward and slowly signed the documents in front of him. Placing the pen down on the table, he straightened and turned once again to his aide, a question in his eyes. The aide spoke quietly, and the Emperor turned and returned to his party at the other end of the stage.

Jake waited a span of seconds, then with great deliberation limped around the table until he also stood in front of the documents. Slowly taking the pen, he leaned forward and signed them as well.

Then, holding the documents in his hand, he turned and walked to the podium at the front of the stage, facing the media. Behind him, in a wall of solidarity, stood Ginger Barnett and the rest of his staff, along with Phoebe and Rob Walker and most of his senior captains - those who had survived Orinoco.

Vitus stood in the back, his skin showing burn damage. Rob Walker's left arm was in a soft cast; many of the rest of Jake's staff showed wounds as well.

Jake raised the document and held it high, so the crowd could see it clearly.

"Eighty-six years ago," Jake began, "We made a promise to make our part of the Galaxy safe from the genocides of the Bat Empire. Today, we have completed that promise. From this day forward, for a period of one hundred years, the Bat Empire will not be allowed to have military warships. They will not be allowed to colonize planets. And they will pay reparations for every planet and culture they have attacked. We have agreed on these points and the Emperor has signed the instruments of surrender."

Jake paused, staring around at the media, the drones, the holo techs in a kind of wonderment. His voice faltered slightly as he continued.

"The price for this peace has been high..."

For a moment, Jake could not speak again.

Behind him, Ginger felt a tear move down her cheek; she knew Jake was thinking about the *Empress Hecate.*

A lone Bat destroyer – one of the survivors of the destroyer squadrons that were out in front of the Bat Fleet at Orinoco - had reversed course and came up behind the *Empress* at tremendous velocity. It performed a kamikaze directly into her engines.

There were no survivors.

"We will not soon forget the sacrifices made, both on the field of battle and by those at home. This morning, in orbit around Nest, First Fleet takes the place of honor in beginning the enforcement of these sanctions.

"We mourn the loss of all the sailors in both First and Second Fleets, and those lost in other actions prior to the recent battles. But we go forward in the knowledge that they gave their lives so that all races in the Rim Federation will be safe from unbridled aggression, now and in the future."

Jake wiped at his eyes, unembarrassed. For a moment, he could not continue. Finally, he wrestled his emotions under control.

"Let's take this moment to remember that the price of freedom is eternal vigilance. I will not be here in the future; my job is done, and I will now retire. But the RDF will continue, protecting the Rim. I implore each one of you to support them now and in the future, and never forget the sacrifice they have made for you."

Jake waited patiently for a minute while the drones and holo techs bustled about, capturing the moment. Then he turned, handed the surrender documents to Ginger, and limped off the stage back to the *Denali*.

At the other end of the stage, the Emperor and his party departed quietly, ignored by the media and the others.

Oakwood, Texas
26 October 2210

I interviewed Admiral Hammett on his birthday, three years after the Battle of Orinoco. Immediately after the surrender ceremony, he had retired and moved back to his little cabin in the heartland of the North American Alliance, where he tended flowers and kept the graves of wives, children and grandchildren who had gone before him.

He was not old, then, in body - his biological age had progressed to only about 50 years - but he seemed much older in spirit. The years - and the losses - had taken their toll. His hair had turned completely white. Due to his war wounds, he walked with a cane, limping as he went.

This was the last interview with Admiral Hammett before he disappeared in November of that year.

I asked him about his two children, the twins Alexander and Ligeia, who were still with Empress Hecate on Aeolis. He told me Andrea had passed guardianship of them to the Empress, and they would be raised in the Aeolian manner, as Andrea had wished. Hammett said he didn't feel that his age permitted him to do them justice as a parent.

I could see the regret in his eyes. The pain of seeing his dead wife, Andrea Iona, in their faces must have been unbearable for him.

During our interview, I asked him for which of his accomplishments he would like to be best remembered. He grinned at me somewhat sadly and told me this.

"We - all of us - every person - we leave only a small imprint on the universe. We all journey down a path, doing the best we can - or the worst we can, in some cases - leaving our imprint. The universe moves on, the stars spin and dance, and little biological creatures live their lives, dancing to the music they hear in their heads."

He leaned back in his rickety old wooden chair, dusted off his jeans and stared out across a field of flowers, toward a distant river.

"I hope some will say that I danced well to the music, and it was good."

EPILOGUE

about 5,000 years later

Pandora crossed the indefinite border, moving from the Core into the Rim. She adjusted course slightly to make for Rio Bravo, an old fortress planet. Rio Bravo was the isolated, end-of-the-line outpost of the 3,000 planet Rim Federation, nestled up against the Core like a forgotten marble rolled against a baseboard.

The planet boasted a small Space Corps outpost for peacekeeping; a research observatory peering hopefully into the Core, hoping to learn something of value from Machine Space; and the terminus end of the space lanes for the Sector. From Rio Bravo, one could only go back Rimward - unless, of course, one desired to enter the Core and disappear forever. Those of the Machine Space did not suffer fools gladly.

Decelerating to a relative crawl, *Pandora* coasted up to Rio Bravo, in High Stealth mode. Inside a small control room reserved for biological passengers, what appeared at first glance to be a rectangular console in the floor started humming an old rock song, one not heard in thousands of years.

The ship came to a high orbit relative to the planet; a crack appeared in the console, and two mechanical legs unfolded from the back. Two mechanical arms pushed the back half of the console upright until - something - stood where it had been. Finally, the top hinged back and become a head, revealing a blocky android which had been stowed in compact form.

In a passable imitation of a once famous singer, the android sang.

"Start me up...Start me up...," it crooned, as it moved to the back of the control room. Approaching a closed door, which slid open at its approach, the android faced a large tank of liquid. Inside the tank floated a male Human body, of approximate middle age. The eyes were closed, and the expression was blank. A harness plugged into the back of the neck.

The android reached up to a small port by the tank and plugged in a finger.

<Are you sure?> asked *Pandora.* <There is no going back. This temporary body will not last long. It will just barely get you there. Or maybe not at all>

<I am sure> said the android.

<I shall miss you greatly> said the Machine Ship.

<As I will miss you, dear one. You will never be forgotten by the race of men>

<Then we part. Goodbye, Jake>

The android remained frozen, plugged into the wall port. Several minutes passed. Suddenly, the Human body in the tank gave a jerk. Its eyes opened, and it thrashed his arms wildly.

The liquid in the tank drained away. With a gasp, the figure thrust its head above the waterline, spewed forth the remnants from its lungs, and took a breath. As the remaining liquid drained, it continued to cough and gasp.

Finally, it reached behind, and with a jerk, unplugged the cable from the back of its neck. It pushed a button and the door of the tank opened. It stepped outside and knelt on the floor, naked and dripping, coughing the last remnants of fluid out of its lungs. Resting for a moment, it raised his head and said softly, "Goodbye, *Pandora*."

*****

Three months later, a small one-man starship approached Earth. It descended until there was enough air for the wings to bite. Then it began a long, roundabout glide down to a place once called Texas.

Jake Hammett came to rest well south of a vast grassland.

North of his location had been the ancient city of Dallas - now gone back to nature, grassy plains with intermittent stands of timber. The land was flat there, like a pancake. A few old ruins stood, crumbled mostly to dust.

But here, more than one hundred miles south of the old city, the land showed a bit of relief - forests of pine trees, scattered oak groves among them, quiet, slow-moving rivers winding their way toward a gulf two hundred miles away.

As *Pandora* had warned, this last body was breaking down quickly. By the time he opened the hatch and stepped out, Jake was weak and dizzy.

He remembered this place where he had once been young, more than 5,000 years before. Now the entire planet was a dedicated nature preserve. Undoubtedly Rangers were on their way to arrest him, a trespasser, landing without permit in this sacred cradle of Humanity.

But they would not find him here. He started walking west, toward the river he knew was hidden in the forest.

The land had changed, had gone wild, but he knew where he was. He spoke, reciting a travelogue to himself, and some long-dead spirits.

"This was just east of Oakwood," he said. "In the late 1800's, there was actually a riverboat landing over there by the river. One of my distant ancestors built them - the riverboats, I mean. They used to go down to the Gulf. And my mother, was born just about ten miles north of here. My father, about twenty miles east. This is where I grew up."

He stumbled. His legs were giving out. It was hard to breathe.

He walked across a meadow, covered in paintbrush and bluebonnet. He had forgotten their existence, until he stepped from the hatch and saw them stretching out in front of him, thousands of them. The memories of Kirsten, and Teresa, and Andrea flashed back to him, then. He saw them gathering bluebonnets from beside the cabin, the little cabin they had kept here for an occasional getaway. Holding the flowers in their aprons, smiling at him as he rocked on the porch at the end of the day.

Kirsten of the wind-blown hair and flashing smile, the happy one.

Teresa with the quick retort and shake of the head when he did something she didn't like.

Andrea who had brought him love at the end, bringing him back to life one last time.

But he couldn't afford to grieve yet. He had to get to the river. The river where his children, and grandchildren, and great-grandchildren, had played for so many years, while he fought among the stars.

Mixed in with the paintbrush and the bluebonnet were patches of clover, although the color was lighter than the blood-red he remembered. How the children had loved to pick clover, looking for the four-leaf variety, never finding one, so loud, so excited, crouching in the grass, looking up at him and asking questions. The tears started then, and his chin quivered.

He fell. Pushing himself up, he looked. The trees were close...maybe twenty meters. He got up and stumbled, toward the muddy, slow-moving river he knew was just ahead. Entering the tree line, he walked across the oak leaves, a carpet covering the soil, crunching in his footsteps. Soon he passed into pine.

"This is more like it," he said out loud. "When we were here, this was mostly pine. The oaks were further north. I guess they moved south a bit."

He felt the ground start to fall away, and he knew he was getting close. Bumping into trees, he wiped tears from his eyes, as best he could.

Before him, the bank sloped down to the water, which flowed gently along, burbling just a bit - a quiet, strong river.

On the riverbank, he stopped, turned, looked back, through the edge of the forest, out to the meadow and the flowers, the paintbrush and bluebonnets, the clover, just as he remembered. Slowly he went to his knees on the ground.

"I'm here, guys," he whispered. He remained there for a few seconds, kneeling, feeling the strength fading out, like wine running out of a broken bottle.

He could hold himself up no longer. He lay down gently on the ground, feeling the pine needles beneath him. He could smell the pine sap from the trees. He felt his heart giving up.

He smiled, and his happiness covered him like a warm blanket. He felt ghosts around him, kind and loving ghosts, waiting for him to finish a long journey.

"I'm home, ladies," he whispered again. "I'm home, my sweet babies. I'm back with you at last."

###

BONUS - EARLY DAYS OF THE RIM

Excerpts from the Orion Arm Wiki, 2230 Edition

Warning: the below section contains spoilers for Book One of the Series. If you wish to go directly to the Preview of the next book, you will find it after this section.

Aeolian Empire

The **Aeolian Empire** is a star nation centered on the Planet Aeolis, in the Beehive Cluster (M44), 580 light years from Earth. Aeolis was originally populated by approximately 212 Humans abducted from Earth by the Machine Ship *Hermes* around 1184 BC and transported to Aeolis, where they were abandoned as part of *Hermes'* bottleneck experiment. The small population survived and prospered, and eventually grew to a star nation of some 55 colonized planets (as of 2230).

The founding population originated in the Greek city-state of Aeolis, on the western coast of Turkey. However, 12 Amazonian prisoners among the abductees took over leadership of the small group on the new planet and established a matriarchal society based on a blend of Amazon and Greek culture and beliefs. The descendants of the original Amazon warriors are known as the House Aronte.

The Aeolian Empire formed a military alliance with the RDF

in 2186 and became a full voting member of the Rim Federation in 2209, due to the efforts of Empress Hecate.

Aeolis (planet)

Aeolis is a planet in the Beehive Cluster, 580 light years from Earth. It is the capital planet of the Aeolian Empire. The capital city, Aronte, is named after the founding house of the Empire, the House Aronte. Aeolis orbits a G2 type star called 'Helios' in the Aeolian language and is similar to Earth in size, composition and climate.

Andrea Iona Satra (Fleet Admiral)

Admiral **Andrea Iona Satra** was the first Fleet Admiral of the RDF from the Aeolian Empire, commanding RDF First Fleet at the Battle of Nest and later at the Battle of Orinoco. On 25 July 2207 at the Battle of Orinoco, Admiral Satra was killed when her flagship, the *Empress Hecate*, went down with all hands after the Bat Empire destroyer *Waspeater* performed a kamikaze attack into her engines. A memorial to Admiral Satra and the officers and crew of the *Empress Hecate* occupies a prominent position in the main quadrangle at RDF Command Headquarters on the planet Kamilaroi in the 36 Ophiuchi C system. The RDF fleet carrier *Satra* is named after her, as well as the primary moon of the planet Haven, Andrea.

Satra was born in 2160 on the planet Aeolis into the Satra clan, a junior branch of the House Aronte. Both her mother and father were killed in battle during the Fringe Rebellion, and she was brought up as a ward of the Imperial Family. She attended the Imperial Naval Academy at Aronte, graduating in 2178 as an ensign. She was first assigned to the destroyer *Mycenae*, where she distinguished herself in the 2nd Battle of Amasya in 2180. In late 2180, she was assigned as the Tactical Officer of the frigate *Chrysaor* and was aboard when it was destroyed off Aegea in the Fringe Ambush of 2182, surviving in a lifeboat for two days before rescue.

Subsequently, Satra advanced to the position of XO of the destroyer *Nemesis*, commanded by Hecate Aronte, the future Empress. She participated in the action at Pestilence Port in April 2185, in which action she first encountered RDF Admiral Jake Hammett of Earth aboard the RDF *Paris*. In July 2185, she was advanced to captain and took command of the frigate *Pegasus*. Satra was further assigned as Naval Aide to Empress Hecate from 2187 through 2191 and then as captain of the battleship *Empress Miranda* from 2192 through 2194. In 2194, Satra was advanced to admiral and served as Chief of Staff for the AEN until 2205. In early 2205, she was seconded to the RDF at Tolleson Base as Fleet Admiral, First Fleet, taking as her flagship the newly commissioned battleship *Empress Hecate*.

Satra married Admiral Jake Hammett in April 2205, shortly after taking command of the *Empress Hecate* and joining the RDF First Fleet.

Satra and Hammett had two children, who were twins:

1. Ligeia Antiope Satra, b. 2206, graduated from the Imperial Naval Academy at Aronte in 2228 and currently a lieutenant in the Aeolian Navy.

2. Alexander Orien Satra, b. 2206, graduated from the Imperial Naval Academy at Aronte in 2228 and currently a lieutenant in the Aeolian Navy.

Antiope (Empress of Aeolis)

Antiope Lysippe Aronte was the 212th Empress of the Aeolian Empire, reigning from 2141 to 2165. She prosecuted an intense military campaign against the Fringe Rebels, resulting in a polarized nation which struggled to understand the unending cost and destruction of the war.

Antiope was born in 2114 to Princess Merope, the second daughter of Empress Asteria. She was raised in the traditional militaristic manner of the Amazonian nobility, attending the Imperial Naval Academy at Aronte, and serving in the active fleet for three years until her first marriage, when she transferred to the Reserves. Princess Antiope first married Prince Hyginus Lysippe in 2135 and immediately gave birth to a daughter, Hippolyta, the future 213th Empress. In 2137, Prince Hyginus was killed while onboard the frigate *Miletus*, which was ambushed by Fringe Rebels while transporting troops to Maia. In 2140, Antiope married as her second husband the Earth-born RDF leader Jake Hammett, who had infiltrated the Aeolian Empire posing as a mercenary named Zeno. She had one child by Hammett, Deinomache. As a result of this birth, per the laws of the Aeolian Empire, Jake Hammett was banished from Aronte.

In April of 2141, her aunt Empress Miranda and her mother Princess Merope were killed by a terrorist attack in the Imperial Palace. Per the laws of succession of the Aeolian Empire, Antiope thereby received the Tiara and became Empress. In response to the terror attack which killed her aunt and mother, she embarked on a prolonged and violent war against the Fringe Rebels, a campaign which drained the treasury, created hundreds of thousands of casualties, and turned a significant part of the populace against her. By the time of her death, Empress Antiope had become increasingly unpopular with the nobility and merchant class of the empire, but was still well supported by the rank and file.

Empress Antiope was killed in the Great Raid of 2165 when a task force of Fringe Rebel warships managed to break through the defenses of the Helios system and bombard the capital, Aronte, killing thousands. She is buried in the Imperial Cemetery near Aronte.

Aronte (city)

Aronte is the capital city of the Aeolian Empire. With a population of well over 10 million, it is the largest city in the Empire. Located on the planet Aeolis in the Helios System, it sits on the banks of the Thermodon River about 4 km from the Pontus Axeinos, the ocean covering most of the western hemisphere of Aeolis.

Basic Rules (RimFed)

The **Basic Rules** are a set of provisions of government which a star nation must follow to be a member of the Rim Federation. Initially adopted by the RDF Colonization Office in 2122 under the supervision of Dr. Kirsten Monk, the Basic Rules were later incorporated into the Rim Federation (RimFed) system of governance and remain the foundational government model for star nations in the alliance. The Basic Rules consist of the Rim Model of Responsible Government coupled with strong sanctions, such as ostracization, for any government which abandons the Rules.

Bat Empire

The **Bat Empire** is a star nation centered on the planet Nest, located 805 light years from Earth on a nearly direct line behind the Pipe Nebula. The Bat Empire was notoriously involved in the genocides of an estimated 9 sentient species before 2207, when it was defeated by the RDF at the Battle of Orinoco and subjected to severe sanctions for a period of 100 years. Since 2207, the Bat Empire has demonstrated exemplary behavior.

Battle of Aronte

The **Battle of Aronte** was an engagement between the Aeolian Empire Navy (AEN) and a rebel fleet seeking to overthrow the House Aronte and install a democratic government in the Aeolian Empire. The battle resulted in the defeat of the rebel force, which retreated to the Aeolian Empire Fringe Worlds.

In 2120, the planet Amasya became the center of a rebel force determined to institute reforms in the Aeolian Empire. Among the reforms they espoused were an end to the House Aronte's rule of the Aeolian Empire, the abolition of slavery, a democratic government based on sortition (choosing political officials by lot), universal suffrage (i.e. the male vote), and the end of laws preventing males from obtaining political office or serving as officers in the Navy. By 2139, Amasya and ten other planets had been taken over by the rebels and a respectable naval force had been accumulated from captured AEN ships and converted merchant vessels.

After several minor skirmishes in and around Amasya, Maia and Barcam, in early 2140 the rebel fleet felt they had enough power to make a surprise attack on the capital city, Aronte, and execute a coup against the Empress. A diversionary attack was launched in the Aeolian system near the gas giant Hypnos, which tied up a significant portion of the Home Fleet. The main rebel fleet then appeared suddenly in the system and charged for the planet, advancing to geostationary orbit over the capital city of Aronte where it prepared for an orbital bombardment which would have destroyed the Imperial Palace, Fleet Headquarters at the Navy Yard, and the Imperial Naval Academy, with the intent of decapitating the Aeolian leadership. A last-ditch suicide charge by the cruiser *Kleitos*, commanded by Captain Ligeia Satra, was able to blunt the force of the attack sufficiently for the Home Fleet to regroup and come in behind the rebels, driving them from the field and destroying most of their ships.

Battle of Nest

The **Battle of Nest** was the first major battle of the Bat War, in which the forces of the Rim Defense Force (RDF) executed a surprise attack on the Bat Empire Navy (BEN) Home Fleet on 3 July 2207 at Nest. The battle was a prelude to the later Battle of Orinoco and was designed to decimate the Home Fleet while the BEN Detached Fleet was enroute to Farpoint (see Battle of Orinoco).

In response to numerous RDF decoy operations (Project Guano, Project Skyhook) that had presented a false scenario that the Human home world was located at Farpoint (HR6497), on 1 July 2207 the BEN split their fleet, sending half of their front-line ships in an attack to wipe out the supposed home world of Humanity (the BEN Detached Fleet). Immediately after the departure of the Detached Fleet, RDF First Fleet struck in a surprise attack at the remaining half of the BEN Home Fleet left behind at Nest, resulting in the loss of 18 BEN warships and demoralizing the remnant of the Home Fleet.

Battle of Orinoco

The **Battle of Orinoco** was the final major battle of the Bat War, in which the forces of the Rim Defense Force (RDF) fought the Bat Empire Navy (BEN) on 25 July 2207 at Orinoco (HIP 94272). The result was a narrow victory for the RDF, but one sufficient to lead to the unconditional surrender of the Bat Empire less than one month later (20 August 2207).

In response to numerous RDF decoy operations (Project Guano, Project Skyhook) that had presented a false scenario that the Human home world was located at Farpoint (HR6497), on 1 July 2207 the BEN split their fleet, sending half of their front-line ships in an attack to wipe out the supposed home world of Humanity in the BEN Detached Fleet. Immediately after the departure of the Detached Fleet, the RDF First Fleet struck in a surprise attack at the remaining half of the BEN Home Fleet left behind at Nest (Battle of Nest), resulting in the loss of 18 BEN warships and demoralizing the remnant of the Home Fleet.

The BEN Detached Expedition immediately turned to pursue RDF First Fleet, which had taken a vector toward the Orinoco system. Joined by the survivors of the Battle of Nest into the Bat Armada, the BEN pursued the Humans in a stern chase that lasted for three weeks, arriving at Orinoco about twenty hours after RDF First Fleet. First Fleet made a run for the system's primary in a planned ploy designed to convince the BEN commander they were dispersing for escape. This illusion of disarray convinced the BEN fleet the Humans were attempting to slingshot around the primary star and flee the system, causing Fleet Admiral Zetun Bruntel to rush his destroyers and faster capital ships ahead of the remainder of his Armada to destroy the fleeing Human ships as soon as possible.

In the event, this was a deception by the RDF, and as the BEN Armada became strung out in pursuit of First Fleet, they were ambushed first by 726 small, one-man Wicked (A40) attack craft and immediately thereafter by the RDF Second Fleet surfacing behind them at the mass limit. In the ensuing battle, the BEN Armada, constituting the main front-line fleet of the Bat Empire, was virtually destroyed, leading to the ultimate surrender and interdiction of the Bat Empire. However, the RDF also suffered significant losses, causing Fleet Admiral Jake Hammett to paraphrase a quote from Lord Wellington regarding the 1815 Battle of Waterloo: "Nothing except a battle lost can be half so melancholy as a battle won."

Charter Debt

Charter Debt is the debt accrued by a colony in return for legal title to a planet or other colony location (e.g. a moon or asteroid), along with the cost of transportation, resources and support required to initiate a new colony in the location. Charter Debt was a concept introduced by the RDF Colony Office in the early days of Earth's struggle to prepare for the coming war with the Bat Empire. In 2121, when Jake Hammett, Teresa Tolleson and Dr. Kirsten Monk formed the RDF Colony Office, the concept of Charter Debt was established to ensure that the resources involved in starting a new colony could be recouped, with interest, in order to build RDF defenses and prepare for the coming war.

Basically, Charter Debt required the 2nd generation colonists (e.g. the children of the original colonists) and the 3rd generation colonists (e.g. the grandchildren of the original colonists) to construct two starships for use by the RDF (or one battleship or fleet carrier). A typical pattern was that the 2nd generation delivered one small starship (e.g. corvette, destroyer, scoutship), while the 3rd generation built upon that expertise and infrastructure to deliver a larger starship (e.g. frigate, cruiser, or carrier). Upon delivery and acceptance of the starships by the RDF, the Charter Debt was expunged, and the colony was free and clear.

In some cases, the RDF allowed substitute payment, e.g. in raw materials, finished goods or labor, to take the place of a delivered starship. For example, the Jovian colony on Europa satisfied their Charter Debt by becoming specialists in low-temperature microelectronics and providing advanced AI cores to the RDF for military use, remaining even today as the pre-eminent AI factory in the Rim. The mixed Earth/Aeolian colony at Eudora satisfied their Charter Debt by providing a long tradition of Marines for duty on RDF ships, and continue to do so today, even though their Charter Debt is satisfied. After the defeat of the Bat Empire and the interdiction of the Bat Home System, Charter Debt was reduced in 2208 to a single starship or its equivalent.

Cold Bay

Cold Bay is a prison planet established in 2125 near Eudora, half-way to the Beehive Cluster. Criminals who would otherwise receive a death penalty in their home jurisdictions or who have been designated repeat violent offenders are exiled to Cold Bay. Once dropped on the planet, individuals are left to their own devices. The technology on the planet is held at an early primitive level (Earth, 1750's) to prevent any chance of escape. Two police actions have occurred at Cold Bay, one in 2198 when a prisoner group attempted to build a crude spacecraft and the RDF intervened to destroy it one day before launch, and one in 2204 when smugglers attempted to carry crude rocket technology to Cold Bay in exchange for gold refined from the planet. This attempt resulted in the destruction of the smuggler's starship just short of the planet, forcing them to use their escape pods to land on the planet where they remained for the rest of their lives. No further smuggling attempts have been made.

Compressed Learning

Compressed learning is a technology provided to the RDF by the Machine Ship *Pandora* in 2121, when she visited Earth to provide a technology boost to Humanity, enabling them to survive their anticipated encounter with the Bat Empire.

Compressed learning allows the direct transmission of knowledge into the brain of the recipient during sleep, with few side effects. This allows most languages to be learned in two or three nights of sleep. It is routinely used by the military forces of most star nations but is shunned by most educational institutions for philosophical reasons.

Core (Galaxy Core)

The **Core** of the Milky Way Galaxy is the area reserved for artificial intelligence creatures such as Machine Ships. This area is off-limits to biological beings. There have been numerous attempts to explore the Core; none of the expeditions have returned. The closest outpost to the Core is Rio Bravo, located at 10,000 lights from the center of the Galaxy.

Daneki (Sentient Race)

The **Daneki** are a sentient race who were virtually annihilated by the Bat Empire in 2185, with only two dozen surviving members escaping. The survivors were rescued by Humans from the early Rim Federation. Their expertise in engineering was put to use by the RDF and they were directly responsible for the development of the A40 "Wicked" attack craft, refinements to the grav deflectors of RDF warships that allowed higher in-system speeds up to 0.6 light, and the shipkiller missiles used at the Battle of Orinoco.

Hermes (Machine Ship)

Hermes is the name assigned by the RDF to a Machine Ship which visited Earth in approximately 1184 BC and abducted roughly 212 persons, along with a variety of plants and animals, taking them to the planet Aeolis in the Beehive Cluster, where they were abandoned. This group of people formed the nucleus of the Aeolian Empire. According to the Machine Ship *Pandora*, *Hermes*'s intention was to conduct a bottleneck experiment, but he was arrested and taken back to Machine Space, where he was sentenced to re-programming for violation of the non-interference directive of the Machine Space society.

Deinomache (Princess of Aeolis)

Princess **Deinomache Andromache Aronte** was a member of the nobility of the Aeolian Empire and the mother of the 214th Empress, Hecate. Princess Deinomache was born in 2141, the daughter of Princess (later Empress) Antiope and Jake Hammett, an RDF Admiral who had infiltrated Aeolis disguised as a mercenary. In 2185, upon the abdication of Empress Hippolyta after her murder of Deinomache's husband Prince Alexander and attempted assassination of Princess Hecate, Deinomache was next in line for the tiara; however, she refused the crown and let it pass to her daughter, who became the 214th Empress.

Farpoint

Farpoint (HR6497) is a planet 475 lights Coreward of Nest, used by the RDF in their deception campaign to convince the Bat Empire Navy (BEN) that it was the location of Earth, the home of Humanity. The deception involved numerous QE buoys distributed in the vicinity of Farpoint and between the system and Nest, which broadcast fake electronic transmissions (EMF) simulating Earth communications (Project Guano). This was coupled with fake AI-driven starships which moved to and from Farpoint, fake cities built on the planet which looked realistic from a distance, and other deceptions, some of which have never been fully revealed by the RDF. As a result of the ploy, the Bats dispatched half of their Home Fleet (the BEN Detached Fleet) to Farpoint on July 1, 2207, which served to split their fleet, allowing the RDF to conduct a surprise attack on the remaining ships at Nest, decimating them and opening the Bat War.

Hecate (Empress of Aeolis)

Hecate Andromache Aronte was the 214th Empress of the Aeolian Empire, reigning from 2185 to 2238. She ended the Fringe Rebellion in 2185 and implemented democratic reforms for all planets in the Empire, including universal male suffrage, the abolition of slavery and the opening of government and the military officer corps to males.

Hecate was born in 2158 to Princess Deinomache, the second daughter of Empress Antiope. She attended the Imperial Naval Academy at Aronte and was commissioned an Ensign in 2176, assigned to the cruiser *Leto*. Serving with distinction during several skirmishes with the Fringe Rebels, she advanced in rank until she was assigned as Captain of the *Nemesis* in 2182. In early 2185, Empress Hippolyta assassinated Hecate's father, Prince Alexander, and subsequently attempted Hecate's assassination as well at Pestilence Port, in which action she first encountered RDF Admiral Jake Hammett of Earth aboard the RDF *Paris*.

After this attempt on her life, Hecate returned to Aronte and deposed Empress Hippolyta, assuming the Tiara when her mother, Princess Deinomache, refused the crown. Hecate instituted numerous democratic reforms over the next decades, including the abolition of slavery, male suffrage, opening the government to males, and accepting males into the Fleet officer corps.

Helios (star)

The **Helios** system is the home system of the Aeolian Empire, located 580 lights from Earth in the Beehive Cluster. Helios is a G2 star, comparable to Sol in all major respects.

House Aronte

The **House Aronte** is the ruling dynasty of the Aeolian Empire and is a direct line of descent from the original twelve Amazons abandoned on Aeolis in 1184 BC.

Hippolyta Lysippe Aronte (Empress of Aeolis)

Hippolyta Lysippe Aronte was the 213th Empress of the Aeolian Empire, reigning from 2163 to 2185. She inherited an Empire divided by the Fringe Rebellion and with a population exhausted by the war. Unable to end the Rebellion, she allowed it to devolve into a "Phony War", in which neither side had the strength or the will to press an attack. Hippolyta was deposed in 2185 after assassinating her brother-in-law, Prince Alexander, and making an assassination attempt on Princess Hecate, her niece.

Hippolyta was born in 2135 to Princess Antiope, the daughter of Princess Merope. She was not expected to enter the line of succession, as Merope was a second daughter of Empress Asteria and the sister of the ruling Empress, Miranda. Hippolyta attended the Imperial Naval Academy at Aronte and was commissioned an Ensign, serving as an active officer from 2153 to 2163. Her career in the Navy was unremarkable.

In 2141, Empress Miranda and Hippolyta's grandmother, Princess Merope, were both killed in a terrorist attack at the Imperial Palace. Her mother, Antiope, then became Empress. This moved Hippolyta to the line of succession. When her mother Antiope was killed in the Great Raid of 2165, Hippolyta ascended to the Tiara.

Hippolyta did not prosecute the rebels in the Fringe with any great enthusiasm and let the Rebellion simmer, resulting in a quiet period called the "Phony War". Instead, she devoted her time to real and imagined conspiracies in the Palace and among the nobility, developing a reputation as a dangerous and somewhat unpredictable ruler. In 2185, she assassinated Prince Alexander, the husband of her sister Princess Deinomache, and attempted the assassination of her niece, Princess Hecate.

Unsuccessful in the latter attempt, she was confronted by Princess Hecate in April 2185 and deposed. She was banished to Selene for the remainder of her life.

Hippolyta died in 2213 at Selene and is buried in the Imperial Cemetery near Aronte.

Empress Hecate (starship)

The AEN **Empress Hecate** was the lead starship of the *Hecate* class of heavy battleships built by the Aeolian Empire in the early 23rd century. She was lost with all hands at the Battle of Orinoco in 2207.

Laid down in December 2201 at Nyx Shipyards in Aronte, Aeolian Empire, the '*Empress*' as she was generally known, was commissioned on 14 July 2204 by Empress Hecate and joined the RDF Fleet at Tolleson Base in December 2205. Her first and last Captain was Hippolyta Melousa. She served as the flagship for Fleet Admiral Andrea Iona Satra in the Bat War. On 25 July 2207 at the Battle of Orinoco, she was lost with all hands when the Bat Empire Navy destroyer *Waspeater* performed a kamikaze attack into her engines. A memorial to her officers and crew is on the main quadrangle at RDF Command Headquarters, Tolleson Base, Kamilaroi. Several RDF starships are named after members of her crew, including the RDF fleet carriers *Satra* and *Melousa* and the frigates *Derinoe* and *Duspera*.

Jake Hammett

Jake Hammett was the first Chief of Naval Operations (CNO) of the Rim Defense Force (RDF). Hammett was born October 26, 2078, in Oakwood, Texas, and grew up in Dallas, Texas, graduating from Dallas Skyline High School in 2096. He was appointed to the U. S. Naval Academy, graduating in 2100, and completed flight training at NAS Pensacola, Florida, and NAS Corpus Christi, Texas. In 2104 he was assigned to VFA-2 'Bounty Hunters' at NAS Lemoore, California, flying the F81 "Dagger II". Hammett served in various fighter squadrons both in the U. S.

and overseas, moving up to the F82 "Stilletto" in 2112.

When the Brush War broke out in 2115, Lt. Commander Jake Hammett was on the carrier USS *Byers* in the Indian Ocean, and immediately began flying missions off the carrier, completing 28 missions and accounting for six enemy aircraft between January and May 2115. On May 1st, 2115, while diving from 38,000 meters to attack a Chinese bomber headed for Japan, recently promoted Commander Hammett was shot down over North Korea but was able to make Mongolian airspace before ejecting. He was captured by the Mongolian Army and interned for the remainder of the war, but the Mongolians refused to turn him over to the North Koreans or the Chinese, saving him from the torture visited on many other captured pilots.

Hammett left the Navy after the Brush War and moved to San Francisco, where he worked in Artificial Intelligence (AI) for SpaceRed, a startup attempting to create a viable permanent habitat on Mars. There Hammett developed AI cores for use in primitive chemical spaceships and early Mars habitats.

Hammett lived and worked relatively quietly in San Francisco until 21 June 2121 when the Machine Ship *Pandora* landed dramatically in the White House South Lawn and presented holographic images of three persons on the outside of the ship: Jake Hammett, Air Force Lieutenant Colonel Teresa Tolleson and NSC Science Advisor Dr. Kirsten Monk. *Pandora*'s message of danger to Humanity, coupled with the message "*If you wish to survive, bring these three*", resulted in a quick parabolic flight in an F90B from Travis AFB, California, to Andrews AFB, Maryland for Hammett. Upon arrival at the White House, Hammett, Tolleson and Monk were directed by the President to proceed to the alien ship and attempt to make contact. The three entered the ship at 7:43 am on 22 June 2121 and contacted the sentient AI *Pandora*. The group came out after four hours to report the disturbing facts of the danger to Earth posed by the Bat Empire. The next day, 23 June 2121, Hammett appeared before the U. N. General Assembly and highlighted the danger to Earth represented by the Bat Empire, the need for the formation of the Rim Defense Force (RDF) and the RDF Colony Office, and the requirement to form an alliance with the Aeolian Empire to present a joint defense against the Bats.

Moving to Geneva, Switzerland, Hammett, Tolleson and Dr. Monk formed the RDF Space Force and began the anticipated one-hundred-year process of preparing for the war against the Bats. Two years later, Hammett formed the first triplex marriage with Monk and Tolleson, creating a new paradigm for use in the RDF where long absences from home base were the norm rather than the exception.

For Hammett's children from this marriage, see the entries for Teresa Tolleson and Dr. Kirsten Monk.

For Hammett's children from his later marriage to Fleet Admiral Andrea Iona Satra, see her entry.

For Hammett's marriage to the Aeolian Empress Antiope, see her entry.

Jake Hammett led the RDF to successfully defeat the Bats at the Battle of Orinoco and placed a 100-year interdiction on the Bat Home System after that battle, but lost his fourth wife, Andrea Iona Satra, during the conflict. Shortly after, in 2210, Jake Hammett disappeared, with rumor that he had departed Earth in a small scout ship to travel to the Rim-Core border and enter the Core. He was never seen again.

Kamilaroi

Kamilaroi is a planet in the 36 Ophiuchi C system, the seat of the Rim Federation government capital New Geneva, and the home of the Rim Defense Force (RDF) Headquarters at Tolleson Base. Kamilaroi is an ocean world, with only two small landmasses and a cooler, wetter climate than Earth. New Geneva sits on an island in the Southern Ocean while RDF Naval Headquarters is located on an island in the Northern Ocean, almost directly opposite New Geneva.

Kirsten Monk

Dr. Kirsten Monk was the first Director of the Rim Defense Force (RDF) Colony Office. Born May 19th, 2087, in Queens, New York City, Monk grew up in Queens and attended Far Rockaway High School, graduating in 2104. After high school, she attended MIT, obtaining her B.S. and M.S. in Physics and her Ph. D in Astronomy in 2112. She worked under Luebmann at Columbia from 2112 to 2115, primarily on detection of exomoons. In 2115, during the Brush War, she was seconded to Applied Engineering Laboratories in Austin, Texas_to develop remote sensing technology for use in the war effort. After the war, Monk remained at AEL in Austin, becoming a primary researcher on asteroid mining. In 2120, based on her general expertise in astronomy, long range sensing and asteroid mining operations, she was appointed to the National Security Council by President Margaret Bolt.

Dr. Monk was at the White House attending an NSC meeting on 21 June 2121 when the Machine Ship *Pandora* landed on the South Lawn and presented holographic images of three persons on the outside of the ship: Dr. Monk, Jake Hammett, and Air Force Lieutenant Colonel Teresa Tolleson. *Pandora*'s message of danger to Humanity, coupled with the message "*If you wish to survive, bring these three*", resulted a directive from the President to enter the alien ship and attempt to make contact. The three entered the ship at 7:43 am on 22 June 2121 and contacted the sentient AI *Pandora*. The group came out after four hours to report the disturbing facts of the danger to Earth posed by the Bat Empire. The next day, 23 June 2121, Monk appeared with Jake Hammett and Teresa Tolleson before the U. N. General Assembly as part of their presentation to highlight the danger to Earth represented by the Bat Empire, the need for the formation of the Rim Defense Force (RDF) and the RDF Colony Office, and the requirement to form an alliance with the Aeolian Empire to present a joint defense against the Bats.

Subsequent to these events, Dr. Monk joined with Jake Hammett and Teresa Tolleson as the initial founding members of the RDF. Monk formed the RDF Colony Office, which had responsibility for locating suitable planets for colonization, conducting the planning and resource collection required for the colonies, transporting the colonists to their new home, monitoring and supporting them until they were fully established, and supervising them through three generations, including the collection of their Charter Debt.

With Teresa Tolleson and Jake Hammett, Monk also formed the first triplex marriage in the RDF in 2123, setting a precedent that endures to the current day in the RDF and throughout the Rim Federation.

Monk and Hammett had two children:

1. Chloe Monk, b. 2129, d. 2207, starship pilot in the RDF, rose to the rank of Captain. Semi-retired from a long career in the RDF as an operational commander, Chloe managed to have herself re-activated as a Reserve Captain and assigned to the destroyer *Antares* as it departed Kamilaroi on 22 June 2207 to meet First Fleet at Orinoco. During the subsequent Battle of Orinoco, Chloe was killed on the bridge of the destroyer as it defended the flagship *Wellington* from the last onslaught of the Bat Armada; she is memorialized with a statue on the Commons at RDF Antiope Headquarters. Chloe is buried in the Hammett Family Plot near Oakwood, Texas.

2. Stephen Hawking Monk, b. 2132, d. 2200, Old Earth politician, member of the New York Assembly, U. S. Senator from New York, and NAA Secretary of State under President James Bolt Jr. Ran for NAA President on the Covenant of God (Saints) ticket in 2184 but lost. He was estranged from his mother and father for most of his adult life, due to his extreme religious paranoia and his writings espousing an Earth government based on a religious dictatorship.

Stephen was a key instigator of the Rule War of 2188; after the defeat of the Saints, he retired to his estate in upper New York. He died there in 2200; he was cremated, and his ashes scattered in the Hudson River.

Dr. Monk also formed a separate, duplex marriage with Commander Lois Vetton in 2124. This marriage was permissible under the rules of the RDF at the time, which permitted a total of four spouses simultaneously if all participants agreed the contracts. This marriage also lasted until her death.

Dr. Kirsten Monk was killed by a stray bullet on July 2, 2134, during a Covenant of God (Saints) coup attempt on Sierra Nevada, while attempting to broker a peace between the warring factions. Her husband, Fleet Admiral Jake Hammett, was enraged and began the process of ostracization for the system; but was convinced by others to defer the process. However, the RDF fined Sierra Nevada two years GDP for the crime, which required them to build an extra starship (the scoutship *Polaris*) before their Charter Debt was satisfied.

Dr. Monk is buried in the Hammett Family Plot near Oakwood, Texas.

Ligeia Iona Satra

Ligeia Iona Satra was a Captain in the Aeolian Empire Navy (AEN) during the early years of the Fringe Rebellion. She was the grandmother of Andrea Iona Satra, the first Aeolian-born Fleet Admiral of the RDF.

Ligeia Satra was born in 2107 on the planet Aeolis into the Satra clan, a junior branch of the House Aronte. She attended the Imperial Naval Academy at Aronte, graduating in 2125 as an ensign. She served on various ships and advanced steadily in rank until 2136, when she was assigned as Captain of the cruiser *Kleitos*. In the Battle of Aronte in 2141, Captain Satra led the counterattack on the rebel fleet which was preparing to bombard Aronte, saving the city, but was killed in the process.

For her actions in the battle, she was posthumously awarded the AEN's highest decoration, the Honor of the Empress, as well as the Star of Aronte.

Machine Ship

A **Machine Ship** is an artificial intelligence (AI) creature with the body of a starship, thus able to traverse the galaxy at will, with nearly unlimited resources of time and energy. The most famous example of a Machine Ship (to biological creatures) is *Pandora*. Also see *Hermes*.

Machine Space

Machine Space is the central part of the Milky Way galaxy, also known as the Core. It is reserved for artificial intelligence creatures only, including Machine Ships, androids and other synthetic or AI-based lifeforms.

Miranda (Empress of Aeolis)

Empress **Miranda Andromache Aronte** was the 211th Empress of the Aeolian Empire, reigning from 2085 until 2141. Empress Miranda prosecuted a lackluster war against the Fringe rebels, never fully committing the military forces of the Empire against them, resulting in a long and lingering rebellion that grew steadily throughout the early part of the 22nd century. Shortly after the Battle of Aronte in 2141, Miranda was assassinated, along with her sister Princess Merope, by the rebel Anicetus on 17 April 2141.

Nemesis

AEN *Nemesis* was a destroyer of the Aeolian Empire Navy (AEN) named after the ancient Greek god of retribution. *Nemesis* was laid down on 6 May 2181 at Nyx Shipyards on Aeolis and was launched on 25 March 2182. After additional outfitting, she was commissioned on 27 October 2182, Princess-Captain Hecate Aronte in command. *Nemesis* took part in several minor actions with Rebellion forces in the Fringe, including attacks on the Rebellion bases at Maia and Amasya. In mid-2183, *Nemesis* was serving as screen for the cruiser *Asteria* when a surprise sortie by two Rebel cruisers and their accompanying destroyer squadrons caught the *Asteria* by surprise as she entered the Aegean system. *Nemesis* destroyed one Rebel destroyer but was struck by numerous cannon rounds, one of which penetrated the bridge and killed most of the bridge crew and severely wounded Princess-Captain Aronte. Nevertheless, the *Nemesis* continued to fight for an additional ten minutes until the action was over and the Rebel ships retreated. For this action, *Nemesis* was awarded the Empress' Ribbon, with Princess-Captain Hecate Aronte and Executive Officer Andrea Iona Satra receiving the Star of Aronte.

Nemesis was also ambushed in 2185 near Pestilence Port by three AEN destroyers as part of a conspiracy by the Empress Hippolyta to assassinate Princess-Captain Aronte, but survived after the intervention of the RDF *Paris*, representing the first acknowledged contact between the AEN and the RDF.

Nest

Nest is the home planet of the Bat Empire, located 805 lights Coreward from Earth behind the Pipe Nebula. The capital of Nest is Raditel. The planet receives about 90% of the radiation of Earth and is famous as the site of the surrender of the Bat Empire after the Battle of Orinoco in 2207.

New Geneva

New Geneva is the capital city of the Rim Federation, located on the planet Kamilaroi in the 36 Ophiuchi C system. It is the home of the Rim Parliament and the seat of government for the Rim. New Geneva was founded in 2136 on one of the two land masses of Kamilaroi, two small islands roughly the size of Iceland on Earth. RDF Headquarters is located on the other island, approximately half-way around the planet.

Ostracization

Ostracization is the Rim Federation policy of withholding all defensive, technological, and logistical support for a colony/ planet which fails to follow the Basic Rules of the Rim Federation. This means the planet is isolated from the Rim Federation and is, for all practical purposes, no longer capable of space travel or space communications. This policy was established in 2122 by the RDF Colonization Office in their initial Basic Rules model, and later adopted by the Rim Federation.

Ostracization implies:

1. The RDF will not defend the colony if it is attacked by an outside force
2. All technology beyond that of the early 20th century, Earth is withdrawn from the colony. No fission or fusion reactors, spacecraft, radio or TV, microelectronics, or other advances from beyond the period of Earth, 1900 are permitted.
3. No deep-space communications are permitted, e.g. no QE boxes.
4. Any person who voluntarily lands on the planet will remain. Accidental landings will be rescued.
5. The RDF will perform periodic checks on the colony to verify compliance but will not land.

Pandora (Machine Ship)

Pandora was the name of the Machine Ship which visited Earth in 2121 and provided a technology boost to bring Humanity to parity with the Bat Empire. *Pandora* landed on the South Lawn of the White House, Washington, D.C., on 21 June 2121. In appearance, *Pandora* was wedge-shaped, similar to an old-style flatiron without the handle. She was matte black, with two linear scribes down each side and crosshatches on top, similar to a tic-tac-toe pattern. She was measured by remote laser at 30 meters long and 14 meters wide at her rear, tapering to a 1-meter blunt point at the front. The impression she left in the ground after her eventual departure was 12 inches deep, indicating a considerable mass. A later report by Jake Hammett stated that the ship was larger internally than externally, which would indicate some type of extra-dimensionality that is not yet understood by Rim science.

After her arrival, *Pandora* posted a message as a hologram on the outside of the ship, consisting of pictures of Mr. Jake Hammett, a former U.S. Navy fighter pilot; Lt. Colonel Teresa Tolleson, an Air Force officer; and Dr. Kirsten Monk, a member of the National Security Council; with the message to bring them to the ship.

The next day, 22 June 2121, the three entered the ship and met the advanced AI who was the mind of the ship. The three were in the ship for four hours. Upon their exit, they walked across the White House lawn to the South fence and held an impromptu news conference with a group of reporters and sightseers gathered there. This short press briefing provided the people of Earth the first insight into the nature of the Galaxy, Machine Space, and *Pandora*. In this briefing, Hammett disclosed the nature of *Pandora* as a total AI construct, with no biological component, and the general purpose of her visit to Earth.

On the following day, while the three were presenting to the U. N. General Assembly in New York a more complete disclosure of the message brought by *Pandora*, she quietly and without warning lifted off from the White House and flew to Geneva, Switzerland, landing in the courtyard of the large office building which became the first headquarters of the fledgling RDF (Rim Defense Force). Over the next two years, *Pandora* sat quietly in the courtyard of RDF Headquarters in Geneva, with no one allowed to communicate directly with her except RDF personnel and no one allowed on board except Hammett, Tolleson, Monk or Atsuko Kawasaki, head of RDF Intelligence. During this period, *Pandora* provided, via the RDF, numerous technological gifts to Humanity, including transcendent fusion drives (tDrives), compressed learning, and the QE box. She also provided the RDF with limited information on the social and military aspects of the Aeolian and Bat Empires.

After slightly more than two years in Geneva, on 26 September 2123, *Pandora* lifted off again and made her way to Mars, where she resided while the RDF completed MarsBase, their first off-Earth Headquarters. In 2137, *Pandora* relocated again to Tolleson Base at Kamilaroi, the new Headquarters of the RDF. On 18 November 2139, *Pandora* declared her mission complete and departed the Sol system. Although she has never re-appeared to public view since that time, rumors persist that she has been seen in various locations throughout Rim space, including once lying quietly on the back side of the Moon. Moreover, in an interview with Dateline RimFed in 2186, Jake Hammett stated that *Pandora* is never far away, and had contacted him from time to time.

Pestilence Port

Pestilence Port is a mining colony in the Eremos system, an A5 class star 125 lights from Aeolis, situated on the large rocky moon Apollymi of the gas giant Epidamos. It is believed by astronomers that Apollymi was once an independent planet of the system which was captured by Epidamos at some time in the past.

Pontus Axeinos

The **Pontus Axeinos** is a large ocean covering most of the Western Hemisphere of the planet Aeolis. Covering an area of 71,288,103 square kilometers, it is slightly larger than the Pacific Ocean of Earth. Its name is identical to the ancient Greek term for the Black Sea of Earth, which further reinforces a commonly held theory that the Amazons of Aeolis originated on the northern shores of what is now Turkey in approximately 1184 B.C. before their abduction to Aeolis.

QE Box

A **QE Box** is a deep-space communications device used primarily by the RDF for military transmissions. Although it has a low bit rate, it has unlimited range and cannot be hacked. Due to the low bit rate, it cannot transmit video, but can send low quality audio and text messages instantaneously across any distance.

Rim Defense Force (RDF)

The RDF (Rim Defense Force) is the military arm of the Rim Federation (RimFed). Originating in 2121 on Earth, the RDF was moved to Mars in 2123 and later to Kamilaroi in 2137 as the number of off-Earth colonies grew, and Earth became more recalcitrant in its objections to meeting the Basic Rules. The RDF is best known for the Bat War, in which it secured the future survival of the Rim Federation by defeating the Bat Empire and interdicting the Bat home planet (Nest) for 100 years .

Rim Federation

The **Rim Federation** (generally known as RimFed) is the central government of the Orion Spur of the Milky Way galaxy. As of 2230 it encompassed 449 states (star nations, colonies, and territories). RimFed is a parliamentary system of government originally developed on the planet Earth; when the original RDF began colonizing planets in 2121, such government was adopted as the only permissible form of government for Human colonies. In 2136, the Rim Federation was established on the same model to act as a top-level government for all systems and colonies defended by the RDF. Since that time, RimFed has been joined by the Daneki and Romish species.

Constitution

The constitution of the Rim Federation is founded upon the Basic Rules, which guarantee individual freedoms and protect the basic rights of the individual.

Distributed Government

In the Rim Federation, individual star nations, colonies and territories retain their own local government, and have the right to control their own territories and peoples, within the scope of the Basic Rules. They may raise, train and control local militias and police forces to defend themselves and their systems. However, local governments are restricted from creating professional FTL navies, as that role is reserved for the RDF. Certain aspects of the Basic Rules have created conflict (e.g. the Rule War) but in general the approach has maintained stability in government for many years.

Rim Model of Responsible Government

The **Rim Model of Responsible Government** is a parliamentary system of government based on the Westminster system originally developed in the Old Earth United Kingdom, coupled with the Bill of Rights from the old United States, used by all planets or colonies in the Rim Federation. The term comes from the Palace of Westminster, the seat of the Old Earth British Parliament. The system is a set of procedures for operating a government. This system was implemented by the RDF in 2122 for all new Human colonies and was subsequently adopted by the Aeolians and Daneki upon their entry into the Rim Federation. RimFed continues to require this form of government for any planet or colony in the Federation, else the entity will be ostracized from all further contact with other Rim members.

tDrive

The **tDrive** is a technology provided to the original RDF (Rim Defense Force) by the Machine Ship *Pandora* in 2121, shortly after her arrival on Earth. A tDrive allows faster-than-light (FTL) travel for starships. An AI interface built into the tDrive is used to control it.

Thermodon River (Aeolis)

The **Thermodon River** is the chief river on Aeolis, the central planet of the Aeolian Empire. The capital city, Aronte, is located at the mouth of the river. The river flows generally west for 3,650 km from the Olympus mountains to the Pontus Axeinos, with a drainage basin of 2,866,000 km2. The estuary of the river forms a prime fishing area and excellent harbor for shipping.

Teresa Tolleson

Teresa Tolleson was the first head of the Rim Defense Force (RDF) Operations Group, leading them for the initial 15 years of their existence. Born February 19th, 2088, in Los Angeles, California, Tolleson grew up in LA and attended Los Angeles High School, graduating in 2106. Appointed to the U.S. Air Force Academy in Colorado Springs, Colorado, she graduated in 2110 with a degree in Aeronautical Engineering. She completed flight training at Sheppard AFB, Texas, and was assigned to the 47th "Hawg" squadron at San Francisco, California, in 2112, flying the F-84 Thunderbolt III. In the Brush War of 2115, Tolleson, by then a Captain, shot down five Chinese J-48 fighters and six Chinese H-42 bombers over the course of six weeks, becoming the first female double ace of the war. Shot down on 27 May 2115, just weeks before the armistice, Tolleson was tortured by the Chinese for several days before the cease-fire was announced. Remaining in the USAF after the war, Tolleson rose rapidly to the rank of Lieutenant Colonel, serving as both a test pilot and training commander; but in 2120, while stationed at Travis AFB near San Francisco, California, she filed sexual harassment charges against the base Commanding Officer. The charges were dismissed by a court of inquiry due to lack of evidence. As a result of these events, however, Lt. Colonel Tolleson was notified she would not be retained in the Air Force. Tolleson made plans to retire in mid-2121.

Tolleson initially planned to accept a job as a pilot for

North American Airlines, but after the dramatic arrival of the Machine Ship *Pandora* in June of 2121, Tolleson became part of the fledgling RDF. Working first out of Geneva, Switzerland, and later out of MarsBase, Tolleson was the driving force in establishing the Operations and Logistic Command of the RDF, arm-twisting corporate and government leaders into supporting the planning and execution of the early ship designs, kick-starting the manufacturing of starships, and recruiting and training crews for the first missions. Tolleson was highly effective in her role, leaving CNO Jake Hammett to concentrate on the development of the long-term strategy for dealing with the Bat Empire.

With Dr. Kirsten Monk and Hammett, Tolleson formed the first triplex marriage in the RDF in August 2123, setting a precedent that endures to the current day in the RDF and many Rim colonies.

Tolleson had two children by Jake Hammett:

1. Granada Tolleson, b. 2127, d. 2217, an actress and author, lived in London, England, and wrote the historical novel "The Princess Takes a Barbarian" published in 2175, as well as dozens of plays and short works. Upon her death, Granada's ashes were scattered at her mother's gravesite near Oakwood, Texas.

2. Scipio (Skip) Tolleson, b. 2130, an Episcopalian priest of the Holy Trinity Anglican Church in Geneva, Switzerland, Earth; his son Scipio II, performed the marriage ceremony for his grandfather (Jake Hammett) and Andrea Iona Satra in 2205, two years before the Battle of Orinoco.

Teresa Tolleson was abducted in Geneva on 2 December 2136 and tortured to death by Covenant of God terrorists in Frankfurt, Germany. She is buried in the Hammett Family Plot near Oakwood, Texas.

Tolleson Base

Tolleson Base is the headquarters of the Rim Defense Force (RDF). It is located on the planet Kamilaroi in the 36 Ophiuchi system. RDF Headquarters was originally located at MarsBase in the Sol System. Due to the recalcitrance of Earth to adopt the Rim Federation Basic Rules and the increasing hostility of the religion-backed government of the North American Alliance, the RDF relocated their Headquarters to Kamilaroi in 2137. Choosing a location next to Terminator Bay, where a moist but mild climate prevailed, the new base grew rapidly throughout the last decades of the 22nd century. The city next to the base, Tolleson City, once known as a rough frontier town, is now considered one of the finer cities in the Rim.

Wicked (A40 Attack Fighter)

The **A40** (*'Wicked' in RDF jargon)* was the Rim Defense Force (RDF) fast attack craft used at the Battle of Orinoco in 2207 to decimate the Bat Empire Navy (BEN) fleet. It is uncertain where the nickname 'Wicked' originated, but it is attributed to Admiral Rob Walker, who reported he accidentally created the nickname due to the A40's speed, stealth and hitting power when he mentioned to his XO that it was a "wicked machine". It is most famous for disabling the BEN Flagship *Pride of Nest* in the first minutes of the Battle of Orinoco, contributing to confusion and delay in the re-grouping of BEN forces. The A40 that disabled the *Pride of Nest* in a suicide attack was piloted by Captain Cassian of the Daneki, a survivor of the planet Danek destroyed by the Bats in 2185. Another A40, piloted by Lt. Commander Vitus of the Daneki, subsequently destroyed the *Warmonger II*, which had taken command of the Bat Fleet upon the loss of the *Pride of Nest*. This destruction of their second flagship demoralized the Bat Fleet and effectively ended the battle.

Zeno

Zeno was an alternate identity used by Jake Hammett during his extended stay in the Aeolian Empire during the period

February 2140 to April 2141. Hammett used this identity to infiltrate the Empire and research methods of enabling an alliance with the Aeolians. The nature of this visit was shrouded in secrecy and few details were ever revealed by the RDF, but it is well-established that Hammett fathered the second daughter (Deinomache) of Princess Antiope (later Empress Antiope), thus becoming the grandfather of Empress Hecate. This chain of events ultimately led to a military alliance with the Empire. Some historians attribute Pandora's cryptic selection of Jake Hammett as the initial head of the RDF to her ability to predict this event, but nearly all mathematicians discount this as an impossible feat of statistical prediction.

AUTHOR NOTES

Thank you for reading this book. I love these characters - they are so full of life (and themselves). That's the great danger for an author like me - falling in love with the people who live on the pages!

For the record, the first glimmer of a concept I had for this series - and the first scene I wrote - was the landing of the shuttle with Hecate's father's body, and the caisson trundling away. Everything in this entire series started with that simple picture in my mind - a princess crying in the sun.

From that initial picture grew a 600+ page novel - a bit too large to publish as it was. Therefore, I split it into two separate volumes - Imprint of Blood, and Imprint of War.

In the final analysis, I think this turned out well. Readers have been quite enthusiastic about this series. I hope you are too. And if you liked the book, please leave a review.

Below, you'll find a sneak preview of the next book in the series, Imprint of Honor. Jake Hammett's children Alexander Orien and Ligeia Antiope, raised by Empress Hecate, are well into their careers. Ligeia's daughter, Miranda, is an Ensign on a scout ship exploring the Arm.

And things don't go well.

You can join my mailing list by dropping into my website www.philhuddleston.com, where you'll get a free book if you wish, and can keep up with things coming down the pike.

If you have other comments, send me a note at sfwritertx@gmail.com - I'm always happy to hear from you, and

I try to answer all emails.

Amazon - www.amazon.com/Author/PhilHuddleston

Facebook - www.facebook.com/PhilHuddlestonAuthor

Website - www.PhilHuddleston.com

PREVIEW - BOOK THREE

IMPRINT OF HONOR

<u>RDF *Kuznetsov* - nearing Delphi Station</u>

Toxie stretched. Her lean, lithe body - the hard-as-nails body of a woman descended from the ancient Amazon warriors of Earth - didn't leave much space at the head of the standard officer's bunk. Just an inch shy of six feet tall, her hair dark as midnight, her eyes a brilliant, flashing, cinnamon-brown, Toxie turned to her husband and threw one knee across his waist. Resting her head on his shoulder, she caressed his chest, loving on him. A slight movement of air from the overhead vents ranged across them, cooling sweaty bodies after their lovemaking.

"What shall we name her?" she asked.

Orien shrugged in puzzlement. "How should I know? Have you talked to your Mum about it? I think you should ask her first. Otherwise, she's gonna be really upset."

"Well…I guess. I'll send her a comm after we dock."

"And let my Sis know, too. She'll be thrilled. But don't let her talk you into anything. Your Mum would be eternally pissed if you let my Sis pick the name."

"Oh, don't worry. I know that. My Mum already doesn't like your Sis. Let's not pour fuel on that fire!"

"I've always liked my mother's name, though. Andrea."

Toxie smiled, rubbing his hair, nipping at his ear.

"I'll take that under consideration."

"Or Toxis Alexia the Second. I like that one."

Toxis Alexia the First grinned, nuzzling Orien's neck.

"I'll add that to the list."

"And how shall we raise her, O Wife of Mine?"

Toxie answered with derision in her voice, pulling back from his neck and giving him a fake slap as she did so.

"The same way we were raised, you idiot! At Aeolis! With Hecate! And she'll go to the Academy! And be a great and famous Naval officer! Much more famous than either of us will ever be!"

Chuckling, Orien reached for his nightstand and retrieved a large glass half-full of clear liquid, downing the remainder in one slug.

Glancing at the clock display on the wall, Toxie frowned.

"You don't need to be drinking right now, Orrie. You have the duty in ... let's see, about an hour. And you should eat something before then. Get moving, sailor!"

She slowly unwrapped herself from his body and pushed him lightly in the side, as if to push him off the bed and onto the floor.

"And Orrie...you're going to be a father now. Think about that. The drinking...if you want advancement to Captain, you have to get that under control. And with the baby coming...it's time, love."

Nodding in deference to his wife, Orien spoke.

"I know. I'll do it."

"I'm serious, love. You have to get it under control - people are starting to talk!"

"I know. I'll do it."

"OK. I won't nag you about it anymore. But get it done, Commander!"

Orien shrugged. "Consider it done, Commander!"

"OK. Then get your ass in gear! We'll be docking in two hours!"

Orien groaned, but grudgingly started moving, sliding out of bed, placing his feet on the floor. Sitting there for a second, his head down, he was clearly thinking.

"What are you thinking about, love?" asked Toxie, with a lilt in her voice, as she lay in the bunk, her skin still glistening with sweat. "How to get out of your watch and stay in bed with me?"

"Exactly," mumbled Orien.

"Well, you can't," Toxie murmured. "So, get up and go do your duty!"

Letting out another loud groan, Orien rose to his feet and stood beside the bed, stretching. Toxie stared at her husband in amazement. Even after all these years of marriage, she never got tired of looking at him. At six feet two inches, one hundred ninety pounds, muscular but still slim, she loved every inch of him.

Like most Aeolians, her skin was golden-brown, a hue like a well-suntanned Cauc. Orien was slightly lighter-skinned, an anomaly for an Aeolian - genes inherited from his Earther father. His hair had gone ever-so-slightly salt-and-pepper now; but in her opinion, it only added to his presence, his command authority.

Toxie loved him. More than she could put into words. And she knew he loved her the same way. They always said they were a matched pair.

But a pair of what? That was the question they always laughed about.

Letting out another groan of displeasure at leaving her, Orien stalked away. Soon enough, Toxie heard the sound of the shower, and knew her husband was finally getting himself pulled together for his watch. Her own duty shift had ended a few hours earlier. Rolling over, she dropped off to sleep.

*****

Two hours later, on the bridge of the *Kuznetsov*, Orien sat quietly in his XO chair, watching young Lieutenant Grimm at the OOD position. Grimm was one of his favorites. Not that Orien played favorites; but it was inevitable that some officers were more capable than others. And those were the ones Orien preferred.

Normally, one would not let a recently promoted lieutenant navigate into a busy port; but Orien thought Grimm was ready. He had asked Captain Sykes, and Sykes had approved it - perhaps not enthusiastically, but approved it. Sykes knew as well as Orien did - developing young officers was part of their command responsibility on the *Kuznetsov*.

Nobody on the crew ever called her the *Kuznetsov*. From the captain down to the lowest rating, everyone called her the *Kuzzie*. It was a term of endearment, the crew's nickname for their ship, their refuge, their home away from home. She was long, wide in the rear, narrow in the front - a wedge. She was black, so black you could not see her in space with normal eyes, not unless you were right up on her, close enough to see her blank out the stars as she cruised by. And that was by design, because she was a hunter, and a killer - a heavy cruiser. And if she were close enough for you to see her blank out the stars, you'd better pray she was on your side.

Few of her current crew knew that the *Kuzzie* was copied after another black, wedge-shaped ship - a strange ship that had landed on Earth one hundred and thirty-four years earlier. That earlier ship had been called *Pandora*; and she had brought the stars to Earth, given them to Jake Hammett and Teresa Tolleson and Kirsten Monk, a box of pain and glory to open for all of Humanity.

But aside from her captain, and her XO, and maybe a few other senior people in her crew, that was a detail forgotten, or dismissed. This crew of Humans and Aeolians and Daneki was generations removed from that event. It was history, something studied in school, not relevant to their daily lives. Humans had grasped the gift of *Pandora*'s technology, embraced it, gone to the stars, expanded beyond all reason. Nobody thought much anymore about how it had all started.

Now, as the *Kuzzie* moved closer to the planet Delphi and orbital dock *Schiaparelli*, Orien could hear Lieutenant Grimm speaking quietly to Engineering, ensuring everything was ready for their approach.

Some said Delphi was the third-busiest port in the Rim now. It certainly looked like it today. In the large orange-tinted holotank at the front of the bridge, ships were everywhere - departing, arriving, entering orbit, leaving orbit, offloading cargo to shuttles - it was a madhouse.

"Lieutenant Grimm, we ready?" Orien asked.

"Yes, sir," Grimm responded. "All systems in the green. We're on the line. ETA eight minutes."

Orien smiled. Grimm had done a good job so far. All was in order; the *Kuzzie* was on a tangential course that would ensure she arrived in the exact spot designated by the Port Authority. In eight minutes, they would dock, and this cruise would be over. And they would go dirtside and disperse to their various destinations for leave.

And while the *Kuzzie* was undergoing refit, he would not have to come back to the Navy for six long, beautiful weeks. Granted, there wouldn't be enough time to take Toxie all the way to their home planet of Aeolis and then get back for the next cruise, not in six short weeks. But at least he could place her in good comfort at their second home, their little military bungalow near Delphi Station.

And being at home with Toxie for six weeks was about as good a deal as a man could get. With a baby coming, Toxie would retire from the Navy now. She had enough time in; she would get full retirement. Orien grinned, thinking about the old Earther saying: *A future so bright, I have to wear sunshades!*

"All stop," he heard from Grimm, and the sound of the mains fell away to idle. They were nearly there. Now Grimm would let her drift in until they were only a few hundred yards from dock - then he would brake with the maneuvering jets to a gentle stop. All was good.

And to return with this good news...Orien would need to

send a QE squirt to Ligeia, to his Sister-Mother Hecate, to all his relatives on Aeolis.

Mustn't forget that...

*****

The alarm was so loud, Orien almost jumped out of his chair.

"What the fuck!?" he heard from Captain Sykes behind him.

Orien scanned his console. The flashing red letters were clear:

COLLISION ALERT - 6 SECONDS

Orien raised his gaze to the holotank. There he saw it - a large freighter, spinning crazily. One of its engines had gone wild as it was braking for dock. Bright red in the holo, the projected course of the freighter ended after only a few hundred meters.

Directly into the bottom of the *Kuzzie*.

Orien instinctively looked at Lieutenant Grimm. The young lieutenant was frozen in place, paralyzed, staring at the holo in disbelief. Orien heard and felt the mains start to come up as the ShipMind reacted first, felt the maneuvering thrusters fire as the AI tried to move them out of the way...

COLLISION ALERT - 5 SECONDS

Five seconds to react. And the *Kuzzie* was large, and heavy, and slow, and her mains were at idle...

Like second sight, like seeing the future, Orien knew what he had to do.

"Helm! Roll us right!" he yelled.

COLLISION ALERT - 4 SECONDS

Even with the best effort of the ShipMind, it would take at least five seconds for the engines to come up to adequate power to move the ship out of the way. The yammering alarm went on and on...

"Roll us right, Helm! To the right! Roll right, dammit!"

Three seconds.

The ship began rotating to the right, the Quartermaster finally reacting to Orien's command. Then it also began to respond to the ShipMind's efforts, slowly twisting away from the oncoming freighter. But Orien knew it wasn't going to be enough.

Two seconds.

Orien turned to glance at Captain Sykes. Sykes nodded, approval clear on his face. It was all they could do. There was no other option.

One second.

IMPRINT OF HONOR - ON AMAZON!

WORKS

Imprint Series
Artemis War (prequel novella)
Imprint of Blood
Imprint of War
Imprint of Honor
Imprint of Defiance

Broken Galaxy Series
Broken Galaxy
Star Tango
The Long Edge of Night
The Short End
Remnants
Goblin Eternal

Generation Ship Destiny
Steele High
Steele Fury
Steele Universe

New books and freebies
www.philhuddleston.com/newsletter

ACKNOWLEDGMENTS

Special thanks to the following people who helped with opinions, criticisms, proofreading, and just general comments like "What the hell were you thinking here?"

Brandon Brown; Jeff Capehart; Ike Eberstein; Richard Edwards; Melissa Huddleston; Clayton Hunt; Karen Hunt; Adrienne Mayor; Rusty Rayborn; Rebecca Smethurst; Susan Summers; and many others...

And to Craig Martelle, David Weber, Ryk Brown, Dennis Taylor, Jay Allan, Joe Haldeman, Jack McDevitt, and Tim Pratt for providing inspiration.

Thank you all!

ABOUT THE AUTHOR

Like Huckleberry Finn, Phil Huddleston grew up barefoot and outdoors, catching mudbugs by the creek, chasing rabbits through the fields, and forgetting to come home for dinner. Then he discovered books. Thereafter, he read everything he could get his hands on, including reading the Encyclopedia Britannica and Funk & Wagnalls from A-to-Z multiple times. He served in the U. S. Marines for four years, returned to college and completed his degree on the GI Bill. Since that time, he built computer systems, worked in cybersecurity, played in a band, flew a bush plane from Alaska to Texas, rode a motorcycle around a good bit of America, and watched in amazement as his wife raised two wonderful daughters. And would like to do it all again. Except maybe without the screams of terror...

Printed in Dunstable, United Kingdom

75917161R10173